THE BAKER'S SECRET

ALSO BY STEPHEN P. KIERNAN

Fiction

The Hummingbird

The Curiosity

Nonfiction

Last Rights

Authentic Patriotism

THE BAKER'S SECRET

Stephen P. Kiernan

HarperCollins*PublishersLtd*

HarperCollins
PUBLISHERS
Since 1817

This is a work of fiction. Names, characters, places, and incidents are products of the author's imagination or are used fictitiously and are not to be construed as real. Any resemblance to actual events, locales, organizations, or persons, living or dead, is entirely coincidental.

The Baker's Secret

Published by HarperCollins Publishers Ltd

First Canadian edition

HarperCollins Publishers Ltd
2 Bloor Street East, 20th Floor
Toronto, Ontario, Canada
M4W 1A8

www.harpercollins.ca

Designed by Leah Carlson-Stanisic

Illustration by mika48/Shutterstock, Inc.

Library and Archives Canada Cataloguing in Publication information is available upon request.

ISBN 978-1-44345-346-2 (hardcover)
ISBN 978-1-44343-889-6 (original trade paperback)

Printed and bound in the United States
LSC/H 9 8 7 6 5 4 3 2 1

To Ellen Levine and Jennifer Brehl
in gratitude

It takes twenty years to bring man from his vegetable state inside the womb . . . to the stage where he begins to grow into maturity. It took thirty centuries to learn something about his structure. It would take an eternity to learn something about his soul. It takes only an instant to kill him.

—VOLTAIRE, 1764

Men are not made for war. But neither are they made for slavery.

—JEAN GUÉHENNO, 1942

THE BAKER'S SECRET

Part One

BREAD

Chapter 1

All through those years of war, the bread tasted of humiliation.

For as long as their nation had possessed a history, the residents of Vergers village had been a people of pleasure, devoted to the senses without shame, and none savored more unapologetically than those of the kitchen. Over a span of centuries, their culture had turned the routine animal act of feeding themselves into an art form. Delectable breakfast morsels with steaming coffee as dark as mud, calming lunches in the shade when haste is the enemy and cheese is the dessert, dinners luxurious, candlelit, and lasting hours—such was the rhythm of their days: Who has a story to tell, and shall we place some flowers on the table?

It did not matter that they lived in a tiny village a kilometer from the chilly northern ocean, their occupations either of the farm or of the sea. If anything, the labors of manure and milking, mending nets or hauling them, only intensified their love of flavor, patience, the company of friends. Therefore the baking of bread, a nearly daylong alternation between active kneading of dough and passive waiting for it to rise, could be as gratifying as deep breathing. In the hearth of the oven, where baguettes basked side by side, making loaves echoed making love.

Then came the occupying army to teach their senses other

lessons: the clack that boot heels make when snapped together at attention, the dull smell of a rifle after the barrel has been oiled. For some, this instruction included a comparatively milder discovery—that even the most pleasing kitchen task, when it is made compulsory, becomes tedious.

Consider Emmanuelle: lovely, gifted in the kitchen, a fawn of twenty-two years. In any other time, the modest bakery where she was employed would serve as a center of commerce and community. In another era she would be distracted, preparing sweets for her Philippe, or taking all day to boil chicken stock down to a reduction so potent with concentrated flavor it could cast spells, all while dreaming of the drape of her someday bridal dress.

Instead, she rose before dawn that day, the fifth of June, to the crowing of her rooster, a belligerent strutting shouter widely known and universally disliked, whose name was Pirate because of the dark patch around one eye. Having slept on the floor beside the couch on which her grandmother now snored, Emma folded her quilt, tucked it away, and tiptoed from the parlor without waking the aged woman or causing the occupying army's captain to stir upstairs. Slipping into her shoes by the threshold, Emma strode with purpose across the barnyard. Pirate charged after her in full lecture—*his* hens, *his* morning, *his* territory—until she found a pinch of feed in her pocket and tossed it by the path, winning his silence long enough for her to reach the baking shed.

Emma stirred somnolent coals in the brick oven her father had built, tossing in chestnut shells for kindling, giving the ashes a single long breath until they glowed awake and the shells crackled. Then began the tedium, the task the Kommandant had ordered her to perform seven days a week, as though she were a cow with milk to be wrung from her straining udder at morning and eve, or a chicken whelping one new egg per turn of the earth. With each passing day Emma's love of baking grew a fraction drier, till what had once been her greatest joy dwindled to barely a husk.

She lifted cheesecloth from several bowls on the side table and studied the dough risen there like white globes. Satisfied with what she saw, Emma punched the rounds, each one contracting with a clean yeasty sigh. Only then, and after a glance out the opening to reconfirm that Pirate was the sole creature stirring, she reached behind a hanging cloth into a bin, five times returning with a handful of golden powder that she sprinkled onto the dough.

Straw. Ground fine each day to supplement the batter. Containing no nutrition whatsoever, its sole purpose was to add bulk. Thus were the rations of flour she received to make twelve loaves daily for the Kommandant and his men enlarged to produce fourteen, two of which she would secret away to divide among her neighbors and whoever in the village was in direst need.

There was never enough. There would never be enough.

Each morning required every crumb of Emma's skills, all of her artifice, to bake loaves containing straw and have neither the Kommandant nor his officers notice. Yet this was only one of five hundred deceits, all conceived during the long strain of the occupation. She learned to sow a minefield and reap eggs. She could wander the hedgerows pulling a rickety cart, and the result would be maps. She could turn cheese into gasoline, a lightbulb into tobacco, fuel into fish. She could catch, butcher, and divide among the villagers a pig that later every person who had tasted it would insist had never existed. And all of these achievements would occur in a land of violence and slavery and oppression.

In a time of humiliation, the only dignified answer is cunning.

It began fittingly, with aroma. One morning three years earlier, when a stalled tank had blocked the paved road down the coast, the Kommandant instructed his driver to use the dirt lane that ran west from the village. Between low tide and the offshore wind, the air that day smelled sour and foul. But as the officer's staff car passed Emmanuelle's barnyard, the scent of baking loaves rose to him like a cloud of comfort. Ordering his driver to reverse, the Kommandant sat with closed eyes until the dust had settled. Then he stepped down from the passenger side, removing his leather gloves one finger at a time. He handed them to his driver and strolled forward.

"What is that glorious smell? You, by that oven. Come forward."

Emma detested the occupying army's language, which sounded to her as though it were created solely to give commands. Whenever soldiers conversed in her vicinity, she thought they were either gargling or preparing to spit. Sometimes she knew from their eyes that the words were lewd; lust sounds the same in every tongue. Hearing a man in uniform now speak her language, and fluidly, Emma was dumbfounded. Forget that she had scavenged flour for weeks to do that day's baking, forget that her grandmother was hungry. She obeyed, marching across the barnyard with a loaf fresh from the oven.

The Kommandant demanded a taste. She held the baguette toward him. He took it, immediately juggling the bread hand to hand, blowing on his fingers, then giving it to his aide to hold. As the junior officer used the gloves to protect his hands, Emma smiling inwardly at her enemies' softness, the Kommandant composed himself. After a moment he tore one end from the loaf.

"At home we call this 'the pope's nose,'" he said, waving the snout of the baguette in the air. It was huge, a pig's portion. He bit hard with his perfect white teeth. Chewing so that his cheek muscles flexed, the Kommandant looked into the distance, as though trying to remember something.

"Excellent," he proclaimed after a moment. "You people certainly have a knack." He turned to his aide, speaking in their harsh tongue for half a minute before facing Emma again. "I told him to establish a flour ration for mademoiselle, first quality. And to order that you proceed here unmolested by our men. They can be eager sometimes. Henceforth you will bake twelve baguettes daily for the officers' mess."

The aide made a note on a paper, and off they drove, still holding the remainder of the loaf.

How had Emma become so accomplished, able to bake with scant rations and yet produce a scent enticing enough to stop an army, having never ventured ten kilometers from the place where she was born?

Ten years earlier, when Emmanuelle was as thin as a willow switch, Mémé had marched her past the barnyard wall, beyond the eastern well, up the lane to the village green, and into the shop of Uncle Ezra. A little bell rang as the door closed behind them. The place was warm and smelled of yeast.

"I've brought you an apprentice," Mémé declared.

Ezra Kuchen had no relations nearby, did not socialize, never joined the rest of the villagers in Sunday Mass at St. Agnes by the Sea. Still, he made the most splendid sticky cinnamon rolls each year on Christmas Day, one for every child in Vergers. From wedding cakes to funeral pastries, no one else would do. Despite his gruff manner, therefore, over the decades he had become family to the townspeople, and thus Uncle.

Now the mole-faced man glanced up from the counter where he was portioning dough into penny loaves, and in less than a second had focused again on his work. "No girls."

As if hired to prove the point, two young men labored away behind him. Emma observed one operating a giant mixer—the metal churning arm turned at a speed she would have slowed to avoid drying out the dough. The other portioned flour, cup by cup, into a large metal bowl—not noticing the slight spill he committed each time. Neither interrupted his work to see who had entered the store.

Mémé dug in her sack, producing a pie tin. She set it on the shelf, slid away the cover, and broke off a piece of crust. "Taste."

Scowling, Uncle Ezra waddled out from behind the counter. Up close, his brow bore beads of perspiration. He took the crust, sniffed it, then popped it in his mouth. He chewed thoughtfully, then slowed. "You made this, Mémé? You're improving."

For reply, she gestured with one hand. Emmanuelle, freckled and twelve, curtsied.

"Is that so?" Uncle Ezra crossed his arms. "Then how did you cause it to flake so lightly? Answer me quick."

"Olive oil with the butter, sir. I melted them together first."

"Bah. How much?"

"Two thimbles, sir."

"Heresy," he muttered. But he reached for another taste.

That was hundreds of baguettes ago, thousands. Seasons had passed, whole years. End to end, the loaves Emma had baked for her enemies would have stretched from her barn through the village to the beach, into the sea, across the salty sleeve of water, all the way to the island kingdom where the mighty Allies smoked cigars and made speeches about courage and did not come.

Now, adding wood to the fire, Emma divided the dough for that fifth day of June into fourteen portions. She spread flour on the counter and began kneading the rounds into the long and slender baguette shape. Faintly she heard a whistling from outside, the high wandering melody that issued perpetually from the puckered lips of Monkey Boy. He would be stopping at the eastern well, just outside Emma's barnyard wall, for his morning drink. Monkey Boy's given name was Charles, but at birth he had been touched by God, was only half sensible, and preferred to spend his days in the trees.

Emma wondered what would happen to Monkey Boy when he turned eighteen. His father was long gone; his mother despaired of so much as keeping the boy washed. Thus far, all he had demonstrated the capacity to do was sell apples, most of which the villagers purchased out of pity. The orchards in that region were solely cultivated for Calvados brandy, crushed in the fall and distilled in winter and far too bitter to eat, but somehow he had found a few trees whose fruit was edible. This discovery was no qualification for laboring far from home in the occupying army's factories. Would the enemy conscript him to work there anyway, as they had Emma's beloved Philippe? Or would they declare him useless, and dispose of him as they had so many others? Monkey Boy's sixteenth birthday was in mid-August, not ten weeks away, and there was no chance the war would be over in two years. Not when it had already raged for four. Probably it would never end. So let him whistle and wander. It did no harm, and a short life might as well be a merry one.

Emma eased the loaves into the oven, fourteen pale babies swaddled in a skin of water to make a crisp crust, using her thumbnail to mark the underside of each one in the shape of a *V*. May you break a tooth on it, she whispered.

No one knew where the *V*s began, or precisely what they meant. But for anyone with eyes open, they were as common as stones: carved into the public benches, scribbled on the chalkboards of summer's empty classrooms, scuffed in the dirt outside the town offices. The occupying army saw, and announced that *V* meant victory, their mighty triumph. They put it on giant flags, flown high. By attempting to make *V* their own, however, they had no idea of the extent to which they committed an act of self-mockery. Proper *V*s did not occur on flags or grand displays, but in secret and only among those who knew: matchbooks left on a café table, folded into a *V*. Driftwood piled upon the beach. Books standing open on their spines. *V*s everywhere, little sprouting flowers of undiminished will.

Nonetheless, Emma's bread would taste of humiliation. Shame flavored the village's food because it had infiltrated the people's hearts.

Twenty-six years after the Great War had devoured nearly two million of the nation's young men, spending them on the countryside's soils like so much fertilizer, a new aggressor had returned with even greater force. This mustached demon had a passion to his righteousness before which all people paled. His hordes swept through Belgium, requiring a mere nineteen days to march from armed border to triumph in the capital, whereupon the tanks turned their turrets in the direction of the coast, and the tiny village of Vergers.

Who could blame the nation's leaders for negotiating? The madman's power was exceeded only by his fanaticism. The linden trees had not yet grown tall enough to shade the graves of those who had died in the last war. There were no lichens yet embroidering the monuments that bore their names. Who volunteers to sacrifice another generation of sons and husbands and brothers, especially for a fight that would be futile?

Thus did life and liberty depend upon a distant ruler who did not speak the people's language but felt at ease commanding them in his. The guttural ruled the elegant, the command replaced persuasion, the shout overwhelmed the subtle.

The invader vowed that he would not repeat the Great War, that this time would be different. His troops would behave themselves, the radio was full of propaganda, and promises of the bright future fell like petals from a bough. They would win the people's hearts, surely, once order had been established.

It was a story people wanted to believe, but they knew better. Village by village the soldiers took down the statues, carting old heroes and artists away in railcars, as if people were too ignorant to imagine that they would soon be melted into armaments, Napoleon into gun barrels, Balzac into bullets. The pedestals on which the bronzes had stood remained in place, however, though now they were monuments to nothing.

Lies collapsed upon themselves like timbers of a barn on fire as the passionate lunatic systematically disregarded every word of the armistice. His troops took the people's guns, confiscated their radios, packed men into cattle cars that were headed to his factories—so that his own nation's males would be available to make new wars on new enemies.

The occupying army spread across the continent with the persistence of a disease. Emma heard it was worse in Spain, where no one was permitted to travel anywhere, for any purpose. She heard it was worse in Belgium, where no one had enough to eat. She heard it was worse in Russia, where the charismatic maniac had besieged one beautiful city and incinerated many small ones.

For two years the people of the coast lived behind a façade that fooled no one, their letters censored, mayors and police chiefs disappearing in the night, any loudmouth jailed or vanished, until the wild-eyed zealot declared it was enough. The nation would become one again, albeit united under identically strict rules. Almost overnight, the village's signposts, alley walls, and storefronts all bore posters listing many forms of conduct—breaking curfew, possessing guns, aiding escaped prisoners, sheltering enemies, listening to foreign radio stations, refusing the occupying army's currency—and under these lists stood a single word that required no translation: *verboten*.

Eventually the truth revealed itself like the sun coming up. Fuel began to run short, battles elsewhere demanded more resources, and food rations fell by half. Fishermen, normally considered smelly and coarse, became a salvation, their catch the village's only meat.

The fastest-growing crop of that season was indignation. When a man has raised a calf, fed it, and milked it, and he sees the full frothing bucket taken away for someone else's breakfast, the woes of elsewhere dwindle and his stomach is not all that grumbles. Only nursing mothers, pregnant women, and young children were permitted to receive a ration of milk. The occupying army insisted that this was an act of generosity. Thus did the people learn that thirsting occurs on many levels.

Some said that the coastal villages had it easier, with mere occupation. Should the Allied liberators ever rouse themselves and come to their aid, however, these lands would be the likely place of collision. No man offers his wheat field to serve as a battlefield. No woman wants her home to be a bunker.

Many days Emma saw the Allies' bombers far overhead, aimed at some destination hundreds of miles inland, her village's predicament so far below it might as well have been the circumstance of ants. From time to time they would cast their wreckage down, tumbling tin caskets that caused destruction so casual she wondered if these pilots might not be enemies after all: the main road to Caen destroyed, four bridges punctured which previously had enabled farmers to come to market, one of the nicest vacation homes on the bluff above the beach blown into a million bits.

The veterinarian Guillaume, a broad-shouldered man with great bushy eyebrows, explained everything to a group in the village one afternoon. Famously a devoted bachelor, Guillaume had later in life found himself a small-boned wife, a considerably younger woman, in Bayeux. Initially people thought Marie was a snob, but gradually they learned it was only that she was as shy as a newborn deer. They had just the one daughter, Fleur, barely a teen but already a staggering beauty. Timid like her mother, she wore a blue apron with patch pockets, in which her hands continuously fiddled with whatever lay hidden there.

Days after hanging the *verboten* posters, the occupying army was away performing maneuvers on the beach, their trucks and tanks and the thud of mortars firing, which enabled Guillaume to speak freely. Still the people formed a tight scrum in front of the row of shops, shoulder to shoulder.

The one exception was the Goat, who listened from the periphery. A ragged young man with a half-grown beard whose actual name was Didier, the Goat sometimes slept on a shelf in Emma's empty hog shed, emerging in the morning steeped in the smell of pig urine, a scent as pungent as ammonia. Also, he would argue over the least thing. Once she had heard him dispute with Yves, an experienced fisherman, over the direction of the wind. Whether it was due to his fragrance, therefore, or his antagonistic nature, the villagers' otherwise close circle gave the Goat ample room. Emma, too, kept her distance from the group—and from the Goat, because of an event in their school days about which she was still angry. She lingered in the doorway of Uncle Ezra's bakery, a mixing bowl in the crook of her arm, a wooden spoon in her free hand. Eyeing something across the square, she stirred and listened.

"The Allies are fighting an intelligent war," Guillaume said. He had a low, calm voice. "It is all quite deliberate. The fuel for our enemy's trucks and tanks comes by rail, for example, and many of the tracks are now destroyed."

No one asked how he knew such things. Since membership in the Resistance was a capital offense, and since the occupying army mandated that villagers report anyone suspected of belonging, likewise on a threat of execution for failing to do so, not asking was a combination of impeccable manners and self-preservation.

In a rural village, moreover, few people were more trusted than a veterinarian. A sick cow could mean disaster for a small farm. The man who came at any hour and stopped the illness, preventing it from spreading to the herd, saved lives. While a physician must understand the human body in great detail, a veterinarian must have comparable knowledge about horses, pigs, goats, dogs. As a young man, Guillaume had even traveled all the way to Ghent, attending for two full years its eminent school for the health of livestock.

Guillaume had famous hands—giant and strong, yet capable of acts of astonishing delicacy—which the villagers had seen deliver a breached calf, resuscitate a lifeless piglet, and remove the worst of boils from the eye of a retriever. They had also watched those hands dispatch an animal beyond saving, the deed done with compassionate speed.

Beyond those credentials, Guillaume accepted payment in whatever currency a farmer possessed: money, food, gratitude. Thus not a villager questioned his knowledge of military doings.

He continued: "Those bridges were stout enough to hold tanks, which now have a nine-mile detour to reach the coast. That damaged road was the fastest way for the enemy to bring reinforcement troops to our beaches. Now there can be no counterattack."

Guillaume drew in the dirt with a stick as he spoke, mapping and explaining, and when he finished he swept it all away with his boot.

As the group straightened, digesting the news, Emmanuelle made a declaration from her bakery doorway. "It is a fairy tale."

Guillaume tossed the stick aside. "What is?"

"This strategy nonsense. All wishing and self-importance. We are far too small to be part of any elaborate scheme."

"Our village, perhaps. But not our location. It is possible that an invasion here would be the tip of the Allies' spear."

"Then we will be impaled upon it," she replied, stirring a moment, and speaking to her bowl. "Train tracks and bridges are diversions, to keep the occupying troops busy building defenses here, to weaken their army in the east."

Guillaume nodded. "That may be, Emma. But how do you know these things?"

"Everyone knows. Everyone with a radio." Emma cast her gaze down at the assembled group. People looked away or at the ground.

"The great Allied tank commander who won in Africa was seen near Calais," she continued. "If we know this, then the invaders certainly know it. At best, we are a decoy." She waved her spoon at the circle of them as a witch would conjure a spell. "The Allies will never rescue us. They will never come."

"Don't say that," the Goat shouted, flapping the arms of his fraying coat. "You are preaching despair. You don't know anything."

Emma considered him a moment, then pinched her nose with her fingers and went back into the bakery. The Goat let his hands fall to his sides.

"Whichever approach they use," she heard Guillaume say, "the Allies are preparing to win. We must be patient."

Patient? It would have been easier for the people to hold their breath for a month. Perhaps slavery is harder for a person who has known freedom. Perhaps it does not matter.

The villagers chafed under so many rules, and found small, perhaps pathetic ways of rebelling. For example, the time of day.

The army's home country lay in a different time zone, sixty minutes ahead. When the occupation began, the villagers were ordered to adapt. Yet without any overt collusion, they routinely arrived at events an hour late. They would claim confusion, or having been misled by the town hall clock, and the soldiers could only conclude that the people of Vergers were exceptionally stupid. No matter how emphatically the officers insisted on punctuality, or how many posters they hung about order, the villagers remained one hour out of reach.

A man could be outwardly obedient, but tardiness revealed his inner determination, proof that slavery affects only the body. It does not include possession of the heart.

The one schedule villagers did obey was distribution of meat rations. Then they became sheep. Even the strongest are humbled by hunger. Odette told everyone that it was only meat that gave bodies strength, that kept an empty stomach from gnawing at itself.

She was likeliest to know. Odette ran the town's sole surviving café—a ten-table establishment that served locals and soldiers without discrimination. A few villagers still had cash, and Odette accepted foreign currency as well. Her supplies came from the black market, to which the soldiers turned a blind eye so long as their plates had decent portions and their glasses were filled to the brim. For locals, her prices were inflated. For the occupying army, they were rapacious.

Odette was mannish despite her prodigious bosom. Short-haired and stocky, her sleeves perpetually rolled up, she made no promises, negotiated without mercy, and bullied anyone who questioned the bill. Odette had no family, both parents dead and no siblings or spouse, so her café became home, her customers a form of kin.

The rest of the people depended on their gardens, and the occupiers' paltry rations. Everything else, the army took for itself. The young soldiers looked ruddy and hale, while the middle commanders developed paunches from too much local Camembert. The villagers grew gaunt, meanwhile, the women's breasts losing fullness, the men's arms hanging flaccid.

Emma's solution was to bake illicit bread.

Chapter 2

F*irst she was Uncle Ezra's washerwoman.* Ranked below Albin and David, apprentices for three and two years respectively, who had never scrubbed pots with enough effort or scoured muffin tins with sufficient digging, Emma swept and carried, cleaned and dried, while Uncle Ezra ranted continuously about how, whatever she did, she had done it wrong.

"Imbecile. If you use soap in a cast-iron skillet, you scrub away years of seasoning unique to that pan. It is like burning a memoir."

Or, on another day: "Dolt. If you use lye on a cutting board, you spoil the natural oils and render it as useless as a plank."

Or, on another: "Numbskull. Must you let the screen door slam as though no one here has ears? Have mercy, and stop it with your heel or head or your beastly backside."

Once she prevented the door from slamming, however, Emma noticed that Uncle Ezra did not throw away the cutting board or the cast-iron pan. He oiled the former, buttered the latter, and went about his business.

Next he taught her how to sharpen a knife, though of course she wrecked the blade, ruining its temper and making it brittle. But later her knives cut well. He showed Emma how to measure, but of course the quantities were unacceptably wrong because liquids cling to the sides of cups, and solids sort themselves out smaller with a little shaking. Yet the croissants turned out flaky and the cookies tasted sweet.

He would ask for a pan, any pan, hurry up, then criticize whichever one she handed him as too small or too large. Yet he used it nonetheless. He would open the oven door, insist that she must have neglected to clean it the day before because it was still filthy, then slide popover tins onto the oven rack anyway.

For months Philippe spent a portion of every afternoon listening as Emma recounted that day's insults. After attending with his customary patience, he would grab her hand and pull her into a hedgerow to steal kisses. Always Emma protested; always she allowed him to prevail.

Gradually, however, she noticed a result from Uncle Ezra's caustic tone: once he had chastised her for a mistake, she never made it again. Popovers, for example, always went into a cold oven; preheating prevented them from filling with air. Right or wrong, name-calling and scorn were his ways of teaching. She began to pay closer attention, observing his methods, eavesdropping on every criticism he gave the boys. They bent under the withering weather, delivered in a daily downpour, but Emma at the sink would stop the running water, silence the blender, pause the giant mixer so that she did not miss a word.

Some days after work, the Goat would be standing at the corner, picking at something or arranging his clothes. Emma turned in the opposite direction although it meant a longer route home. Or, if Philippe had come for her that day, she would seize his arm and walk especially close as they passed on the sidewalk. Philippe would say hello to Didier but Emma held her tongue. Her sweetheart smelled of motor oil and she of soap. The Goat wore an atmosphere of filth.

In Emma's third year at the bakery, Albin's father fell from a hayloft and broke his leg. Despite six years of investment in apprenticeship, Albin seized on the excuse to return to the family farm. Six months later, David dropped a twenty-kilo bag of flour, which made a small cloud when it burst. As Uncle Ezra delivered his predictable berating—the boy was a buffoon and an idiot and a true horse's ass—David removed his apron in a sort of slow motion. He hung it on the hook in back with similar ponderousness.

"Where are you going?" Uncle Ezra cried. "We have unfinished work today. The mayor has requested a napoleon."

David left without bothering to prevent the door from slamming.

The baker stood with hands on his hips, fuming. Emma, having interrupted her scrubbing in order to hear the lecture, stared into the soapy water. Uncle Ezra worked his lower lip back and forth as though he were chewing it. Beside an oven that held three cheesecakes, a timer ticked away. The two of them were alone for the first time.

"He was lazy," Emma said at last. "I watched him drop a bit of eggshell into a cake batter, and not bother to spoon it out."

"What? When?"

"Yesterday. I removed it when he was in the cooler." She pulled the plug from the drain, which choked loudly as it emptied, and continued, "Albin sneezed with his mouth open."

"What? Disgusting."

She shrugged. "I always replaced the recipe he did it in front of."

"How long have you been helping them?"

Emma stared into the gleaming sink. "Since I began here."

"Damn it," Uncle Ezra said, punching his fist into his other palm. It was the first time Emma had heard a man swear, and she blushed. "And now I suppose you will be leaving soon too?"

For Emma, the moment was fragrant with opportunity. She scanned the shop, pies cooling in the front window while rolls and loaves and one unsold breakfast croissant sat in the display case. David's broken bag had not yet been swept up, which could only be done after saving as much unspilled flour as possible. Normally, that would have been her duty.

Meanwhile on the main counter there stood the mayor's unfinished napoleon—also known as thousand-leaf cake because of its many thin layers of alternating puff pastry and pastry cream, a test of any baker's patience—and all that remained was to frost the top. Uncle Ezra had been preparing to do exactly that when he paused to rain invective upon David: the frosting sleeve was already filled, a medium gauge nozzle at its tip, a bowl of melted chocolate alongside for dripping a design onto the frosted top.

The baker remained with hands on hips, his question hanging in the air. Emma wiped hands on her apron, strode to the counter, picked up the frosting sleeve, and turning it gently clockwise, began to wring a stream of white confection out the nozzle in exact sympathy with the pace of her movement around the cake.

Uncle Ezra came to stand beside her, watching. She could hear him breathing. When she pinched three fingers together to dip in the chocolate, he opened his mouth to speak, but as she drizzled the dark brown in a rosette on the frosting, hovering the bowl near in her free hand so no errant drip would mar the white, he said not a word. When the napoleon was completed, she drew the back of a knife across her design, an X in three directions to give it flair. Uncle Ezra sniffed and crossed his arms.

"Yes? Did I do something wrong?"

He chewed on his lower lip a moment before answering. "Two years."

"Two years until what, sir?"

"Until you become my competition."

Chapter 3

F*rom that day forward they were equals,* the grouchy baker and his apprentice of sixteen, seventeen, and more. Production increased. The shop's reputation grew. People traveled from Caen, from Bayeux, from Honfleur, saying they had heard of this cake or that pie, this bread or that pastry.

The story of the shop was part of its appeal. Nearly every customer had heard about the pie crust made with butter and olive oil, about the baker who wanted no women but took as apprentice a young girl. Yet no tale would make Emma an expert. Talent was but one ingredient in a lengthy recipe. She knew enough to make mastering the basics her first goal. Also she continued to pay attention, interrupting herself midtask to watch Uncle Ezra whisk sugared cream of tartar violently into a gentle meringue, or fold one batter into another to make a third, new thing. Soon enough she began to intuit how to apply basic principles in new circumstances. She started to improvise, baking raisin muffins, adding a flourish to frostings, making sauces and reductions for Odette's café.

One Christmas Eve—Emma was nineteen, taller than Uncle Ezra, more confident every day—she stood in the shop doorway beside him, helping distribute the fabled sticky cinnamon rolls. They had shared the work equally: him baking, her toasting the pecans, him kneading the dough, her blending brown sugar with butter to make the glaze, and both of them pouring the sweet nectar over finished rolls for the village children with so much care it could only be an act of love. He gave the treats on squares of wax paper while Emma kept track, making sure no clever boy managed to get himself more than one.

Up skipped the Monkey Boy, whistling and wearing an elfin cap. His mother prodded him to say thank you. "Happy Christmas, Aunt Emma," he said.

"Never," she shouted, surprising herself. "It will not be."

She turned and bolted back into the shop. Uncle Ezra frowned at the tray of rolls in his lap, then groused at the next child to hurry along. Emma did not speak of it until she sat with her father and Mémé that evening at Christmas dinner.

"I will *not* become Uncle Ezra," she declared, balling her hands into fists.

"Of course not," her father said, but then he coughed into his sleeve.

"You have vastly more talent," said Mémé, which Emma felt missed the point entirely.

After the big meal she met Philippe for a stroll on the sea path, along which young men and women had meandered since the time of the Romans. The ocean lay flat in December cold. Three large vacation homes on the bluff sat dark and empty, as if the windows were scanning the horizon for summer's return. Below, a retreating tide seethed against the beach.

"I will not become Uncle Ezra," she said. Philippe was trying to kiss her neck but she squirmed out of reach. "I refuse to be solitary for all of my life."

"And what if you are?" he teased. "You will always have a score of admirers, as long as you make that raspberry trifle."

"Oaf," she said, giving him a swat. "I will be alone and you will laugh."

"Of course you will not be alone," Philippe said, going suddenly still. "It is out of the question."

"It is not out of the question." Emma stamped her foot. "I am working his early hours. I am slaving in his shop. I am learning his skills as if they were devotions. Yesterday I spent whole minutes deliberating between two eggs, trying to decide which one suited a recipe better." Emma's breath rose as a cloud in the darkness. "For seven years I have skipped down this path like a foolish schoolgirl, without a single moment's foresight that I could wind up in the exact same life. What is to prevent that from happening?"

He took both of her hands. "I am."

With that, she calmed. Emma accepted his kisses, allowed him to pin her against a tree trunk, and as an immodest Yuletide gift, permitted one of his hands a brief entry within the folds of her cloak. His fingers were cold against her waist and her skin surprisingly warm.

Mémé disliked Philippe because she thought he was short. In fact he stood an average height but Grandpère, her husband, had been nearly two meters. As Emma's father, Marcel observed how quietly the young man talked, wondered whether a repairer of engines by trade could support a family, and kept any opinions to himself. He had married against his parents' wishes, their pressure and ire serving only to drive their son away. When they refused to attend the wedding, the break was permanent. Therefore Marcel vowed on his late wife's soul that whatever his reservations, he would not inflict that suffering on his daughter. She could give her love to an octopus and he would not object.

Emma, however, knew things her family did not: Philippe listened to her as attentively as she did to Uncle Ezra. While other boys pawed at their girlfriends without respect, Philippe walked with a hand around her waist only when they were alone. Emma was serious to a fault, whereas he laughed and his eyes became dangerous. When she confessed one day that she could not remember her mother's face, Philippe held her close and his hands did not wander.

Afternoons, he met Emma after work at the bakery and leaned near. "You smell like sugar."

"Go away," she laughed, but gave him her knuckles to kiss.

The sole time he felt fickleness from her came when they encountered the Goat. Philippe could not help wondering what history was between them, that the sight or scent of that young man some days made her ardent, and other days turned her temporarily into stone.

Philippe had been eleven when his family moved to Vergers, and her enmity was already fully established—as was the Goat's perpetually lingering, apologetic presence.

Emma refused to tell the story. A tale in which one is mortified does not bear repeating. However, that is not the same thing as saying the events never occurred.

He did not call himself the Goat, of course. Didier desired to be known as the Wolf. That was the title he invented for himself, instructing villagers, insisting that people elsewhere knew him by that name alone. Which people? Which elsewhere? Emma knew he was no traveler, with friends in other places, merely a farm boy gone adrift, no more wolf than she was field mouse.

Kinder villagers were indulgent, though, and called him the Wolf in his presence. Behind his back was another matter. From adolescence on, Didier had sought to be manlier than his nature. It always backfired. He volunteered for the national army, only to be dismissed for weak eyesight. He attempted to join the fishermen, but injured his back hauling a loaded net. He tried to grow a beard but it came in thin and only on his chin. One afternoon at the weekly town market, Odette joked that perhaps Didier had no onions, and Emma wisecracked that he looked like a goat. The gossiping biddies cackled and the nickname stuck.

Once upon a time, however, Emma and Didier had been classmates, their mothers dear friends. Yet he teased her all through childhood, and not playfully. He pulled her hair, stole her papers, called her names. One day his mother sliced her thumb while butchering a leg of lamb, and the resulting infection killed her in a fortnight. Adolescent Emma found that the funeral and sympathy made Didier oddly interesting.

His annoying behavior, meanwhile, only increased. One afternoon at recess when she was climbing the ladder to the slide, he ran up from behind and yanked down her bloomers, revealing her bare bottom to the entire schoolyard. Although he was punished—a ruler fifteen times on his backside in front of everyone—it did not absolve the shame Emma felt as she jerked her underwear back into place while all of her classmates stood laughing.

Years later she still wondered what had possessed him to do such a cruel thing. From time to time she turned the question over in her mind, as though it were a stone in her pocket. Now he was grown and ambitious, yet still he struck her as pathetic, his attempts at manliness not genuine but a compensation for something missing. The Goat wanted to rouse the citizens, to incite rebellion. But if he had a fist, he kept it in his pocket.

Somehow the occupying army had overlooked Didier at conscription time. Probably a census error by the old town clerk, Émile, doddering between his filing cabinets, which no one was in a hurry to point out. The army ordered the Goat's father and brother to report, loaded them onto the train, then moved a dozen officers into their farmstead. From the upstairs window, they flew their red-and-white flag with its ugly black emblem. They smashed antique chairs for kindling, fed heirloom mahogany wardrobes to the flames. After that, no one knew where Didier called home.

Philippe did not need to hear the Goat's story to observe Emma's reaction to him, and to steer her wide of wherever he happened to be. Though it perplexed him, Philippe noticed that her affections were most ardent when they had seen the Goat and gone another way. Her kisses made a persuasive compass.

See Emma then, in the dim hour of dawn on the fifth of June, years later. The yearning for Philippe felt so similar to the hunger of her belly each day, she did not know which want was which. Given time enough, perhaps one can grow accustomed to all pains. So she baked—to save her life, and Mémé's, and all the others in the village who depended on her secret network of food and fuel.

The skies threatened rain, the wind blew harshly, but the Kommandant's expectation of baguettes remained as certain as the tides. Emmanuelle slid on quilted gloves, placed a bowl of water in the oven to harden the crust, and turned the loaves on their sides. They were brown and crisp, the *V* thinner but visible for anyone who looked.

Removing her mitts, Emma began her next task: preparing the following day's straw. The oaken pestle spun quick in her hands, grinding against the marble mortar until the grass shafts became a soft powder the color of her hair.

The idea had come from the animals, and their departure. The occupying army requisitioned one species after another, cows, then pigs, then sheep, so that the demand for dry straw dwindled to nothing. The soldiers also confiscated all dogs over forty-five centimeters in height, though for what purpose Emma shuddered to imagine. Nonetheless, with no animals needing bedding, straw sat in the lofts unused.

One afternoon Monkey Boy wandered by, whistling his familiar tune, but shy when he reached the barn door.

"Are you going to lurk there all day?" Emma asked. "Because I have nothing to feed you."

Monkey Boy's shoulders dropped. He stumbled across the barnyard to the wall of beige bricks that separated Emma's farm from the eastern well, flopped down with less care than a dog takes to settle on the dirt, and fell instantly asleep. Observing through the open door, Emma rose and crossed the grassless barnyard. As she stood over Monkey Boy, for once considering him with something other than dismissal, it became clear that he had collapsed not from fatigue but from hunger. He looked like a clothed pile of sticks.

Emma considered the thousands of hours her hands had spent cooking under Uncle Ezra's critical eye, dicing onions or pinching salt or adding the tiniest soupçon of dry mustard to sharpen a broth. Wasted luxury, pointless education. What good was finesse in the face of starvation? It would be like needlepointing while the barn burned. She needed to do something. Her training, and yes, she could admit it, her talents, demanded better use than frosting cakes or sugaring muffins.

Emma turned from the emaciated boy and marched back into the barn, her hands in fists. Dough for the next morning's baguettes sat in metal bowls, three rounds taking their rise on the sunlit sill. She rested a palm on one as if on the brow of a sleeping baby. Outside Monkey Boy whimpered in his sleep. At that moment, her gaze fell on the heap of straw sitting in the loft unused.

So it began, one pinch ground fine and stirred into the twelve-loaf mix. Emma baked as usual the next morning. She slid the arms of warm bread into the green canvas bag the Kommandant's aide used when he came to fetch them. She wrung her hands as he motorcycled away with the bag over one shoulder, wondering if she had just sentenced herself to death.

Emma barely slept that night. If she were found out, who would look after Mémé? She rose before dawn, as ever, and when the dough was ready for final mixing, she added that pinch once again. Later, when the aide motorcycled into the barnyard, he held the canvas bag toward her without a word. No praise, but more importantly, no complaint.

Soon one pinch became two. Every few days she added slightly more, until a morning several months along when the aide asked in broken words if she had changed her recipe, because lately the crusts were tough. That was the ceiling, therefore, five handfuls, beneath which she remained ever after.

Now each day Emma scooped powdered straw into a mass of dough the size of three melons, adding salt to aid with concealment. She baked the Kommandant's twelve loaves, and portioned the extra two among Monkey Boy, or Madeleine whose eyesight had gone bad, or Fleur the veterinarian's beautiful daughter, or the newly married Argent couple, or Pierre, the cowman too affable to comprehend a time of war.

"I give them my milk and they leave me alone," Pierre confided in Emma one day. He removed his pipe from his mouth. "I am not being disloyal to my country, I am protecting my girls." He blew a kiss to the trio of bovines grazing in his dooryard, with their long eyelashes and bashful ways.

Emma handed him one third of a loaf. "I only want to keep as many people alive as possible."

"Yes, until the liberators come." Pierre tucked the bread in his coat pocket.

"They will never come."

"Emmanuelle, my dear." He chomped on the pipestem. "Of course the Allies will free us. At this very moment they might be massing and preparing to attack. Or do you have no hope at all?"

"You cannot eat hope." Emma fidgeted with the harness straps on her wagon. "You cannot trade it for butter."

Pierre patted his chest. "I fought in the Great War. I know the world will not stand by idly. Therefore I am filled with hope. The day of our liberation will be a great moment in history."

Emma turned away to continue her deliveries, calling back over her shoulder, "They will never come."

One morning Emma was busy kneading when she heard a noise in the yard. Pirate came charging out from behind the rain barrel, crowing like the last defender of civilization. She slid the mortar and pestle for grinding the straw under a table. Then she gathered her skirts and hastened to the wide barn door.

Beside the opening in the barnyard wall stood a man dressed entirely in black. At Emma's approach he turned his head only, glaring back before strolling away toward the eastern well.

She hesitated. If she did not follow, though, the rooster would awaken half the village. Pirate sought constantly to escape the barnyard confines; Emma thought he probably imagined whole harems of hens on the other side of the wall, each of them eager to be bred.

She had seen pictures of hedgerows elsewhere, the demure

low walls of Ireland, the fence with a gate in England's Lake District. But in the region of Vergers, hedgerows were something else: thick warrens of bracken and root that stood twice the height of a man, arched over the lanes like a chapel roof, dividing properties as impenetrably as any wall. Those bushes contained all manner of predators that would make short work of a three-pound bird.

Emma shooed him away, and he quieted once she had passed through the wooden door in the barnyard's brick wall, pulling it closed behind her.

The man now stood on the far side of the well. He wore a dark beard, trimmed thin along his jaw, and heavy black glasses. "That infernal rooster should be served for supper," he said.

"He makes an excellent watchdog," Emma replied evenly, wiping her hands on her skirts. "You never know who might be sneaking up."

"I was not sneaking," the man said. "The scent of your baking is a torment."

"You know I am following orders."

"Emmanuelle." He shook his head. "Emmanuelle."

"That is my name."

"Who would know better than the man who baptized you?"

Emma crossed her arms. "Why does the Monsignor visit me on this rainy morning? Surely my obedience to the Kommandant commits no sin."

"I dare not speculate about you and sin," the priest said. "That is for God alone to condemn. It is for me only to pity and lament. But I am here to make a request. Actually, two."

"I have nothing to offer you."

"Do I seem that much of a fool?" he said, wiggling his fingers at her. "I know all about your little network."

"I have no idea what you are talking about, Monsignor."

"Your neighbors tell a different story in the confessional booth. You have woven a web with deceptions. By preying on their desperation, you compel them to bear false witness as well."

"If I am guilty of deceiving anyone, it is the occupying army. In my opinion, they deserve much worse."

"You are guilty of many things, of course." The Monsignor sidled out from behind the well. "The question is what I ought to do, if I am to obey my conscience."

"Your conscience is not my business."

"I suspect you are concerned enough with your own."

"I sleep well," Emma answered. "Aside from hunger, fear of the officer upstairs, and worry about Mémé's mind going foggy."

"Poor Mémé, at the moment when she is most vulnerable, to be attended by a sinner."

"'Judge not, lest ye be judged.'"

He rolled his eyes heavenward. "She quotes Scripture at me." The priest sighed, circling the well, one hand trailing on the stones. "Tell me, Emmanuelle, when did you last attend Mass at St. Agnes by the Sea?"

She leaned against the brick wall. "Last October. When I realized that my prayers were all for an enemy's death."

"But you know, too, that prayer could remove that hatred. Why did you stop at that time in particular?"

"I knew that God had forgotten us."

The priest stopped in his circling. "Blasphemy. God is always present."

Emma pushed up her shirtsleeves. "If God exists, He is resting comfortably on the ocean's far shore, reclining in plump chairs beside our so-called Allies, who have perfected the art of watching us suffer and doing nothing about it."

The priest shook his head. "Proud as your rooster, and it is my fault. I should not have permitted you to apprentice with a Jew."

"What? What did you say to me?" She advanced on him, hands balled into fists.

"You will show respect, Emmanuelle." The priest raised one finger in rebuke. "At once. I have friends among the officers. Indeed they worship the same Christ as you, and come to Mass accordingly. I imagine they might frown on your secrets."

Emma paused, calculating. Pirate stirred behind the brick wall, growling like an underfoot cur. She approached the priest, quieting her tone to match his. "If you have been hearing those villagers' confessions, you know I am keeping half of them alive."

"Perhaps," he conceded. "But your ministry of the pragmatic is performed without faith."

The priest peered into the well, addressing his words to the darkness. "I did not come here to preach, Emmanuelle. But I must say this, which I know with all my being: to live without faith is to make a hell on earth."

Emma threw her hands up. "Why did you come here, then? What do you want?"

"Two things, as I said. The first—" He straightened, tucking his hands into the wide opposing sleeves of his tunic. "Bread."

Emma's eyes went wide. "You are so corrupt it is comical."

"The broken rail lines mean I have not received Communion wafers. You have extra loaves, don't deny it. Your pride is a sin before God, and your penance is to provide me with half a loaf each day, henceforth."

She snorted. "For you to feed your face."

"For the holy sacrifice of the Mass, Emmanuelle. For my

flock, which in this dark hour hungers more than ever for the bread of life. And yes, young lady, though you scoff at me, my second request concerns the salvation of your immortal soul." He lifted the crucifix that hung around his neck and kissed it. "Attend Mass this week, and be saved."

Emma strode to the door in the barnyard wall, where she paused. "You know, Monsignor, I still remember the day I made my first Holy Communion. I thought you were a living prayer, a direct connection to God. But I am older now. And it turns out that you are merely selfish."

"I say again: Life without faith is a hell on earth."

"Please." She passed through the opening. "Don't come here again."

"A hell on earth," he yelled after her.

Out of the Monsignor's sight Emma pressed a palm to the bricks to steady herself. Would he actually betray her to the occupying army? Should she return to the Church? Life was difficult enough without these questions.

"Bastard," she whispered.

Chapter 4

Did Emmanuelle feel afraid? Of course. No one in the village was immune. Fear, they learned, did not live in the heart or mind. It inhabited the stomach like a bad oyster. There was nothing to do but endure it. Neither could anyone deny it, because everyone had witnessed what the occupying army did to Uncle Ezra.

First they made him wear a star. They ordered it, commanded it on one of their posters. Odette was certain he would refuse. This thorny man who showed contempt for his best customers, who bowed to no one, who held himself and all to the same impossible standards? Never.

But there he was, the day the order took effect, with a six-pointed star sewn onto his tunic. It was yellow, the size of the palm of his hand. He stood in front of his shop, giving everyone an unambiguous view. Others wore the same star, of course, people who villagers might have known were of another faith—had they ever thought about it—because they did not worship at St. Agnes by the Sea. For some reason, the compliance of Uncle Ezra mattered more.

"Yes," he barked from the doorway of his shop, slapping the star on his chemise. "Here it is. My mark of David, the house of David. Look all you like."

Though his neighbors were obviously not the source of the star regulation, Uncle Ezra directed all of his indignation at them. He paced in the street flexing his fists, spitting in the dirt. In response, people were never kinder: praising his baked goods, buying extra, calling a greeting from down the lane. One day after a thick fog rolled in off the ocean, when he locked his shop for the evening, someone had left a new lantern on his stoop.

"Here it is," he nonetheless proclaimed to the square the next morning, slapping his star. "I am doing what I am told. I am an obedient knave."

Soldiers entered the library and confiscated all books by Jewish authors. Jews had to carry papers and leave jobs. They would realize that they were under surveillance. Then they would vanish. No one under surveillance was ever found innocent. First you were identified, then you were watched, then you were arrested. A plus B equals C.

"Here I am," Uncle Ezra railed in the street, his apron stained with butter, dusted by flour. "Son of Abraham. Child of Isaiah. Here I am."

One day soldiers came to the shop. Emma, busy at the giant mixer, did not hear them until one put his rifle butt through the front door's window and the shattering glass startled her. She switched off the mixer and hurried out front. Soldiers stood on all sides of Uncle Ezra, hollering at him in their harsh language.

"I don't understand you," he said. "What are you saying?"

The men continued to shout until an officer swaggered into the shop and they silenced. The captain wore his helmet angled forward, hiding his eyes. His mouth was pinched, as though he had bitten into something sour.

"Unless you are going to buy something, please leave," Uncle Ezra told the men. "You make my life hard enough, with the flour rationing. You have already emptied my bank account."

The captain studied the shop without haste. "We will search," he said. He barked a word to his men and they began ransacking, breaking shelves, spilling bowls, knocking a cake to the floor. He spoke in a bored tone. "You have nothing to fear, if you have done nothing wrong."

"Go home," Uncle Ezra called to the back of the shop. "Leave now, Emmanuelle."

He had never before used her name. But before she could take one step toward the back door, all of the soldiers made the same loud sound: *Ahhh*. Feigned surprise and genuine joy. One of them had punctured a sack of flour, and from it he seemed to have pulled a pistol—though Emma could see that the gun was as black as a locomotive.

"What is this?" the captain asked Uncle Ezra, dangling the pistol in front of his face. "What have we here?"

"I've never seen it before," Uncle Ezra said. "Please leave my shop."

"Never seen it? What are you making imply? Did I put it there? Or one of my men? Which one? I will punish him at once."

"I don't even know how to load a gun. What use would I have for possessing one? I know the laws."

"I'm sure you do," the captain said, shaking his head, as if hurt with disappointment. "The penalties as well."

He handed the gun back to the soldier who had found it. The others seized Uncle Ezra and pulled him from the store.

"Go home," Uncle Ezra called to Emma, but a soldier jammed a rifle into his belly and he said no more.

They dragged him away. Emma followed at a distance, as did others from the village. This was something wholly new. Although eventually there would be so many incidents of this sort the villagers would lose count, this day was a first, and they were ignorant about what might happen. Naive. Along the way someone had tied Uncle Ezra's hands, and though the soldiers buffeted him about, he held his head high. Emma saw that his lips were white with rage.

The crowd arrived at the churchyard, where a row of poplars stood with their pale bark and heart-shaped leaves. The soldiers shoved Uncle Ezra back against one tree and stepped away. Suddenly the people knew, could not believe that they hadn't known, felt ugly and wrong for being there.

The captain stood to one side, smoking a cigarette with the rich odor of real tobacco. He had wanted an audience, obviously. The whole event was theater. Emma kept a hand to her mouth as though she might be ill.

"Have you anything to say for yourself?" the captain asked.

"I have never seen that gun before," Uncle Ezra said. He tried to use his best gruff voice, the one the villagers knew and feared, but he was nearly stammering. "If I had hidden it in the flour, it would have been white."

The captain laughed, smoke dragoning from his mouth. "Are you defending of yourself? In the face of clear evidence, are you protesting of your innocence?"

"Of course I am innocent," Uncle Ezra cried. "I am a baker, a danger to no one. I make bread. Let me go."

"Of course you are innocent," the captain mimicked. He dropped the last of his cigarette on the grass, grinding it with his heel. He sauntered closer to Uncle Ezra, unclipping his holster, pulling out a pistol.

"I am Captain Thalheim," he said. "By the way."

"For God's sake," Uncle Ezra pleaded.

"Let us pause for a moment here," Captain Thalheim said, raising the pistol till the barrel was an arm's length from Uncle Ezra's face. "Contemplate your mortality."

And he waited. The wind blew, just then, pressing Uncle Ezra's apron against him so that everyone could see the spreading stain and know that he had wet himself, that his last moment on earth would be one of humiliation, the fierce expression gone utterly from his face as his head lowered and all the people saw the bald spot on top.

"That's right," Captain Thalheim said, and he pulled the trigger.

Part Two

WANT

Chapter 5

The *he following morning,* for all to see, someone had carved a *V* into the poplar's bark. It was undeniable, an arm's length above the blood spatter. Revealed, the green wood within wept and then hardened.

Captain Thalheim gave an order, and a private whose trousers were rolled at the cuff because he was too short for them came and stood before the tree, pondering. Later he returned with a stool and a chisel, peeling away the dappled bark until the *V* became a carved square. The next day the poplar bore a new *V*, half a meter higher. Word spread through Vergers like fire through a wheat field. Who had dared? Villagers snuck past, confirming it for themselves, in part to honor Uncle Ezra, in part to see what would happen next.

The small private fetched a stepladder, reaching up to chisel away another square. A second private stood guard over the tree that night. Yet somehow in the morning a new *V* appeared, more than two meters up the trunk from the bloodstain. People gossiped about it before Uncle Ezra's funeral began. Following the execution, the Monsignor had come with a wheelbarrow and brought the body inside St. Agnes by the Sea, wrapped Uncle Ezra and placed him in a casket at the front and center of the church, performing a memorial service as though they had been of precisely the same faith. Normally the villagers would have discussed this oddity for days, but the new *V* on the tree took precedence. It gave a strange electricity to their grief. On the way out of the church they stared, confirming it for themselves. Emma alone could not bring herself to pass that way.

"Not as long as that tree wears its badge of cruelty," she declared that afternoon to the locals gathered at Odette's café—by which she meant the reddish-brown blot on the light gray trunk. She had come to deliver a beef reduction which had low-boiled on her home stove the entire night, a bucket of gruelish bone juice concentrated down to one jar of fat and flavor. "I don't care who is responsible for the *V*."

"It must be Monkey Boy," Odette told her customers. "No one else can climb that high."

"Oh yes," Emma scoffed. "Our clever young rebel. He is the linchpin of the Resistance."

Four days after Uncle Ezra's execution, Emma had yet to venture back inside the bakery. Sympathetic neighbors had boarded up the front window, which the soldier's rifle butt had shattered. They had cleaned up the glass. Otherwise the place remained untouched. The cake that soldiers had knocked from the shelf lay yet on the floor, its frosting mottled with mold. Rolls on the counter had staled into stone.

People were already making inquiries, however, not out of heartlessness but because Easter was coming and thus the need for hot cross buns—however gritty they might taste with low-quality flour and without Uncle Ezra's trusted touch.

"Now, Emmanuelle," Odette said, wiping a table. "Be gentle with us."

"He is highly skilled in symbolism," Emma continued. "For a boy who cannot write his own name."

She strode off into the street. No one spoke for some time. At nightfall, when Odette went outside to light the torch—her café now crowded with officers from the occupying army, their booming songs and well-fed gusto, their ruddy skin and strange currency—she spied a light across the way. With the bakery's front window boarded, Odette could not snoop. But a woman with no family bears extra concern for her neighbors. In a reconnaissance farther down the lane, through the side glass she saw Emma with a broom, sweeping flour from the floor into a trash bin, slowly as if it were a sacred act, slowly so as not to raise a cloud.

Early the following morning Emma stood at the barn table kneading loaves for the Kommandant, when she heard boot heels clack together.

She startled, whirling to see Captain Thalheim in her barn. The man who had murdered her teacher raised one boot to rest it on a chunk of wood, as if he were posing for a portrait, helmet low to conceal his eyes, his face shaved as smooth as a grape.

What means of retaliation did she possess, other than insolence? "Yes, Sergeant?"

He bristled. "I am a captain."

He spoke her language, but clumsily and with his chest puffed out.

"Of course," she said. "Sometimes I am as dumb as my feet. What brings you here?"

"You are the one baking for the Kommandant."

In response, Emma raised her floury hands like a surgeon awaiting gloves.

"So possibly you might be a reasonable to help me."

Inwardly Emma boiled with rage, but the pistol remained on Thalheim's hip and she contained herself enough to shrug as if unconcerned. "Possibly."

"Who owns tallest of ladder in this town?"

"I don't know," Emma said. "Why do you ask?"

"I do not explain my reasons."

She turned back to the kneading board. "I have no idea . . . Sergeant."

The captain opened his mouth to speak, then paused, weighing his options. At last he started for the door.

"Wait," Emma drawled. "I know."

Thalheim paused at the doorway. "Yes?"

"I should have thought of it immediately." She dawdled, picking a clod of dough off her thumb. "Silly me."

"Yes?" he said, tapping his foot. "Out with it, then."

"The Monsignor must have the tallest ladder. How else would he change the lightbulbs in the nave of his church?"

"Thank you," the captain muttered. A moment later she heard his motorcycle start with a rattle, then growl as he rode away.

Emma seized the dough and kneaded as though it had disobeyed.

If she had intended to throw suspicion on the priest, however, she did not succeed. Instead the private obtained a means of reaching the most recent *V*, higher in the tree, to carve it out of existence. Now the poplar bore three large squares carved in the bark, all above a splatter of brownish red. Two guards stood sentinel that night, with a light trained on the tree as though it were a prisoner who might escape.

For several days there was no change, until the Kommandant overheard two soldiers complaining about the tedious guard duty. He sought Thalheim personally, finding him in the square outside Odette's café.

"There is work to be done," he snarled at the captain, who hung his head like a scolded schoolboy.

"Yes, sir. But the people must also be made to respect—"

"Real work, Captain. War work."

Nearby, Odette wiped a table indifferently. Although her mother's family hailed from Mainz, and she had grown up in a household that spoke the occupying army's language, she concealed her fluency. By eavesdropping she learned about troop activities, the contents of railcars, and when a senior officer might be visiting.

Odette recounted the conversation to her neighbors the next day as they lined up outside the schoolhouse for rations.

"Vee can't spare gutt men to guart a tree," she said in exaggerated imitation of the Kommandant, earning the villagers' laughter. Odette wagged a scolding finger at an imaginary Thalheim. "Vee must prepare for zee invasion."

"Which will never come," Emma whispered to Mémé, who swayed at her elbow in the queue.

Mémé snapped her teeth. "Shoot."

"Shoot who, dear one?"

"Thalheim."

Emma hid a smile. "Let's not say so in public, all right?"

Mémé did not reply. She was frowning at her fingers, tangling them together as if they were tied in a knot.

With the tree guards reassigned, the next morning a new *V* appeared—above the reach of any ladder, extending into two branches like an embrace of the whole churchyard.

Everyone agreed that Monkey Boy was not only the sole person capable of such acrobatics, but he was also the least likely to perform them. People saw him wandering the meadows, one arm raised as he called to a passing crow. They saw him on a bench in the village green, sulking like a toddler because his mother had forced him to wash his filthy face. No, someone else was being clever at the occupying army's expense. The villagers' speculations made a low buzz, like a hive in a tree branch.

At last it rained, an all-day seaside downpour that washed the bloodstain away. All that remained was a splintered area where the bullet had lodged after shattering Uncle Ezra's head.

Yet Captain Thalheim could not resist one last blow against the rebellion. After the storm passed he dispatched a corporal, a strapping blond with strong arms and a square jaw who brought with him a long-toothed chain saw. The Monsignor monitored the proceedings from the rectory, his cottage across the lane from the church. When the engine snarled to life, the priest marched across the churchyard, one arm raised with the finger pointing at heaven—a sight that would have cowed the stoutest villager. But his shouting about God's house and the sanctity of church property was inaudible as the corporal revved the chain saw and approached the tree. The soldier never acknowledged him. The blade took its first bite, bark chips flew, and the Monsignor flinched.

The machine howled while sawing and grumbled while idling as the soldier cut a wedge from one side of the poplar, sliced another from the opposite side, and the tree dropped unceremoniously onto the churchyard grass. By then the priest had repaired to the rectory, where he scowled behind a half-closed door. As efficient as his tool, the soldier methodically reduced the tree to a stump, the stump to a flat knot on the ground, so low one could stub a toe on it. The poplar had required perhaps fifty years to attain its height, but the soldier's job took no more than twenty minutes.

When the muscular corporal shut off the motor, he paused to sit on the downed trunk and smoke a cigarette—few things expressing leisure and indifference more visibly than the expert making of smoke rings—then hoisted the chain saw on his shoulder like a gun and marched back to his unit. He left the fallen limbs and greens behind like litter. Watching him go, the priest lifted the rosary around his neck, kissed the crucifix, and closed the rectory door.

In those days the villagers let nothing go to waste. Poplar, though a poor burning wood, had other uses, lumber and such. People soon came and hauled everything away.

That evening the veterinarian's beautiful daughter, Fleur, knocked on the door in Emma's barnyard wall, then retreated a few steps. "Is anyone at home?" she piped.

Emma set aside her chore of the moment and crossed the yard to open the door. Leaning against the bricks was a cross section of the poplar, a circular slice from the tree. "What's this?"

But Fleur only curtsied, stuffed her hands into her apron pockets as ever, and trotted away up the lane. Emma examined the slab of wood. From that day forward she used that board for her kneading and rolling, and none other would do.

Still Captain Thalheim did not have the last word. One day later, all of the churchyard's remaining poplars bore *V*s in the upper branches. So did four ancient oaks that arched over the village green. It was like a story, told in hieroglyphics. Seven days after Uncle Ezra's death, trees all over town wore tattoos of defiance. No one knew who was responsible. Years later, people who survived those times debated with fervor who had done the carving.

Emma had her suspicions, but found them contradicted a few afternoons later when she spotted Monkey Boy, high in the special sycamore on the edge of the bluff by the sea. He was giggling like a three-year-old while his political self-expression arced out of the high branches in a long golden stream.

Chapter 6

Despite the *Vs,* Uncle Ezra's execution caused Emma to weep daily in the arms of Philippe. While others tried to comfort or distract her, he attempted nothing of the kind.

"Terrible," he said as she bawled against his chest. "It is a crime."

Emma was a messy crier, nose running and eyes red, yet he seemed not to care. Philippe came to the house, asked Marcel if his daughter would like to take a walk, brought her somewhere private, put his arms around her. And she would gush.

Philippe spoke softly, telling her it was a huge loss. Unlike her father, Mémé, and the Monsignor, not for one sentence did Philippe attempt to beguile her out of grief. "An enormous wrong has been done," he said, tucking her head under his chin.

Sometimes Emma slid her hands inside the back of his shirt, skin touching skin. Sometimes when she was done weeping, Emma lifted her face to be kissed.

In another day, these touches may have flowered into intimacy. Infatuation might have grown into mature love. Instead, in October, the occupying army uprooted Philippe, ordering him to present himself for conscription. He would report in five days, then work in a factory making weapons that the mustached fanatic needed for his hordes.

"You cannot go," Emma said, clinging to his arm the night before he was to depart. "It will kill me."

"You know the accord as well as I do." For once he was turned away from her, standing sideways. "Every three of us who work earn the liberation of one man in a camp. Plus I have been ordered." He leaned closer to take a deep breath, inhaling the scent of her hair. "There is no choice."

Come next morning, Philippe stood in the chilly rail yard with others his age and older, brothers and uncles, fathers and cousins. Albin and David, the former bakery apprentices, milled around as if they were tourists needing directions. Even Émile, the aged village registrar, joined the crowd as ordered, and he a trembling twig of a man who had spent his lifetime sitting at a counter in the town offices where he stamped papers, filed birth notices, and certified that marriage licenses were filled out properly, dandruff flaking all the while from his thick white hair.

The conscriptees' faces were as stoical as stone. A soldier with a clipboard called names, mispronouncing them so horribly, under other circumstances it would have been comical. Regardless, people recognized which name was theirs. They left their suitcases and valises where instructed, and formed a silent line beside the huge black locomotive.

The soldier with the clipboard studied Émile, grabbing one of his hands for inspection before waving him away as unsuitable. The old man tottered away without looking back.

All that time Emma hid behind a pillar, trying not to weep in public, and failing. Before they parted the previous night, she had permitted Philippe all sorts of liberties, enough to stoke their imaginations and warm their memories till they could see one another again. When the train sounded its shrill whistle and strained away, she felt as though her heart were being ripped from her body.

The locomotive left a cloud of diesel exhaust that offended her mouth for the rest of the day. It tasted of longing.

There was no address to which she might write. Nor were there letters home. The village saw new posters, though, hung on seemingly every blank wall. DADDY IS WELL, the blond mother in one of them told her blond toddler. HE MAKES GOOD WAGES IN THE FATHERLAND'S FACTORIES.

Another, with an army marching in neat rows: ABANDONED CITIZENS, TRUST IN THE PROTECTORS OF JUSTICE AND ORDER.

Still another contained an idea so offensive and perplexing, Emma did not understand—nor would her father, Marcel, consent to explain—with cartoons of bespectacled men, fat and effeminate and wearing the British flag for neckties, while all over them crawled rats with long noses and twisted whiskers on whose side was written the word "Jew."

The losses did not end with her teacher and her lover. A week after Philippe departed, four soldiers appeared in the barnyard, demanding to see Marcel. Emma called to her father, who emerged from the house drying his hands on a dish towel.

"How may I be of assistance, gentlemen?" he asked.

The lead soldier struck him backhanded, knocking him to the ground. Emma rushed forward but Marcel waved her away, and stood by his own power. Then, while he twisted the towel on itself, three of the soldiers ran into the barn, knocking and kicking things.

Her father did not look injured, but Emma had never seen him nervous before. The last time she had seen his face wear that morning's expression, he'd had a stomach illness that made him vomit for two days. Noises continued from inside the barn, and Emma had an inkling.

As calm as a pond, she turned to the officer. "May I request your name please, sir?"

"How dare you to ask?" he replied, gargling her language.

"If your men spoil my dough for the Kommandant's bread, he will surely ask me who was responsible."

The officer deliberated a moment, then yelled to his soldiers. He was interrupted, however, as two men burst out the barn's side door, cantering into the field across the road.

Emma knew those men, farmers from the outskirts of the village. Ordered to report for conscription, they had obviously disobeyed. Far from being reckless or rebellious, such a decision was understandable: in their absence the crops would wither, their families starve, their fields turn to weeds.

The soldiers spilled out of the barn's chicken-coop entry. The officer said a few words, after which one soldier dropped to a knee. Raising a rifle to his shoulder, he brought his cheek to the stock with the familiarity of a violinist tucking his instrument under his chin. The farmers gamboled and dodged, the distance shrinking between them and the field's far hedgerow. Emma found herself unable to look away as the soldier became perfectly still. He breathed out, squeezed the trigger, and one of the farmers fell. Settling himself, he took another deep breath, released it, fired his gun, and the second man dropped.

The officer said a word of praise to the marksman. The other two dragged Emma's father away.

By midafternoon, the Monsignor had come twice with his wheelbarrow, removing the farmers one at a time. The first funeral would take place the next morning after seven thirty Mass, the body wrapped and at the front and center of St. Agnes by the Sea, the second funeral identically and immediately following.

That evening, two more soldiers pushed open the door of the house without knocking. They stood at attention under the lintel, guns ready. Emma sat on the couch holding Mémé, who rocked forward and backward and kept asking what day it was.

"Tuesday," Emma told her grandmother. "It's Tuesday, Mémé."

"Yes, but what day is it today?"

Captain Thalheim entered and wrinkled his nose as if the room had a smell. Emma recognized him, despite the helmet pulled low over his eyes.

"There is no man in this house now," he announced. "There should be a man here, for your safety and security."

Emma held Mémé and did not reply.

Thalheim snapped at the soldiers. They began rummaging through the house, poking their rifles under cushions and into drawers.

Mémé stood, inching toward the captain and wringing her hands. "What day is it? What day?"

The soldiers barged past her without a word, pounding up the stairs with the captain following at a measured pace. A moment later they were back in the parlor.

"I will take the room with the southern window," the captain said in Emma's language. "It has superior light."

"But that is where Mémé sleeps," she told the floor.

"It will do nicely." He turned to his men. "Bring my things."

That night Mémé slept on the couch, as confused as a fresh-shorn lamb, while Emma lay close on the rug. The next morning's baking was marred by a banging from the house. Leaving her kneading board to peer out the barn door, Emma saw Thalheim on a chair, hammering a two-meter pole into a bracket against the house. From that pole, in red and white with a black icon that resembled a man running, hung the occupying army's flag.

Her stomach turned, and she stumbled back to work. She missed the stability of her father. She missed the patience of Philippe. There were no flags for these allegiances.

Soon the captain began performing what he called inspections but she considered interruptions. He would sidle across the barnyard to smoke a cigarette, stand in the baking shed doorway, and complain. "Are the peoples of this village truly the dullest on earth? I've seen more of spirit in mules. And how can you be standing the heat of that oven? It is a vexation."

Emma did not answer, but not out of fear or respect. Through self-possession, she was denying him whatever it was he wanted. She considered silence an eloquent form of rebellion.

Thalheim spoke her language like a mathematics textbook. But his eyes never stopped surveying the barn's dusty interior, as if he expected to find a cannon hidden among the hay bales, a tank concealed in the chicken coop. Eventually he would tire of his own voice, climb on his motorcycle, and rattle away.

With a soldier in the house, making extra loaves required twice the cleverness. Soon, however, Emma discovered that she could tell from the barn when he had wakened because he was both noisy and vain. He shaved each morning with as much care as if he were performing surgery. He kept his fingernails pared and curved, leaving the cuttings for Emma to clean. He thought nothing of standing at the mirror for full minutes, adjusting his helmet to the perfect angle. These doings gave her time to hide whatever needed hiding.

Emma's extra flour ration was snow white and fine, in contrast with the half-ground brown that ordinary folk had to accept. Bread became her clock, her rhythm, her means of survival. Like Scheherazade pleasing the Sultan with a new tale every night, each batch of loaves purchased Emma another day, another round of the village, two baguettes to share among the starving.

Before the occupation Emma had worn her thick locks loose, graced by a green ribbon. Philippe had loved her hair, loved loosening that ribbon. One thing she admired about him was that he played no games about love. Her role was to remain coy, and safeguard the virtue of them both. Philippe trusted her with that power, because it allowed him to make no pretense of concealing his desire.

The occupation, however, had taught Emma that wanting was dangerous. She had only to consider what had happened to Michelle. At one time she had been the village beauty, the person against whose allure adolescent Emma had most often compared herself, and always found herself wanting. Michelle had skin both smooth and radiant, hair so blond it shone white in summer. Her bosom matured early and generously, her lips were as full as fruit. As she grew up, first boys made fools of themselves around her, then teens did, then grown men. She became the village's schoolmistress, expert in grammar, arithmetic, and deflecting the attentions of her students' fathers.

Then Michelle took up with a junior officer in the occupying army, one Lieutenant Planeg, handsome like a gelding with icy blue eyes. Sometimes after maneuvers he directed his truck to stop by the schoolhouse, children's faces at the windows, soldiers in the truck razzing while he stole a kiss before driving on to the garrison. That summer, when the troops took Sundays to swim in the sea, Planeg's motorcycle could dependably be found standing outside Michelle's cottage at the top of the knoll.

Now the villagers turned their backs on her in the rations line. Some spat on the ground as she passed. Only the priest would speak with her publicly. The working men, Philippe told Emma during an evening stroll, called her "concubine." People worried about when school recommenced in the fall. Would parents allow their children to attend? For Emma, no comparison with Michelle would be necessary again.

Most soldiers were far less gentlemanly than Planeg, Emma knew that, too. There were rumors that a trio of them had forced several women who had been foolish enough to walk alone at night. Whatever the gossip, the women's bruises were genuine, though that could have been the result of interrogation, or as little as a passing soldier's bad mood. If anyone was going to ask those women what had been done to them, it would not be Emma.

Whatever the truth, rather than anticipating the loss of her maidenhood to Philippe, as Emma had imagined before the occupation, now she expected to die in the act. In wartime, beauty is a weakness. Be it by one soldier or many, sooner or later an attractive girl of twenty-two will be ground like straw.

Therefore Emma braided her hair in knots, and no longer washed her face in the morning. Yet somehow hunger had made her all the more arresting. Mémé said as much, and so often that the girl determined never to look in a mirror. She wore her grandmother's skirts like curtains around her waist, careful to offer nothing to a soldier's suggestible imagination.

How suggestible? Consider the Kommandant. Once he had tasted her bread and pronounced his love for it, not even straw would alter his devotion. And yet, despite her contempt for him, never had Emma wished to please a man more. As long as he and his officers feasted on pope's noses, it enabled her to divert crumbs to her neighbors, thereby extending the string of life in that village one day longer. Thus she made the bread as fastidiously, as expertly, as possible. Emma had found a form of concubinage after all, mastering the art of satisfying a man while deceiving him.

When she was found out—and Emma never doubted that eventually she would be found out—the only question was what her punishment would be.

Chapter 7

E*veryone had jumped* when Captain Thalheim pulled the trigger on Uncle Ezra, but pistol fire was not unfamiliar. Before the occupation, no one would dispute it, the best shot in Vergers—and the surrounding towns as well—had been Guillaume the veterinarian. First, he was about at all hours, finding the shortest distance between a farm where he'd been treating an animal and his home, where Marie and Fleur slept. The countryside had rough hedgerows, however: a maze of brambles, webs of branches and roots, a fierce natural fence that lengthened any journey and made visiting a sick cow, or a piglet that refused to nurse, no casual jaunt. Within these tangles, trees stood dark like a sultan's guardians—huge, mute eunuchs.

Clever villagers knew a few shortcuts, openings a farmer had cut for horse, wagon, or plow, just wide enough to give a person access to his own fields. Later Emma learned all of the openings, but until then Guillaume was the master, and it showed most in his marksmanship. He might cross a horse turnout at dusk and surprise a buck at his watering place, or skirt the edge of a wheat field at dawn and flush a covey of doves. Whether he was on foot or astride his dependable blue bicycle, out would come his swift pistol, the aim of his sure hand, the focus of his sharp eye, and the man would arrive home with breakfast or supper or a month's good meat. He had no rival.

Second, his gun was an instrument of mercy. A dog might be dragging its hindquarters, a horse limping on a fractured leg, a cow shaking its head over and over in the confusion of skull worms, and the farmer would send for Guillaume. Promptly he would arrive with his pistol and do the work of God.

At the insistence of his wife, Marie, Guillaume had hired an apprentice: Étienne DuFour. He was a pale, sniveling weasel, weak in every way that the veterinarian was strong. DuFour's job was to maintain the doctor's apothecary, carry salves and bandages, and sometimes sit the night with laboring cows or colicky horses. People wondered why the veterinarian had hired such an insubstantial man, until one day Emma asked him directly.

"Why are you wasting your breath and time on that fool?"

Guillaume was angling a claw hook into a horse's hoof, digging out a twisted nail. It was farrier's work but the farrier was itinerant and would not arrive for a fortnight. Guillaume chuckled, resting the hook on his thigh. "Marie believes I can help him," he answered. "The man tries my patience. But she says I am capable of healing more than animals."

Then came a week the veterinarian spent away from town. He had offered no explanation, nor warned anyone, nor arranged for anyone to serve in his stead. People knew that his blue bicycle was gone, nothing more. Marie volunteered no information, and beautiful Fleur was too young to be asked.

In the week's middle, Neptune, one of Pierre's immense draft horses, caught herself in a hedgerow. He had left the corral gate open in a moment of absentmindedness, and she wandered off into a tangle. Trying to turn in the narrow space under the hedges, she snagged her hoof in some roots, and in yanking on it had managed to wedge herself deeper.

That would have been a surmountable problem, requiring a few minutes' patience by Pierre as he sweet-talked in her ear and used a rope to work her powerful leg free. For all her size and power, Neptune was a compliant beast. But on that day a thunderstorm blew up from out to sea, swift across the fields till lightning struck close to the hedgerow, and the giant horse panicked. In the attempt to bolt, she managed to break her shin.

When Neptune did not return during the storm, Pierre pulled on his oilskin and went searching. The rain had ended by the time he found her, standing sideways across the path. He knew what the injury was without touching her. He pressed his head to her flank, weeping for a minute, then calming, then ever so gently, as if he were helping a baby to be born, easing her injured hoof free. Much as he hated to abandon Neptune in her pain even for a moment, he strode off, faster than his old man's balance truly allowed, till he found a boy at a neighbor's farm, and with a penny for his labor, sent him to fetch Guillaume.

DuFour arrived instead, nose running, shoes and pant legs wet from hurrying through drenched fields. In one hand he held an umbrella, half of its ribs inverted. In the other he carried a satchel of bandages and salves.

"This animal needs no ointment," Pierre lamented. "You must end her misery."

The farmer tried to lead his horse from the path into the open. Neptune gimped and squealed, tossing her head until he relented.

"Perhaps I can heal her," DuFour told Pierre.

"Perhaps I can fly like a crow," the old man responded. "She has a broken leg. Do what you must, I prefer not to watch."

Pierre hobbled back toward his house, bent with grief. It was a slow and quiet walk across two wheat fields, which gave him time to think about his other draft horse. Apollo and Neptune had pulled beside one another, cutter and tedder and plow, for fifteen years. As Pierre's strength had dwindled over time, and the land he farmed therefore diminished, those two animals made his life possible. He had not needed to steer them at the plow in years, for example. They knew when to turn and how to follow the previous row.

But one horse? Worthless. Apollo would eat and require medicine, he would wallow and sicken and resist, the whole time missing his work twin, imbalanced as if a leg had been amputated, not trained to work by himself, not strong enough to pull alone. And in wartime the odds of finding, much less affording, a partner horse were as low as a repeat of the miracle of fishes and loaves.

There was, too, the inescapable reality of age. That winter Pierre had been unable to draw the wood-splitting ax higher than his shoulder. It was as clear a signal as the bell ringing in the spire of St. Agnes by the Sea: he simply did not possess enough remaining life to train a new animal. Neptune's mishap aside, a draft horse typically lived beyond twenty years. The farmer knew he himself would be lucky to survive another five, and that was without considering the effects of the occupation, which were unlikely to lengthen the count of anyone's days.

Pierre approached the barnyard across from his tiny stone house. Sorrow over Neptune pierced him. He imagined an identical pain would afflict Apollo once he came to understand what had happened—and do not tell a farmer that animals do not comprehend death; they know it as fully as any human, and often mourn with greater dignity.

Now Apollo stood before him, a deep-breathing giant. The horse scratched his flank on the fence, which leaned from his weight, then he ambled nearer to be petted.

"Funny thing, Neptune getting in this scrape," Pierre told him, scratching along the horse's mane, under his massive jaw. "You were always the one who wandered."

The last of the thunder rumbled from the east, and an idea came to him. The very notion gave him a sense of relief. Biting down on his pipe, Pierre slipped the loop of rope off a fence post and opened the gate. And that was that. He turned away, leaving the gate wide.

At first the enormous animal did not move. Pierre took his sadness and shuffled into the house, closing the door quietly. That way he would not hear the pistol shot for Neptune. What an admission for a man, to acknowledge that his days of horses are done. His mother, rest her soul, had often made a point of telling people that he had learned to walk by holding a mare's tail for balance. Now, at long last, the time had come to let that tail go.

Apollo ventured two steps out of the corral, turning his huge head to survey in all directions, before crossing the dooryard to a temptation he had desired countless times from inside the fence: Pierre's herb garden, which flourished behind a circle of small rocks. Rosemary, lavender, thyme, all sweeter than ordinary grass. Bending his long neck, and with dainty bites, Apollo began to eat.

Back in the hedgerow, DuFour could not bring himself to finish the animal. It was like felling a tree: in which direction would Neptune tip? Probably into the path, blocking the way. And what was he to do with the carcass? He had no idea. Taking out the pistol, he opened it and loaded the chambers. Then, reasoning that he would only need one round, he unloaded it completely. Over the hours he repeated these actions several times while rain dripped from the leaves and a pair of finches chased one another down the path. The horse whimpered and shook. DuFour marched off, stopping a few hundred steps away before returning to stand beside Neptune. She had closed her eyes, holding her broken leg bent at the knee.

As the sun set, still DuFour had not acted. When night fell and no one could see, he took his broken umbrella and went home, returning at dawn to find the horse still there, of course, still suffering, of course. Traffic along that hedgerow was nil, such that no one came along to share DuFour's hesitation, to commiserate, to buck up his courage or help him do the job.

Neptune had drawn within herself, silent and unmoving, as fixed as a commandment, and DuFour began to hate the horse for its predicament. The torment continued for two full days, the veterinarian's assistant keeping vigil without taking action, until the blue bicycle returned.

"Where have you been?" DuFour demanded as the veterinarian pedaled up the lane. "It has been an agony here."

"Did I not leave you with my gun?" he replied.

"Here it is, the vile thing." DuFour held out the pistol. "I did not know what to do. You told me not to treat anything."

Guillaume ran his gaze along the horse, her lowered head, the broken leg now drawn high against her haunch. He murmured to Neptune, then turned to speak through clenched teeth. "You are no longer my apprentice."

He took the satchel of medicines away from DuFour's feet, finding a round and loading the gun. "Your empathy for a creature in pain should have overcome my orders."

"I did what you told me. I did what you said."

"Neptune," Guillaume called loudly, the huge horse lifting her head out of a fog of pain. "I am sorry you suffered so long."

He pressed the pistol to the horse's ear and fired. She collapsed knees-first, then fell on her side with a sigh. DuFour stood there, not making a sound.

"You are in exile from me," Guillaume said, pressing two fingers under Neptune's jaw to confirm that there was no pulse. "Never come near me, never speak to me." He stood to his full height. "You have one last task, though. Go fetch Odette, and tell her to bring butchering tools. We shall all have meat tonight."

Chapter 8

Within a month of Neptune's death, old Émile, the town clerk who had avoided conscription at the last moment, died in his sleep from heart failure. Immediately DuFour took his place. His title was assistant to the acting mayor, himself a puppet from another town installed at the Kommandant's direction. Now all papers passed through DuFour's hands, all requests landed on his desk.

At first people considered this change an improvement, because Émile—might he rest in peace, but truth be told—was afflicted with savagely bad breath, as though he breakfasted on rotted garlic, and wore black coats whose shoulders were always distractingly snowed with dandruff. Also Émile moved at the pace of a snail, laboring out of his chair with a sigh, bending over a filing cabinet with one hand at the small of his back, and maintaining a pace such that a job which required at most three hours' work would instead occupy the entire day.

By contrast, DuFour was as sharp as a map pin. Stamping forms and filing papers, after each transaction he rang a little bell. His efficiency compensated for his lack of charm.

Soon enough, however, the people of Vergers realized that DuFour was the worst sort of person to install in this position, because it gave him power. A request for increased rations because a child had been born, an application for permission to travel, formalization of a marriage license—everything passed within his bureaucratic jurisdiction. He was the waist of the hourglass, the throat of the bottle, and one thumb could stop the entire flow. After Mass one Sunday, Marguerite the tobacconist remarked that not even Saint Peter in heaven made so stinting a gatekeeper.

But there were consequences. A rations paper delayed meant hunger for a child, a travel form ignored thwarted the opportunity to visit an ailing relative before death arrived, and DuFour calculated with expert accuracy the villagers' desperation for such things. He extorted shamelessly, scorned personal appeals, proved impervious to pleas for mercy or haste.

One Monday morning when he arrived at work, Odette stood at his office door, wanting compensation for damage three drunken soldiers had done to her café on Saturday night.

"Wait," he said with a sneer of superiority, turning to fumble with keys and unlocking his office door with a flourish. As Odette followed him through the open door, DuFour stopped in her path. "Wait."

She paced in the hall, though there was no one ahead of her, while he pulled the door nearly closed. After some minutes passed, she peered through the opening. DuFour stood over the piles of paper on his desk, moving this stack here and that one there, then rubbing his hands together as if warming himself by a fire. More documents cluttered the windowsill.

"You worm," she cried, throwing the door wide so that it banged against the wall cabinet. "These drunken oafs broke five of my chairs. Who the hell made you prince? I knew you before you wore trousers."

DuFour drew himself up with a haughty sniff. "The compensation solicitation form," he drawled, offering a long sheet of paper. "Complete it in triplicate and it will be processed in due course."

"I see how it is." Odette nodded. "Each of these pages is a little game for you, isn't it?"

"The mayor and his advisers are pleased with my work."

"So I fill out your form, and you take your sweet time processing it."

He tented the fingertips of one hand on the fingertips of the other. "Naturally we give priority to the most urgent requests."

"Naturally." Odette tugged down on her shirt, by which she intended to convey a businesslike air, but which also inadvertently emphasized her large bosom. She leaned forward, palms atop all of his collected papers.

"Careful," he warned. "These are my responsibilities."

She lowered her voice to the range of a man's. "Here is an invitation, you crawling beetle. Come to my café sometime, if you please. I will give you fine food and strong drink, free of charge, on the house. And when you are most at ease, full, drunk, most smug in your little power, I will plunge a knife into your neck."

As she left the town hall, Odette passed Guillaume bicycling homeward, probably from some all-night vigil with a stricken animal. He studied her expression, then stopped, calling out to her, "What on earth are you so happy about?"

Chapter 9

O*dette was not alone* in having wants. In fact Emma began to suspect that the single animating energy of Vergers was want.

The spiral of desire included every villager—but the origin, the starting place, was Emma herself, who, on the anniversary of Philippe's conscription date, found herself missing him so desperately she struggled to breathe, she could not sit still.

It was October, normally an interval of backbreaking labor as each farm brought in its harvest, but that year a quieter time for the villagers, and one of melancholy. With the beach forbidden by the occupying army, Emma could not visit the places she and Philippe had whispered and kissed. Because of an officers' tent, she could not sit on the bluff where he had held her while she wept over Uncle Ezra. Due to mine placements, she could not hide in the gulch where on his last night she had allowed him parting favors—his hands on her skin, her softness at his touch a discovery only the two of them knew—that recurred so often in her daydreams.

As if she were the most confident woman who ever lived, that night Emma had opened the upper buttons of her dress to display herself for him. Philippe's eyes bulged, but then he surprised them both by leaning forward and kissing her breasts. Her head swam with pleasure and surrender, and the ocean crashed at their feet. The memory still made her blush, though in the many months since then, the thrill in her heart had been replaced entirely by longing.

On that particular anniversary of remembrance and desire, Emma was meandering by the harbor, a stork soaring past without one flap of its wings, her yearning broadcasted like a beacon across the landscape, because when it comes to the ache of love, few places are superior to the seaside in October. Yves the fisherman trotted down the dock in her direction. In no mood for conversation, she began to move away, but he called out.

"Emmanuelle, one moment please."

Everyone knew that Yves had the best singing voice in the village. Early risers heard his shanties as he set out in the gray dawn. Afternoon strollers eavesdropped on his humming while he repaired his nets. Odette confessed to entertaining unreligious thoughts when he rang the rafters during hymns at St. Agnes by the Sea. Thus his call from the docks was musical enough to hold Emma in place. He hiked up his foul-weather overalls and hurried down the gangplank to where she stood.

"How may I help you?" Emma asked, more out of manners than desire to assist.

"Well, that's it, you see." His cheeks were raw from the sea, his hands thick and callused. "Help is exactly what I need."

Emma could not imagine how she could possibly aid a man such as this, his life rough and hardened. But after a glance over his shoulder, Yves continued.

"Each day now the soldiers are waiting when we come in, to confiscate our catch. They leave us only enough to live for another day, so we can continue to supply them." Yves leaned closer. His forearms were huge. Somehow he managed to have no smell of fish on him, only rubber and faint motor oil. "If I had a bit more fuel, I could try a second haul later in the day, keeping all of the catch for our village. Every fin and gill."

"How am I to help?" Emma asked, crossing her arms. "I have no fuel."

"No." Yves smiled. His teeth were bright and straight, a rarity in a town whose dentist had been conscripted with the others. "But you are friends with Pierre, the dairyman. He receives a ration for his tractor, though I have not heard it running in years. Also I passed by there the other day. He is down to three cows, so the crop work must be minimal." Yves spied down the docks again before leaning closer still. "If he could spare a jug or two, it would mean cod for him, haddock for you, bream for the rest of us. On a good day, anyway."

Emma heard her stomach growl. She knew an excellent recipe for tarragon cod. She also knew that Pierre had a fuel tank behind one of his barns, though she had never considered how much it held. "What do you want me to do?"

A soldier swaggered down the dock, rifle at his hip. "What's the delay?" he snapped. "Leave your sweetheart and we finish the counting."

"Right away." Yves stepped back. "Bring fuel, Emmanuelle," he whispered. "If I can fish, we can eat."

The next morning Emma visited Pierre as he milked Antoinette, perched on his stool and all the while chewing on the mouthpiece of his pipe. Mémé sat on a huge rock in his dooryard, picking at the lichen that yellowed its northern side. Emma waited to ask—the yoke for draft horses wearing a cobweb, the ladder to the loft on its side like a man on vacation, the sack of chicken feed dusty from lack of use—until Pierre's bucket was sufficiently filled that it no longer rang with each squeeze, but made a satisfying frothy thrum. Fuel? Why, yes, mademoiselle, his tank was nearly one quarter filled.

"It is my bank account," Pierre explained. "My savings, in case times become more difficult before our rescuers come. The army gives me a tiny ration, mere drops, but over time it accumulates. Just like milk does, from a good girl." He caressed the flanks of Antoinette, who flicked a fly from her ear with an expression as if she had winked. "However."

Emma waited, rubbing the cow's long nose. One quarter of a tank would not catch many fish. "Yes?"

"I might consider trading a portion, for a pouch of tobacco." He paused his milking to frown into the bowl of his pipe. "You've no idea how I long for a decent smoke. It aches all the time, like a sore tooth."

Next Emma sat in the parlor of Marguerite the tobacconist, her store long closed for lack of inventory. She nodded her aged head, confiding in Emma that she had heard rumors about a smuggling operation in Cherbourg. British tobacco, in small leather pouches to prevent mold. Strong, peaty stuff. Marguerite was an obedient citizen, though, whose law-abiding ways extended to include the whims of the occupying army.

She sighed and smiled, displaying the gaps in her grin, tobacco stains on the remaining teeth. At age seventy-seven, she explained, her eyes were beginning to fail. It was to be expected, it was to be endured. However.

Her need was for a combination of light and faith. Marguerite could not last the long week between the Monsignor's Sunday sermons. She needed her daily verses. But a candle flame was no longer sufficient for reading the Bible after supper. Could Emma somehow, miraculously, find her a lightbulb?

It was a circle of want. Emma pondered on these things as she wandered the village and missed her Philippe. Like a sad song, walking sharpened her sorrow, yet soothed it as well.

During her travels Emma came to notice that no one was wearing yellow stars anymore, and not because the occupying army had relaxed any regulations. The grocer, the rail-yard worker, two of Yves's fellow fishermen, they were all gone.

She saw Monkey Boy, though, ambling along the hedgerows and whistling his little tune. She saw the draft horse Apollo, a huge-hooved giant wandering the world in search of Neptune, his partner under Pierre's yoke for fifteen years, exerting identical power, at the identical pace.

Apollo stood observing at the edge of a ditch while five soldiers of the occupying army shoveled under a sixth one's supervision, and Emma thought the horse did not look well: large-eyed, his ribs showing, his slow breathing as he took it all in. She came up and patted his giant flank, saying, "I know exactly how you feel."

Later that day Emma passed a field above the sea, where barbed wire coiled not only along the top of the bluff, but in a long arc out to the dirt road. A soldier was nailing a sign to a thin post, then using the side of his hammer to pound the post into the clay. The sign bore a skull and crossbones, and a single word which provided as complete a declaration as any literate person would require: MINEN. There were four more signs, identical, in an arc around the field.

No one had fuel. No one had tobacco. No one had lightbulbs. The occupying army had taken everything of value—including this land along the sea, with its lovely view of the beaches, now appropriated for minefields. There was no denying it: all of her neighbors' desires were impossible.

Yet somehow Yves had opened a floodgate, like the locks at Honfleur which kept harbor boats afloat under full moons, when the tide could drop fifteen meters overnight. Everyone lacked something; everyone asked Emma for help. This person needed soap, that one shoes, this one medicine, that one a pane of glass.

There were a few exceptions. First, DuFour, whom no one trusted, and who knew it, and who therefore did not dare make a request of any kind. Second, the priest, who announced that he would offer the holy sacrifice of the Mass regardless of who partook of the blessed sacrament, and thus did not ally himself with either faction.

Amid all of this activity—a request for razor blades awaiting Emma at the eastern well, another for skin salve as she followed the hedgerows—she spent her days mentally kneading a single question: Why, of all people, were they asking her?

The question followed her everywhere, even as she made her weekly trek to the village laundry: a metal shed roof over a marble pool, each side long enough for three women kneeling hip by hip to scrub at a time, water supplied by a hand pump at one end, drying racks and clotheslines at the other. As a place for the women of Vergers to gather, the laundry placed second only to the weekly market. But Emma deliberately came at an hour when she could expect to be alone. Afternoon light angled through the trees, dappling the dense hedgerow to the west.

It was here that Philippe had ventured one noontime when Emma was sixteen, lurking in the bushes while she and the other women scrubbed for their families. He and Emma had been glancing and flirting for so long, she was as aware of his presence as if he had been playing a tuba. Perhaps the women perceived as much, those mothers and aunts and grandmothers, because they finished all at once, as if by some shared understanding. Once they'd departed with their clean loads, Philippe sashayed into the open, stepping on the marble rim of the washing pool and balancing along its edge. Soap had made it slippery, of course. He was halfway across, Emma studiously ignoring him while watching every move, when his foot slipped, his arms windmilled, and her suitor fell face-first, flat into the shallow pool. For a long moment he did not move. Was he hurt? Emma jumped to her feet, tossing aside the shirt she'd been washing, not wanting to get wet, not sure how to help, when Philippe burst upward, shook himself like a dog, took two bold strides across the basin, and kissed her on the mouth.

Six years had passed since that day. Philippe was far away, no one knew where, and the occupying army had encamped in the village for the rest of time. Kisses were for dreamers, and people with too little work to do. Emma dumped her basket of clothing unceremoniously into the water. Romantic memories were an indulgence she could not afford.

Washing had become a frustrating chore, too, because of the scarcity of soap. Emma's clothes did not accommodate this deprivation, her blouses nonetheless growing dusty with flour, her skirts accumulating dirt as usual. Meanwhile Mémé managed to soil every garment within minutes of donning it, spilling from spoons and sloshing her mug. Emma decided to provide her grandmother with one set of clothes per day, and if she made a mess at breakfast, the old woman would have to spend the day in unclean wear. Otherwise the washing would be constant.

Emma caressed the garments back and forth in the water to help the stains soften. Was every act some version of kneading? For a person commanded to make bread, it might seem so, just as a policeman over the years begins to see all of his neighbors as suspects, a physician notices strangers' symptoms, a farmer measures a place by the quality of its soil, a merchant is concerned with nothing before an item's price, and a person living under military occupation seeks perpetually to be free.

"Pardon me, mademoiselle."

Emma jumped in surprise.

"I am sorry, I did not mean to startle you." It was Michelle, the woman carrying on with Lieutenant Planeg. Once she and Emma had been rivals in beauty, but there was no comparison anymore. Emma struggled merely to stay clean, while Michelle's hair was lustrous and blond. She wore a snug chemise with two buttons open at the top, as if she had forgotten to finish dressing herself, or was inviting someone to help complete an undressing, and a crimson bloom of a skirt. Her skin was lucent like a pearl.

"Mademoiselle." Emma gestured at the washing. "Forgive me for not standing."

"On the contrary, forgive me for not kneeling with you. I failed to dress properly for the occasion."

Emma spoke to the water. "You look lovely, as ever."

"It is all illusion."

Emma raised her eyes. "I think not."

Michelle took a long breath, in and out. "Whatever you may have heard, whatever you believe, I am here to ask your help."

"A common request lately, although I am ill equipped to help anyone."

"You have managed to gain the favor of the occupiers without compromising your honor. That is an achievement."

What sort of an admission was Michelle making? Emma wondered while the young woman continued. "You have fed your family. You have kept your household intact. You have done these things without the aid of a man."

"I would rather have relied upon my father and Philippe."

"I would prefer that for you, too, friend."

Emma pondered that sentence a moment. Had they ever been friends? In school, or since? She could not remember.

"I know I do not look it," Michelle said. "But I am starving."

"You are right. You appear to be very well."

"Oh, but if you could see—" She reached to unbutton her chemise further.

"No, no." Emma waved her wet hands. "That isn't necessary."

"I am all bones. I have sores on my skin."

"I'm sorry to hear it, Michelle. Of course I have sores, too."

"Yes, but you do not depend upon your skin as a means of survival."

Emma turned and began churning a dress in the water. Michelle was being too familiar. Philippe had always shown Emma's skin such respect. It was part of her, but the lesser part of what he desired. Or so she believed.

Michelle knelt in the dirt after all. "I beg of you."

"What do you want from me? Stand up."

"You have ways of getting things. Everyone knows. Everyone is talking about it."

Emma flipped the dress over and spanked a stain out of it. "I have no such ways."

Michelle wrung her hands. "If only I had some eggs—"

"What?" Emma spun at her. "My Mémé is hungry every day. I might actually grow a bit peckish from time to time myself. If I had eggs, do you think I would give them to a whore?"

Michelle jumped to her feet. "I am no whore. How dare you?"

"You said your own self that you survive by your skin."

"With a man I love. A brilliant lieutenant who is an engineer, who accompanies me to church, who shows me kindness. Something my fellow townspeople cannot manage."

"Because you chose him, of all men. An enemy of our people."

"You have no idea what it was like. Being beautiful was going to be my doom."

Emma scoffed. "I am so full of sympathy it is spilling out of my ears."

"Men were circling my house like dogs who have cornered a rabbit." Michelle had begun to pace, her skirt billowing at each change of direction. "I know what soldiers do. We have all heard the stories. What defenses did I have? I had spent so many years keeping the hounds of our village at bay, all those men with their attentions and appetites, regardless of my honor, regardless of their wives. I could not trust any of them to protect me, not one. But then, my lieutenant—"

She stopped pacing, composed herself, folded her hands as if attending a cotillion. "Lieutenant Planeg behaved decently, a proper courting gentleman. He brought me flowers. He called me lady. On the day I finally allowed him in for tea, all the rest of them went away. The soldiers gave me peace. Besides . . ." She paused, seeming to wipe away a tear with the tip of a pinkie. "Who knows how we choose, Emmanuelle? Do you remember choosing Philippe? Or did you simply accept one day that there was a feeling, so powerful and right, and you could not resist?"

Emma's hands went still in the water and she did not speak.

"I am no strumpet." Michelle adjusted her bodice. "I love this man. I believe he will keep me safe, because our liberators are never going to come."

"On that, I happen to agree with you."

Michelle wiped dust from her dress where she had knelt. "If you can give me eggs, perhaps I can provide you with something in return. The benefit of his protection, perhaps."

Emma drew a blouse up and down the scrubbing board. "I

am already safe, thanks to the Kommandant's infatuation with my bread."

"You see?" Michelle said, softening. "We all make deals to stay alive."

"This conversation is moot." She took up a new dress, plunging it under and back. "I have neither eggs, nor any means of obtaining them. But I do wonder what made you think that I might. Why did you come to me?"

"Because Uncle Ezra helped me."

Emma paused in her work. "He did?"

"Eggs, if he could spare them. Butter. Whenever you made something too botched to sell, he would give it to me. That is how I first bought favor and delay from the soldiers. Lieutenant Planeg in particular loved your éclairs."

"Too botched to sell?"

"He couldn't bear the idea of you being ashamed."

Emma laughed. "Are we talking about the same Uncle Ezra?"

"We will never know his equal." Michelle sidled to the edge of the washing basin. "But with all my heart, I hope that you will come close."

With a bow, she swept away.

Emma sat back on her haunches. Uncle Ezra had been helping people all that time? How had she seen only a gruff disciplinarian, a baker more exacting than a physician? And had he aided the others, too—Yves, Pierre, Marguerite?

It was all too much. In the past she could have discussed a quandary like this with Philippe, depending on his patient listening and quiet practicality. Instead she was utterly alone.

Emma frowned at the chore still ahead of her. Clothes drifted in the shallow pool like so many floating bodies.

Chapter 10

S*ome days, the bread turned out perfectly.* The dough was responsive, the oven consistent, the results superior. Some days, events conspired to help Emma's purposes succeed. That morning she felt the slightest sensation of ease, of generosity.

Perhaps want was not a catastrophe. Perhaps it was foreseeable, a predictable result of necessity, a remembering of when life had been easier.

She stepped out of the baking shed into northern glory: a pale October morning sun, the verdant landscape awaiting harvest, a meek breeze scrubbing the air of all but the fragrance of sea. A bumblebee labored close in curiosity before flying off on his noisy errands.

Emma heard Mémé humming tunelessly in the kitchen. The baguettes were baking, ready in time for the Kommandant's aide. Here was a moment of calm, a pause, and Emma lingered in the barn doorway, indulging in an arched back, a full wingspan stretch. Which was when she heard a horse flutter his thick lips.

There, his neck craned over the door in the barnyard wall, stood Apollo. She felt an impulse to rub his nose, and she surrendered to it. He held still at her touch, calm and gaunt.

"You, too?" she whispered. "You want something, too?"

The enormous animal did not move, except to cup both ears

in her direction. Emma reached to rub Apollo's withers while her eyes inspected his body: the once-powerful legs now drawn with hunger, the visible ribs, the great warmth that remained to him.

"Somehow the world provides for you, doesn't it?"

Apollo remained mute. But he leaned forward, pressing against the door. At Emma's feet there grew a clump of clover, flowering and summer-sweet beside the stone wall, probably the last of the season. The horse stretched his neck toward it, lips smacking, but he could not reach. He tried again, then lifted his head and looked at her with both eyes.

"You are just like all the others," Emma said. "Everyone."

She bent and picked a handful of clover, and held it under the horse's nose. He smelled it, cropped the bouquet with his foreteeth, and chewed thoughtfully. She held the rest on her open palm.

Maybe it was that simple: she helped the hungry, she fed an animal. One creature's weed was another creature's breakfast, and thus could the village be fed.

"All right," she told the horse, bending to pick, then offering him more clover. "All right."

Part Three

CUNNING

Chapter 11

This was how the network began. She let them in, one by one. Drops into a bucket of need, poured out in providing. Every day it grew: a candle here, a sliver of soap there. Each person traded in his or her own currency, had his or her own wants, and Emma bested them all with her method for bread. And her occasional willingness to steal.

Only from those who supported the occupying army, however. And in a manner so expert and patient, afterward it remained in doubt whether a crime had actually occurred.

The first victim was that sniveling DuFour. Emma studied his work habits at the town hall, the lazy pace, the arrogant displaying of keys as he locked and unlocked his office, the long lunches he took at home each day. This in a time when most villagers lived with hunger of one severity or other. She could have emptied his office entirely, files, fixtures, and furniture, in the time he lounged and ate. But that would have brought suspicion, arrest, execution.

Instead she waited for a day on which it rained. After DuFour puttered homeward for lunch, she snuck into his office as quiet as a deer. Rolling his chair to the hallway, she partially unscrewed the overhead lightbulb. The long corridor went dark. She placed the chair precisely where it had been.

DuFour minced back to work, one hand on his belly, smacking his thin lips. When he entered the darkened hallway, he threw the switch and nothing happened. He tried repeatedly, then rolled the chair himself and tightened the bulb. Of course it lit right up.

The next day of foul weather, Emma made sure her rounds passed town hall at noon. She needed less than one minute to loosen the bulb and make a retreat. Later the clerk pondered his dark hallway a moment, before bringing his chair over again.

The third time, he strolled outside, a pantomime of bewilderment as he examined the roof and scratched his pate. Emma sat in the doorway of Uncle Ezra's bakery, not looking behind herself, not dwelling on the boards still covering where soldiers broke the glass. She pretended to repair her boot, a stockinged foot on the step. DuFour glanced at her, his face pinched and wrinkled like a walnut.

"Nothing," he snapped. "Mind your own business."

As he waddled back into town hall, Emma bit the inside of her cheek to suppress a smirk.

It took two more days of rain, five in all, before DuFour flicked the switch, glared up at the dark ceiling fixture, and marched with his many keys off to the locked storage closet. He returned with a fresh bulb. After screwing it into place, he tossed the old one onto the papers in his tall metal wastebin.

The next day, Emma with her own fingertips spiraled that discarded bulb into the lamp beside Marguerite's sewing chair. She wished Philippe were there to share the moment, her little triumph.

But the aging woman had furrowed her brow. "Did you steal this lightbulb?" she asked. "Because if you did . . ."

"It was given to me," Emma reassured her. "Someone didn't need it anymore, and made a gift. My idea was that one generosity might lead to another."

"I had not forgotten." Marguerite opened the drawer in her side table, removing a packet of tobacco that she pressed into Emma's hands. Next she reached for the Bible and switched on the lamp. "Let there be light."

The other invisible crime was one that preyed upon the Monsignor. Emma had not intended to involve him in her barter and trade, but Pierre's fuel supply was limited, and Yves's second daily fishing would burn through it like a young man with his first paycheck. Already sixty people had eaten some of his catch. The villagers depended on Emma. She needed an alternative before a quarter of a tank became none.

The occupying army possessed fuel, but none of it within Emma's reach. Captain Thalheim rode a motorcycle, and the Kommandant's aide used one when he fetched her bread, but neither machine spent any time unattended. Likewise the occupying army kept its trucks and tanks in a motor pool under the snarling supervision of the quartermaster, a growling hogshead of a man, the largest human Emma had ever seen. Pulling her wagon along the bluff one afternoon, she recognized Yves's boat plying the waves northward, and knew she needed to find another source.

The next morning she became fortuitously aware of a private matter that the priest had concealed from the entire town. Because her deliveries took her everywhere, at all times of day, Emma had grown better informed than the worst gossips. Thus she spied the Monsignor scuttling behind the rectory in the early hours carrying a bucket of something, and peering in all directions to be sure he was not seen. Emma was no more able to overlook those signals than she could ignore an air-raid siren. She returned while he said morning Mass, sneaking in back by the tall grass. Emma was greeted by a clutch of clucking hens, all delighted by the incorrect supposition that they were being fed again already. The priest, bless his miserly soul, had chickens.

It was a treasure, nothing less: chickens each produced an egg each day, self-regulated their quality by pecking to death any among them who grew ill or showed weakness, and when their productive time came to an end, they made several meals and soup. No wonder the Monsignor was fat in a world of slender.

Stealing was out of the question. A missing chicken would bring investigation, with the potential to unmask her entire network. Oddly enough, among Emma's calculus, the moral prohibition on coveting—particularly the possessions of a priest—did not enter.

On Sundays the Monsignor said Mass for the villagers at St. Agnes by the Sea at nine o'clock, offering a separate celebration of the blessed sacrament for the occupying army at ten thirty. No one attended both services, but everyone wondered whether he used the same sermon for both Masses, or tailored his homilies to the different congregations. More than once in the rations line, Odette speculated aloud about whether the Monsignor might slant the gospels for the occupying army, downplaying the salvation of all humanity by a Jew.

On the six other days of the week he performed the liturgical rites once, at seven thirty, as regular as a metronome. Therefore Monday through Saturday, Emma could meander past his coop, performing reconnaissance without fear.

There were five hens, all good layers. They lived in a small pen for them to wander in the day, plus a hutch in which to sleep securely at night when foxes slunk out of the hedgerows to feed. No rooster stood guard, to make a racket should any person draw near. Chickens, she knew, ate everything, so on each visit Emma brought nibbles of meal or an end of bread, which she arrayed in a figure eight by her feet. Soon the birds grew calm in her presence, puttering around and between her legs. One day, as a hen pecked at a bit of lettuce by Emma's shoe, she bent slowly, slowly, then snatched the bird up squawking and ran for home.

Emma did not need to leave the hen loose in the barnyard for long. Pirate woke from his slumber atop the hog shed. Cawing, crowing, a rumpus of feathers and strutting, he swooped down, and proceeded to plunder the surprised hen with the vigor of the long deprived and innately unconscienced.

After morning Mass, the gossiping biddies liked to stay late with the Monsignor, Emma had learned from her espionage, in order to debate later whose soul he seemed most assured would enter the gates of heaven. Therefore she left the bird to Pirate's lustful clutches for a full thirty minutes, bouts of breeding so brutal they made a blur, before hurrying the traumatized hen back to the rectory.

On her way to repeat the maneuver the next day, Emma wondered how she would identify which birds were unbred. Discerning proved simple, however, as one hen kept to itself, preening its bedraggled feathers and starting at the least noise. Emma snared one of the others, rushing it to the barnyard and the waiting rapist.

So began a rotation, with three ingredients. First, a bird took its turn in the arena of violation. Second, Pirate became intolerable, his aggression and arrogance evidenced by crowing at all hours of the day, greater verve when harassing Captain Thalheim, and a peacocking stiffness to his walk that in a human might be considered swagger.

Third, Emma searched for the priest's eggs each morning, held them one by one before a lit candle, and in the space of a week found six instances in which a dark blot cast a shadow within. Those eggs immediately enjoyed a place of honor in her baking shed, beside but not too near the wood-fired oven, incubating. She had to keep them a secret from everyone, even Mémé, because the temptation to eat one would be too great to resist. It required a certain coldness of Emma's heart, knowing that her grandmother was starving, but denying her one of these fragile jewels of protein because of the larger potential within.

Meanwhile Emma turned the eggs as regularly as if they were loaves, and in precisely twenty-one days the homestead was proud parent to six yellow chicks.

The birds would not freshen for months. During the waiting, Emma pilfered from the occupying army several coils of barbed wire, which she hid in the hedgerow behind the eastern well. She returned, too, to the mined land where she'd seen the soldier hammering warning signs, and helped herself to one. Then, in a remote and fallow patch of Pierre's property, an area long in neglect, she created a false minefield.

Should Pierre discover her deception, Emma intended to inquire whether the flavor of the tobacco in his pipe was to his satisfaction. But she predicted there would be no objection. In fact she had asked weeks before if she could remove his huge sack of chicken feed, which hung in the barn like an engraved invitation to mice. Without asking why, Pierre replied that it would be a relief if she took it, as the sack reminded him too sorely of the days when he had kept chickens and idly thought himself a rich man, not knowing how abruptly such things could come to an end.

A passerby presented even less of a risk. Anywhere in that region, upon seeing barbed wire and a MINEN sign, no sane person would dare to explore. As for the occupying army, Emma reasoned, any soldier would assume some other corps had mined the area, and happily swerve wide of the danger.

Within her minefield Emma erected a small wooden box with a drop-door to serve as coop, a pen with wire fencing for wandering space, and a wooden water trough that the rain would refill. One morning after Captain Thalheim left to report for duty, and after the Kommandant's aide had come for the baguettes and motored away, she tucked the six chicks into her shirt, their tiny hearts thrumming against her skin, their fragile wings aflutter, and carried them to their new home.

The test of her patience had not ended, however. Every day for five months, Emma came to feed the chicks, using different points of entry each time. She did not want to trample the grass into a trail, which would sabotage the deterrent powers of the MINEN sign. Thus did she grow incrementally expert in the hedgerow shortcuts, learning countless ways to journey from field to field without using roads whatsoever.

Periodically Emma would stumble across a machine-gun nest or mortar emplacement, one occupying soldier intent in his place at the weapon, while his sleepy fellows paused in their cigarette smoking to inform Emma that she should take a different route next time. Sometimes they snacked, especially the young units, whose average age was perhaps seventeen. The youths in one pillbox discovered a cache of Camembert—some cave for aging cheese abandoned when its owner had fled at the war's commencement, back when people believed there was somewhere safe to flee—and had so gorged themselves, Emma mused that she could have disarmed them all without a fight. She found other, equally unimpressive soldiers: weak men, injured and tired, veterans of the brutal war on the Eastern Front, sent here to heal, and to guard the coastline against an invasion that would never come.

Some soldiers did not speak the occupying army's language. Had they been captured? Was their presence another form of conscription? Emma refused to dwell on that possibility, because it raised the idea that her Philippe might likewise be manning the enemy's guns far away on the Eastern Front. A few times the soldiers she happened across were sharing a stolen bottle of Calvados, which tasted as sweet as springtime but kicked like a startled horse.

None of these warriors were her object. Emma had sworn off all things political, and she kept her vow. Her purpose was to feed chicks, day upon day, all steps in her larger plan, which unfolded at precisely the pace of the maturing of a bird. One bright morning, the chicks clustered in one corner of their yard, busily, as if to distract her from the opposite side. Emma followed her curiosity in that direction, knelt, parted the greenery, and there on a clutch of grass as if on a throne: the first egg. Brown and round and silent, the treasure was now hers.

Chapter 12

Only a few weeks into Emma's new profession, Mémé began calling it "Gypsy," after the Roma people whose wagon caravans had passed through the village once a year or so for most of her life. Once the occupation began, those people had vanished—into the eastern woods, some said. Also Emma was not some minstrel or dancer, wandering out of Bohemia. She was of the village, from birth forward.

Yet somehow, like the Gypsies, she became a traveling hub of barter and exchange. Somehow she became a deal maker, a keeper of secrets. When did she acquire the wooden-wheeled cart, its horse harness adapted for human pulling? How had she outfitted it with trick suitcases, hidden drawers, a watering can with a false bottom that concealed other liquids beneath? When did this young maker of bread become so circuitous and sly?

The villagers were not the only clever ones. One afternoon Emma was pulling her cart through a crossroads, harnesses over her shoulders and her day of exchanges nearly complete, when she encountered soldiers from the occupying army replacing the road signs.

They were doing it deliberately wrong. One of them was removing the existing signs—BAYEUX 11 KM., with an arrow to the right, CAEN 29 KM., with an arrow to the left. The other soldier hammered replacement signs onto the same post, but saying BAYEUX 9 KM. to the left, CAEN 51 KM. to the right.

The soldiers were not laughing, or joking, or speaking at all. They were entirely matter-of-fact while they posted falsehoods that would misdirect any traveler who was not a local.

"You." One of the soldiers pointed his hammer at her. "Move along. You go now."

"Yes," Emma said, shouldering the harnesses and pulling her way home.

Of course they wanted to mislead people, she thought. They—with their maps, communication wires everywhere, convoys all in a line—had no need of directions. Changing signs was propaganda of the most subtle and brilliant sort. But who thought of sowing this confusion? Who sat around all day, dreaming up such lies?

Above all questions, this: How could any reasonable person retaliate?

Exhausted at the end of her day, Emma was carrying the last of the laundry in from the cart when she heard a scuffling by the door in the barnyard wall. The moon hid behind scudding clouds, so she crept nearer to see what was making the noise. Something harmless, she hoped: a fox, a coypu, so she could finish this final chore and curl up on the floor beside Mémé's couch. Knowing that the bread task awaited at dawn, she had been imagining that horizontal moment for hours.

Instead of something small and wild, however, the Goat stepped out of the shadows. Emma put down the basket, trying to summon the energy to deliver a statement of unwelcome that would scour his ears. But he was bent with fatigue, his knapsack appearing to be loaded with lead. From his lowered head down, his gait an old man's shuffle, Emma recognized her own tiredness, and hesitated.

That night in the moonlight, long past curfew, and the occupying army would shoot anything moving at that hour, the Goat did not survey his surroundings at all. He scuffed across the barnyard, opened the hog-shed door, and stumbled inside. She heard him drop the weight of that knapsack.

Although the occupying army had confiscated the last of the pigs years before, the shed still contained a horrible stink. That explained why Didier's skin was filthy, why no one could bear to stand beside him. The scent clung to him like a garment.

Was there always to be someone who, by comparison, made your circumstances seem fortunate? Emma had thought so after her conversation with Michelle. Imagine romancing an officer of the occupying army because it was your best hope for survival. And now imagine sleeping in a hog shed because there was no better place to lay your head. It made the parlor floor, snoring Mémé an arm's length away, seem like luxury.

Emma did not have the heart to evict the Goat that night. Nor did she have the energy. She hoisted the basket of laundry, heading into the house and the ever more appealing prospect of her pillow. The moon threw shadows across the yard, a painter expert exclusively in the palette of gray and blue.

Come morning, Emma rose before the sun to bake the Kommandant's bread, her body hungry, her spirit fatigued. Pirate harassed her ankles while she crossed the yard. As ever, a pinch of feed purchased his silence. Working the dough roughly, she peered outside before adding straw.

The Goat was sneaking toward the barnyard door. The knapsack hung empty on his back, so he must have moved things in. He was planning to stay in the hog shed. The presumptuousness. Emma would gladly have evicted him, with a salty dose of scorn for the pleasure of it, but it was early and she could not risk waking the captain. Of all things, too, Pirate goose-stepped along beside the Goat, not crowing or attacking, but clucking and bobbing his head.

The world was a mystery which each day slid further from Emma's understanding. Was she supposed to help the Goat, along with everyone else? The wants of her fellow villagers were like the ocean, miles wide and the other side beyond sight. Emma already had all she could handle with Mémé, her own hunger, the Kommandant's infernal bread. Didier was one person too many. Or perhaps he offered a convenient receptacle for her frustration at being overwhelmed. She rushed through the barnyard door, catching him by the eastern well. "What do you think you are doing?"

Didier had reached the rise of hedgerow across the way. He paused there, glancing back at her and at the path ahead.

"Don't think about running off," she continued. "Or I'll take your mess from the hog shed and throw it down the well."

"That would be a fragrant little chore, wouldn't it?" He skipped down the embankment toward her. "With the pig memories so strong in that place?"

"How can you bear to sleep in that stench?"

"I rest easily in any room the enemy ignores. And your captain—"

"He is not mine in any way."

"Perhaps." Didier sidled closer. "But the officer would not deign for one moment to soil his hands, would he? I could stockpile mortar rounds in there, and the scent would be all the guardian I need."

"Mortar rounds," Emma scoffed. "You live in a fairy tale."

"More like a nightmare, don't you think?"

"I think," Emma said, rolling up her sleeves, "that you have one whale of a nerve, playing house on my land."

"Perhaps so," he answered again, and was he suppressing a grin at her? The cheek of him. "What if I said that I have your father's permission?"

"You have no respect for anything. He has been jailed these eleven months, and you know it."

"What courage he shows us all," the Goat said, shaking his head. "Such a shame that his daughter is so fearful."

She put her hands on her hips. "You know nothing."

"I know that you have tolerated his imprisonment for nearly a year, without once inquiring about his situation, much less demanding his freedom."

Emma took a step backward. Should she have done so? "Of whom should I inquire?"

The Goat swept an arm toward the house, the upstairs room where Captain Thalheim slept—or more likely, at that hour, where he was shaving with his customary vanity and precision.

"You would have me indebted to that murderer?"

The Goat shrugged. "He comes to court you nearly every day. I can hear him, abusing our beautiful language for your benefit. You never exercise your power over him."

"You sound worse than Mademoiselle Michelle."

"I *am* worse than Mademoiselle Michelle. I have compromised myself far more than she. But unlike her, I have purposes greater than my own survival. I have large reasons."

"Oh yes." Emma rolled her eyes. "You'll tell anyone who loans you a cup to pour your self-praise into. The Wolf is busy with all sorts of intrigue. Please spare me."

Now he did smile, openly. “Actually, Emmanuelle, you ought to join us.”

“Fairy tales, I told you,” she scoffed. “There is no ‘us.’”

Still smiling, the Goat shook his head. A noise from the house took their attention. An upstairs window casement opened, a bare arm reached out holding a basin, and it poured soapy water out on the ground.

“Love to stay and chat,” the Goat said, “but I prefer to continue breathing.”

He ran then, rabbiting away up the trail. Emma was surprised to see how fast he could go.

Blast him, though: Emma returned to the baking shed with a head full of questions. Should she have been asking about her father? Was the captain seeking her favor? Could she manipulate him to anyone’s benefit? And how had the Goat so distracted her, that she forgot to evict him from the hog shed? Pondering, she bent to work on the kneading board—her souvenir from the tree against which Uncle Ezra had died.

An hour later Emma had made the baguettes, wet their skins, and laid them parallel in the oven like the beds in an orphanage. They were brown and ready when Thalheim presented himself at the door. “Do you have a whetstone?” he asked.

Emma was removing loaves, one in each hand. She turned, and the captain was holding an open straight razor. What was he intending? She glanced at the rolling pin, her only ready means of defense, but no match for the small sharp blade.

The soldier frowned at his razor. “If I don’t sharpen this soon, I will be slitting of my own throat.”

“No luck,” she said with relief, calming herself by laying

the baguettes on the cooling rack. "We always used Uncle Ezra's."

The captain did not leave, however. Reaching for two more loaves, Emma studied him sidelong: uniform immaculate, so impressed with himself. She imagined snatching that razor and slashing him. But then she remembered being a little girl and watching her father shave, how casual he was with his face, how familiar with it, shaking the blade in the water before taking the next stroke, putting a dab of soap on the tip of her nose, stretching his chin to shave his throat smooth.

Damn that Goat, though. He had awakened in Emma a want, which was a feeling she had learned to distrust. Desire always led to sorrow. And now it swept over her like a breaking wave.

"I have something else for you," she said.

"Some other kind of sharpener?"

"No." She removed the oven mitts and lifted a baguette. "Yesterday my rations were larger than usual. So I made extra." By one end, Emma held the bread toward him.

Thalheim's eyebrows raised. "For me."

She nodded, unable to speak.

"Mademoiselle, if there are errors with rations you should report them, not cook them."

"You don't want this? Because plenty of other people—"

"Of course I do." He marched forward and took it from the other end. "The Kommandant's praises have made your bread legendary. He does not sharing with junior officers."

"I hope you enjoy it. And next time I will report the error."

The captain seemed to freeze for a moment, still as a statue, weighing, calculating. Then he broke his pose, and for the first time in her presence, he smiled. "Or perhaps not."

Emma felt a flush of power. His smile lasted barely a second, but she had seen. The Goat was right. She could play this man. It was an entirely new and agreeable feeling. For the moment she was immune to thoughts of danger.

"Perhaps not," she agreed. "And in return . . ."

"Yes?"

Remembering the other loaves, she slid on mitts and bent to the oven to lift them out. "Never mind."

"Please," Captain Thalheim said. "Continue."

Emma marveled at her coquettishness. She had never been anything but frank with Philippe, direct as an arrow. Where had she learned the wiles she was using now? "I don't dare say."

"I have made ask for you to continue. Please."

Emma placed the last baguette on the rack. "It is about my father." The captain stiffened, but she had embarked, and would not stop now. "I worry about his health, if he has enough to eat, whether he will ever be free."

"It is not always so good to ask. A man overlooked may live longer."

"It has been almost a year since his arrest," Emma persisted. "We have had no news of any kind."

Thalheim bowed. "I am ordered to Calais for several days. But if you insist, I will make inquire."

"I would appreciate that . . . Captain."

He lifted his eyes when she said his correct rank, opening his mouth, but no sound came out. He tucked the baguette under his arm.

"I hope you enjoy the bread," she said.

Thalheim clacked his heels together, leaving without another word.

Chapter 13

One rations day—when the war was old enough that, had it been a child, it would have been walking and talking—the army uncharacteristically overlooked something of value: Emma spied a hock of ham and seized it. Reduced, it would flavor meals for weeks. A bit of meat clung to it, too, where the army's kitchens had butchered in haste. Emma showed it to Mémé for an instant, then stuffed the hock into her bag before anyone else might see. She tugged the old woman's elbow, drawing her back into the street, when a few steps ahead she noticed a new couple departing.

"Who is that?" she asked of the women standing in line.

"The Argents," answered Odette, a basket on her hip. Bringing a basket for rations was the definition of optimism.

"I don't know them," Emma replied.

Mémé observed the couple as well. "Strangers."

Odette cleared her throat and spat expertly. "The woman's family owns the center villa on the bluff."

"The big stone place? Why didn't the army take it over, like the others?"

"No electricity. But look at the fancy shoes on them," Odette muttered. "You'd never know there was a war on."

"Why would anyone come here? Especially people with money?"

"They're in no danger. Wars are always fought by poor folk, on behalf of the rich folk." Odette switched the basket to her other hip. "Her family's in banking, or was, anyway. Argent, the husband, is a philosophy professor. I heard they walked all the way from Paris. How rich they must be, to have those shoes waiting here for them."

"Must be nice," Emma agreed, wending away from the line.

"Baby," Mémé declared, knuckling her ear. "Baby."

Odette smirked, making eye contact with Emma. A more tactful neighbor would have ignored Mémé's nonsense, Emma thought, steering her grandmother away.

"Baby," Mémé repeated in a whisper, pointing with her chin.

Emma glanced back at the Argent couple. The woman walked with a sway in her hips, duckfooted, while the young professor hung by her elbow in a visibly solicitous way, as if she were fragile. Her belly might not be showing yet, but their manner was. Perhaps Mémé was not as batty as she seemed.

The answer to Thalheim's inquiry arrived within a week, but in an unexpected form. Odette came running into the barnyard, her giant bosom heaving.

"Emma," she cried out. "Dear God, Emma."

Pirate charged at her like a division of tanks, full throttle and engines roaring.

"I'll make you into soup," Odette threatened, aiming a swift kick, though the bird was too quick and dodged away. *"Emma."*

"What's the matter?" she said, coming to the door, having left Mémé at the table with a bib and a plate of soggy bread. "You would think the invasion had arrived."

Odette tried to swallow but her mouth was too parched. She

tugged the front of her blouse out and back to fan herself. "Your father," she gasped. "All this time they've been holding him in the basement of town hall. Now they're taking him somewhere."

"Dear God," Emma said. "Where?"

Odette's face contorted. "The train station."

Untying her apron, Emma poked her head into the house. "I'll return as soon as I can," she called. Not answering, Mémé played patty-cake with the bread on her plate.

For a few moments Emma strode beside Odette, but the heavyset woman was too slow, and begging pardon, she dashed on ahead. A crowd had already gathered by the time she reached the station. The black locomotive's engine was rumbling.

She saw a group of soldiers, half a dozen with their rifles lowered, staring at the ground and shifting their weight from foot to foot. Two were smoking to pass the time. The station was crowded with villagers, as though someone famous were due to arrive.

Then Emma spied her father, hustled into the waiting area by two more soldiers. He had a long beard, tangled and gray; his clothes were in tatters.

"Papa," she called out, waving her arms. But he did not respond. "Marcel," Emma cried, using his name for the first time in her life. Yet it caused him to lift his head and scan the crowd.

But Guillaume had placed himself in the way. "You should not be here," he growled. "You are in danger, too. And you cannot help your father now."

Somehow she squeezed past the giant veterinarian and Emma and her father saw one another across the mayhem.

"My dear girl," he called, the soldiers pulling him toward the train. The chubby man began to weep. "My beautiful girl."

An officer with a pencil-thin mustache came with a truncheon from behind, and clubbed him between the shoulder blades. Marcel fell to his knees, but the officer gave the soldiers a command, and they dragged him toward the train.

"You are a good man," Guillaume called out. "A good man, Marcel."

He turned his head as the soldiers hoisted him into a cattle car. "Emmanuelle, my love." They slammed the sliding door shut.

"Father—" Emma rushed forward, but Guillaume caught her, pulling her away. The crowd surged toward the train as he took her arm, half carrying her down the lanes toward home.

They did not pause for more than two kilometers. When Guillaume stopped beside an orchard, Emma was panting. While she caught her breath the veterinarian checked up and down the path. He returned with a grim expression. "Do you want to know why your father was sent to a labor camp?"

"Because I inquired," Emma said, her throat raw. "The captain warned me, but I was a fool and made him ask."

"No," the veterinarian said. "It's because he was one of us. He was a member of the Resistance. A great leader."

"Then I spit on your Resistance, and your deadly games."

"He knew this could happen someday. Emma, your father was nothing less than heroic."

"He was a *farmer,*" she snapped. "A good man, but simple. And lonely since his wife died. Did you snare him into this war business?"

Guillaume lowered his voice. "Actually, he was the one who recruited me. We could use your help now, too."

"I am not interested."

"Did you know that our Kommandant is considered one of the lenient ones? The policy in other places is that if one of their soldiers is killed, thirty citizens are rounded up and shot."

"That has nothing to do with my father. And today they hit him with a club because of me."

"There is a town south of here," Guillaume continued, "Oradour-sur-Glane, where someone kidnapped an enemy captain. No one knows who or why, the occupying army could not find out, nor make anyone confess. So they killed everyone, Emma. Man, woman, child, all. Six hundred and forty-two of them. All."

"I despise you." She pushed the man's huge chest with both hands. "You have sent my father to die."

Emma burst away under the archway of trees, dodging through hedgerow shortcuts to reach home before anyone else could infuriate her.

Odette was there, mopping Mémé's brow with a damp cloth. Somehow the news had managed to outrun her.

"What is your name?" the old woman murmured, pivoting back and forth on the couch as if the room contained a crowd. "What is everyone's name?" But gradually her energy ebbed, and Mémé curled into herself, sniffling. The only other sounds were Odette dipping the cloth in a basin, and the water falling when she wrung it out.

People gathered in the courtyard, which for once was quiet because Odette had thrown a basket over Pirate. But no one dared enter the home. Guillaume found a place by the barnyard wall. DuFour narrowed his eyes at the veterinarian, who did not so much as notice, before slinking away up the lane. Eventually the Monsignor arrived, and they parted to give him a path.

He wore black vestments, with a white stole that hung from either side of his neck, and he strode slowly, as though he were leading a long procession. The priest paused outside the house, shaking holy water on the open door. "May the soul of Marcel be protected by the Almighty so that he arrives in a place of peace."

Emma glared at him from the floor, where she sat at Mémé's feet. "Peace? Do you actually believe they are taking him to a place of peace?"

"God understands suffering," he answered. "Because He sacrificed His only begotten Son."

"Are you actually saying this to me?"

"Emmanuelle, I hope you will draw close to the comfort of the Lord. There is peace through prayer."

"Go mount yourself."

Everyone in the room gasped. A murmur passed through the people outside as her curse gossiped outward like rings from a stone hitting a pond.

"God forgive you," the Monsignor said, making the sign of the cross.

"Thank you, but I decline," Emma said. "All I want now is to help our people survive." She wiped her face, though it lacked a single tear. "All I want now is to make the occupying army die."

Chapter 14

The next day Emma made bread without seeing, handed baguettes to the Kommandant's aide without hearing. Numbly she loaded the wooden-wheeled cart with her tools of deceit: the carpetbag, the watering can with a false bottom. Weaving her web had become routine regardless of circumstances. Too many people depended upon it. As with a dairyman who must milk his full-uddered cows the morning after his wife has died, certain kinds of life allow no pause.

"Gypsy?" Mémé called from the doorway. "We Gypsy?"

"Not today, dear one," Emma answered. "Today, me alone."

Marguerite stood at Mémé's elbow; she had arrived just after dawn and refused entreaties to leave. "Go about your business," she told Emma. "We'll be fine."

Emma slid her arms into the straps of the wagon, which she had adapted after the occupying army took their last horse. She could pull and steer, but when the wagon was full she had to lean back with all her weight to make it stop.

It was a short march to Pierre's, where the old man dozed on a chair in the sun. When Emma placed her large glass jug beneath the spigot of his tank, a few drops dribbled out and the flow stopped.

"That would be the final bit," Pierre said, sitting up and pointing with his pipestem. "There was more than I'd expected."

Emma shook the jug to hear the sloshing of its contents. "Most good things do not last long."

"Maybe so." He reached over to rest a hand on the flank of Curie, his youngest and most docile cow. She swished her tail as a princess might wave her fan. "Personally, I would like my life to stretch long enough to see the Allies come. That will be a fine, fine day."

Emma straightened. "None of us will live long enough to see that, because it will never happen."

"You have no hope, Emmanuelle."

"Can that be eaten?" she said, capping the jug and placing it on her cart. "What does it taste like?"

Next she went to check on her chickens. She left the wagon at a break in the brush, approaching their pen from a new direction. Emma did not see the dead bird until she had nearly stepped on it.

The hen must have shown weakness of some kind. It lay in the dirt, eyes hooded, its flank hollowed where the others had pecked it to death. Despite all the effort it had taken to bring that bird into existence, despite all the value it held for Emma and the villagers, on the morning after her father's injury and exile it caused her no emotion whatsoever. She picked up the hen, examining the small body, how little it weighed considering the worth of what it produced, then wrapped it in a cloth to tuck it away in the carpetbag.

The other hens puttered about in their usual manner, wary, single-minded. Emma scooped their dish into Pierre's old feed bag, then set it full by the trough. They gathered and bent to peck away, and she suppressed the urge to slaughter them all.

Two dodges through the hedgerows later, she arrived at the bungalow of Mademoiselle Michelle. Relieved to see that the soldier's motorcycle was absent, she knocked on a front door which was newly painted blue. As Michelle opened the door, Emma took several steps back. She had no desire to be invited in.

"Emmanuelle!" Michelle exclaimed. "What a surprise."

"I remember our conversation at the washing," Emma said.

"As do I." Michelle hesitated, stepping out of the house. "I am sorry to hear about your father."

Emma waved both hands, as if there were smoke in front of her face. "Your rabbit, is there a regular time that he visits?"

"I told you already that I am no strumpet."

Emma kept her eyes averted. This was all so distant from the chaste desires she had shared with Philippe. She knew now that they were innocents, they knew nothing. "Do you have a routine? Has he assigned a certain hour for you? That is what I am asking."

"Why?"

Emma fidgeted with her dress and said nothing. She ran a hand along the wagon wheel, then pulled it away. A glance told Emma that Michelle looked radiant, whereas she was wearing the same dress she'd had on since Monday.

"Most days he cannot come here at all," Michelle answered. "But when he does, it is in the early afternoon."

"Always by motorcycle?"

"Otherwise it's an awfully long walk." She smiled. "Though I suspect Lieutenant Planeg would crawl if he had to."

Emma scanned the surrounding field. The bungalow sat atop a steep rise. She had never considered the prospect from here, a place one could watch the roads and know people's business, the sea a distant northern glimmer. "Do you have a bright cloth of some kind? A colorful shirt, perhaps?"

"My mother left me a red scarf, you might remember seeing me wear it at church last Easter."

"No, but that will do."

Michelle leaned on one leg. "What mischief are you up to?"

"From now on, when your rabbit comes, hang that scarf from the upper window." Emma stepped closer. "You will keep him inside the house for one solid hour. Can you do that?"

"What is your purpose in all of this?"

"After he leaves, you may find an egg in the crook of that tree." Emma pointed at a chestnut beside the bramble downhill. "Not every day. But some days. Most days, if all goes well."

"How is this possible?"

"If you do not know, then you cannot be forced to tell."

Michelle beamed. "But an egg? Every day he visits?"

"Most days, as I said. But this machine has many moving parts. You must keep him in for the full hour, I don't care how."

"I believe I can manage that," Michelle said, in a tone that caused Emma to regard her directly. She seemed taller, more confident, less a fool than a survivor. Michelle knew something, Emma realized, about which she herself was wholly ignorant.

"Here." She dug in the carpetbag and handed Michelle a bundle of cloth. "Unwrap this after I've gone."

Emma slid the harness straps over her shoulders, pulling the wood-wheeled wagon away and down the hill. Michelle watched until it had turned at the bottom of the lane, heading neither right toward home nor straight toward the village center, but left, in the direction of the harbor.

Then she unfolded the cloth, carefully, to discover that she held the broken body of a chicken. It was strange to receive a dead thing, and Michelle gazed with some puzzlement in the direction Emma had gone, before realizing that for her and the lieutenant, this gift would make an unexpected feast.

Chapter 15

E*mma spied Apollo a distance ahead,* ambling up the dirt road above the harbor. In her wooden cart she carried the last bit of fuel for Yves, whose boat sat becalmed in the tween-tide waters below. But the old horse rounded a corner out of sight, so that in following, Emma nearly stumbled into a truck of the occupying army, broken down in the middle of the lane. Its hood was open wide, like a great metal mouth, while something black dripped to a puddle in the dirt beneath.

A corporal with red hair stood alone near the rear of the truck, all of his attention on Apollo. Emma watched him reach under a fence to dig a ground-fall apple from the grass, holding it toward the giant horse. His flattened palm told Emma this soldier had grown up on a farm. Then he nuzzled Apollo from the side, and she was sure of it. He knew enough not to put his face before a draft horse's head; one toss of Apollo's neck to shoo a fly and the man could have a broken nose. Also he appreciated the comforting scent of horse, his face close to the animal's flank.

What Emma smelled, however, was opportunity. Slipping out of her harnesses, she ducked to the front of the truck. With one step onto the front bumper, she peered down at the engine. The front portion hissed, a thread of steam rising from an open reservoir of some kind. But there—she spied the thing she was seeking, a length of hose, and grabbed it with both hands. The rubber was hot but not unbearable. It required several pulls back and forth before one end released. Then she tugged and twisted till the other end came free.

Emma was stuffing the hose under a cloth on her cart, when the red-haired soldier cleared his throat.

"Why, hello, m'mselle," he said. She turned and he had both hands on his hips. He wore a wide smile, but it was not a friendly one. The corporal spoke her language well enough that she could hear the menace in his voice. Had he seen her hiding the hose? "Hello say I to the pretty girl."

"Good day," Emma replied, sliding one arm into its harness.

He was at her side in an instant, holding the remaining harness so that she could not slip it on. "Why such a rush, m'mselle? Doesn't she like soldiers?"

Emma kept her gaze to one side. "My grandmother is ill. I must go help her."

"Your grandmother." The soldier nodded, strolling his eyes up and down her body without concealment, assessing as if she were a cow at auction. He smiled again, the same sick grin. "I know this one. You are Thalheim's girl, eh?"

"I am no one's girl."

"Aw. And such a pretty face." He reached one finger up to touch her jaw, and then to press it till Emma's head turned. "Pretty profile, too."

Emma could feel heat coming off the back of her neck. Her mouth filled with the taste of acid. She risked a glance. He wore a pistol on his belt. "Actually I belong to Philippe. My fiancé."

"Eh, but you forgot him for one moment there. When you said nobody's girl."

She needed a different track, something to turn him. "I saw you were skilled with the horse. Did you live on a farm?"

While wrapping one hand around her wrist, as if to measure its circumference, the corporal nodded with mock sadness. "So far from everyone. So far from the nearest pretty girl. And now this m'mselle shows up, right here." He stepped back abruptly, jolting her away from the cart so hard that she stumbled. "And we are far from everyone. Just like the farm."

Emma recovered her balance and tried to pull her arm free. But he had a grip like a vise. "Let me go."

He dragged her toward the back of the truck. "The other corporal went for us a tow. He won't be return for hours."

"I mean it," Emma said, twisting. "Let me go."

The corporal yanked her against him, chest to chest. "First, one little kiss. Then we discuss."

"That's enough." The voice came from the front of the truck, turning them both. Guillaume stood there, seeming as large as a tree.

"I order you to leave," the red-haired soldier said.

Not answering, Guillaume strode the length of the vehicle with an iron look in his eye. Emma pulled away, realizing that she could do so because the corporal had released her wrist. He reached to unclip his pistol, but Guillaume slammed him against the side of the truck. Emma heard the wind go out of him like a punctured tire.

Guillaume twisted the corporal's arm till the shoulder dislocated. The soldier cried out feebly, his wind still gone, wheezing as he fell to his knees. The veterinarian took the pistol, emptied its bullets into his hand, then stuffed them in his pocket. He grabbed the soldier's arm and lifted, making him scream.

"Can you hear me, you mouse?" Guillaume said. "Can you understand me right now?"

The soldier moaned but nodded.

"You have an army, so you can be any kind of damn fool you want. But you do not trifle with this one, do you hear me? This woman, you leave alone."

The corporal gritted his teeth. "I will have you shot."

"No. I could kill you now with your own gun, and there would be no witness to speak against me. But I am showing you mercy, because I believe you will obey." He pointed at Emma. "This one you do not touch."

Guillaume shoved the soldier on his back; he writhed in the dirt. The veterinarian threw the pistol, tumbling end over end before it fell in the tall grass. He nodded to Emma. "Come."

Mutely she followed him back to her cart. He waited as she slid her trembling arms into the harness. Apollo ambled up, standing there blinking.

"Which way were you headed?" Guillaume asked.

Emma gestured with her chin.

"The harbor." He lifted his blue bicycle, which was lying on its side. "I'm headed that way myself."

She felt wobbly in her knees, but after a few steps Emma recovered her balance. Fear was swiftly displaced by heat. If Guillaume had given her the pistol, there would be one less soldier on this earth. Her mind boiled with how she might have shot him, while the ground passed unnoticed beneath her feet.

Apollo let them go, wandering off in the direction from which Emma had come. The veterinarian matched her pace, not speaking, his bicycle clicking as it rolled alongside. Soon she had resumed her usual clip.

At last he broke the silence. "You know that it is not safe—"

"The one person." She cut him off. "The one person on earth permitted to lecture me is my father."

"I think I know why you travel our roads every day."

Emma increased her pace. "You have no idea."

"Perhaps. But I know that you could be safer—"

"If I stayed at home. But I will not be staying at home."

"I would never suggest such a thing, mademoiselle. Some animals cannot live in a cage."

Emma felt herself softening. This man had healed her father's livestock many times. And had just rescued her. "What is your business, then? I am glad you saved me, thank you. Though it is a fraction of the penance you owe for my father's exile."

"But of course," he said. And with that, Guillaume stopped walking. Emma did not notice for a few steps, but then slowed the cart by turning sideways. He stood beside his bicycle; it looked like a toy compared with his bulk. "I had something else in mind."

Emma looked down her nose. "Yes?"

He surprised her then by smiling. "That expression on your face. I can't decide if it comes from your father or Uncle Ezra."

"Both men I loved, one who the occupying army murdered and the other who they took away in a cattle car."

"One day this army will pay for its deeds."

"How nice to think so," Emma said, scanning the harbor below. A pair of gulls chased a third, who cried and squawked down the shore. "The Monsignor says that when I die I may go to heaven, too. But neither belief will fill anyone's belly today."

"Exactly," Guillaume said. "That is why I want you to have this." He reached into the satchel in his bicycle's basket, producing a long black sheath. "This is a thigh harness," he explained. Leaning the bike against his hip, he slid out a bright steel blade. "You can strap the weapon safely out of sight. A person would have to grope you to know you carried it. But if the need arises, this knife is high-quality steel, with a gutter along one side for the blood to flow without splashing you."

"I, well . . . hmm," Emma stammered.

"You might think to stab in this area," he continued, gesturing at his chest. "But ribs make a surprisingly protective cage. It is more effective to plunge the knife lower, here." He pointed below his sternum. "No protection. And if you can, hook the blade upward so it punctures the important things."

Emma's mouth went dry. It was as though her bluff were being called. Was she capable of stabbing someone? The red-haired corporal had made her think so, not five minutes before. But the steel reality of this weapon far exceeded her angry fantasy.

"I don't want it," she said at last.

"If you embark on activities that cause people to depend on you, then you have a responsibility to protect yourself." Guillaume slid the blade into the sheath, placing it in her hands.

The weapon was heavy, and the leather smell reminded Emma of saddles. "I told you." She spoke more firmly, holding the knife back toward him. "I don't want this."

"Yes you do," Guillaume answered mildly. He threw a leg over the seat of his bicycle, gripped the handlebars, put one huge boot on a pedal. "I heard you tell the Monsignor yesterday with my own ears."

"What did I say?"

He leaned closer. "That you wanted to kill."

Chapter 16

T*hey had been ordered to assemble,* everyone, no excuses, that morning in April. It was a bluebird day, whole hillsides of apple trees in blossom, pinks and whites and the hum of bees. New ration cards would be issued. Anyone in Vergers failing to attend would therefore no longer receive a share of the permitted food.

Often the occupying army traveled with its dogs, large, unfriendly, brown-and-black animals. At rest they were pretty, with bushy tails and ears that rose and curled like tulip petals. Around the villagers, though, the dogs snapped like wolves, curling their lips to show their teeth. Sometimes the soldiers took the animals for walks in the lanes, and if they passed a villager the dogs would lunge at their leashes. Odette said she would gladly kick one of them, except that it would probably bite off her leg.

That day the dogs were tethered at the edge of the square, one private standing by as they growled and paced as far as their constraints allowed. Leading Mémé to the opposite side, Emma passed Marie and Fleur a step behind the bulk of Guillaume, who was discussing with the Goat whether the soldiers deliberately tormented the animals, to keep them in a constant snarl.

The veterinarian bowed to Emma but she did not greet him. Nor did she tell him about the knife strapped to her leg.

"Cage an animal," Guillaume was saying, "train it in frustration, teach it subservience when all its breed has ever known is freedom, and you will cultivate creatures like this."

The Goat nodded. "Maybe they are doing that to us, too."

Yet all was orderly as the villagers assembled. The Argent couple made a late arrival, but that reflected how they generally kept to themselves. They only left their stone palace on the bluff—mansions on either side commandeered by the occupying army, communications wires webbing in all directions from their rooftops, their home exempt because it lacked electricity—when it was time to join the queue for rations. Everyone observed as the husband became more solicitous to his wife, and her belly grew round as though a half-moon had affixed itself to her spine, which caused Emma to bask in the remaining wisdom of her grandmother. As they joined the crowd now, the young woman's visible pregnancy inspired the village's gossiping biddies to draw aside a few steps—so that their queen bee could scold about indulging during wartime in pleasures of the flesh, and the others could tsk and cluck.

At last the Kommandant appeared on the top step of town hall, as stiff as a fence post. Officers flanked him in descending order of rank, Thalheim lowest on one end, the pencil-thin mustache officer on the other. Those two, Emma mused, all swagger and display, but in truth they were pawns.

An officer midway up the ranks came forward and called for quiet. Once the crowd settled, the Kommandant began.

"The rations process has become disorderly," he said in their language, his pronunciation excellent. "Also there is the potential for corruption. You people do not follow directions."

"Or choose not to," Odette muttered, causing a titter among people in her vicinity. The Kommandant raised an eyebrow, and soldiers turned in the disturbance's direction. Silence returned.

"Today you receive new cards, which will improve our efficiency. One person shall carry the card for a family. We will have order in their distribution this morning, and—"

Another noise interrupted from the far corner, dogs snarling, then a woman's scream. The Kommandant frowned. Now several dogs were barking, and the woman wailed. The crowd began to murmur, people shifting in place. Thalheim drew his pistol and fired a single shot into the air. The crowd silenced instantly, at which the Kommandant nodded to his captain in approval, but the quiet made one last yelp sound twice as loud.

"What has happened there?" the pencil-thin mustache officer called, standing on tiptoe to peer over the crowd.

Two soldiers came forward, each holding one of Guillaume's arms. They looked like dwarfs beside him, but the veterinarian did not struggle or resist. "This one, sir," one of them said. "He killed one of the dogs."

A gasp went through the crowd. "This is bad and going worse," Emma said to Mémé, taking her arm. "We need to leave."

"The animal broke his leash," Guillaume said. "He bit Marguerite, and was not letting go."

"Snapped its neck with his bare hands," the soldier marveled.

"Those animals are the property of our great nation," Thalheim said. "You have killed the wrong animal."

"I ask permission to treat the old woman," Guillaume said. "She is bleeding heavily and you took our physician away last year."

The Kommandant was frowning at the entire scene. His speech had been disrupted, when the whole point had been to emphasize order. These bumpkins were so annoying. If not for their bread and brandy, and a few of their whores, a man would be tempted to slaughter them all. The officer to his left leaned closer. "What shall we do, sir?"

"We cannot be permissive," Thalheim called from his lower step. "They must learn obedience, through punishment."

"This fellow is useful, though," said one on his right. "He has treated our animals repeatedly. He saved my horse."

"We already tolerate that tree-climbing fool," Thalheim persisted. "Also the old woman with no mind left. Any waste of resources invites disrespect. Sir, here is an opportunity—"

"I am tempted." The Kommandant raised one hand to quiet his headstrong captain. "I am inclined to excuse this incident as a significant error—but a forgivable one. The property of our army must not be harmed by any person, in any way."

He waved one hand in dismissal. "Jail him for two weeks. And as for the ration cards—"

"But he has a gun."

The Kommandant turned toward this new interruption. It came from DuFour, that busybody he had installed in town hall to monitor the villagers. "Who dares to speak out of turn now?"

"In his bicycle saddlebag," the clerk continued. "A pistol."

"You worm," Guillaume growled. A few steps away, Marie clung to Fleur and began to weep. Emma pulled at Mémé but she resisted. She wanted to see.

In a moment a private had wheeled the blue bicycle forward, dumping the satchel in the dirt. He squatted to spread the contents wide: the pistol, two knives, a bag of ammunition, and tight rolls of paper.

"Maps," DuFour yelped. "He has maps as well."

"You will pay for this, cockroach," Odette called from her side of the square.

"Silence," the Kommandant ordered, though nearly all the

other villagers were already quiet. He turned to face Thalheim, whose pistol was still drawn, and gave a curt nod.

"No," Marie cried, a hand to her mouth. "No."

Afterward there were many versions of what happened next. The villagers in front of Marie crowded together, which they later said was to protect her from a horrible sight. The people behind her also saw the crowding, but from their perspective it was an act of selfishness that prevented them from seeing. Odette observed nothing, because she had gone to help Marguerite, who herself later insisted that Guillaume had not killed a dog at all, but rather a soldier, and no one contradicted this account because the villagers understood her need to absolve herself from responsibility for his punishment. Ultimately there was no definitive history. Each person told the story that each person needed.

On certain things, everyone agreed. They all saw the Goat slinking away through the crowd. They watched villagers close around Guillaume's wife and daughter as bees surround a queen.

Thalheim raised his arm higher than he was accustomed, till the pistol was inches from the veterinarian's face. "Contemplate your mortality," he said.

Guillaume thrust his chin forward. "What took you so long?"

After the firing of a single shot, after the large body collapsing in the dirt, after Marie wailing on her knees, the Monsignor appeared with his hand-pushed jitney for the dead. He pointed at both soldiers who had been holding Guillaume's arms, and even with their help it was still an effort to load the veterinarian into the wheelbarrow. The priest paused then, head bowed, making a sign of the cross over Guillaume's body. His hand trembled in the air.

"What is the trouble?" Thalheim said, wiping his pistol with a cloth.

"No trouble," the Monsignor answered. "It's only that I baptized this one."

"You are not nearly old enough," the captain sneered. "What kind of fool do you think I am?"

"Not at birth," the priest explained. "On the day before he was married."

"Well, he's in the way now." Thalheim holstered his gun. "Move him along."

The Monsignor nodded. "I don't mean to be a nuisance, but this one is too big. I need help."

"You people." Shaking his head, the captain pointed at Pierre. "You. Step in and help here." As the old man waddled over, Thalheim half turned before checking himself. "A little fewer of backtalk from now on, eh? That collar and cross are less protection than you think."

The priest opened his mouth to speak, but Pierre had bent to grab one of the wheelbarrow handles, so he took the other and lifted it without saying a word, and together they rolled the dead man off to church. As with the others, Guillaume's funeral would take place in the morning, right after seven thirty Mass, his body at the front and center of St. Agnes by the Sea.

But there was a final impression for those still present as the wheelbarrow creaked out of sight: that was the first moment that anyone could remember seeing the Monsignor move with a limp.

Emma bent and picked up a stone at her feet, wrapping her hand around it and squeezing. She wanted her memory of this day never to escape her mind, to remain as certain as a rock.

The Kommandant ordered a stricter curfew, which brought groans from the remaining crowd. Limited travel at night was less an oppression than an insult. When people have known free passage through their town, at all hours, under every version of moon or stars or weather, curfew announces that the place is no longer theirs.

Odette helped Marguerite down the lane to her café, to wash the wound in hot water. The crowd dispersed, Thalheim ordering people away. A group of women ushered Marie homeward, her body racked with sobbing, her daughter, Fleur, silent and a few steps behind.

All that time, the soldiers who had helped to load Guillaume's body remained standing by, watching Marie go, giving the new widow a thorough appraisal. One of them whispered to the other, who did not reply, only stood closer and nodded in agreement.

Sometime that night, despite fences and searchlights and guards, someone poisoned all of the occupying army's dogs. They died howling. Word spread among the villagers like a bad rash. Who had dared?

The occupying army gathered nine women at gunpoint, one for each dog, and forced them to dig a mass grave on farmland outside the village. Unused to shovels, the women needed all day for their task. No one had ever taught them how to work a spade around a stone, or where to press their heels to drive the blade deeper. Unfamiliarity with the tool made the job twice as hard.

The soldiers allowed the women no rest, so that even those with farm-hardened hands watched them grow blistered and raw. No food, no water. Toward sunset the hole in the earth was deep and wide enough. By pointing their rifles, the soldiers communicated to the women to throw the carcasses in.

In groups of four they lifted the animals by their paws, the bodies stiff and heavy. Once the dogs lay side by side, the inverse of puppies piled on one another to nurse or sleep, the soldiers ordered the women to fill the grave.

Several wept as they took up their shovels again. The job lasted into the night, past curfew, so that the gravediggers went home with a military escort. Their hands curled into themselves, brittle and dry as autumn leaves. On the march through town they could hear singing from the garrison, lusty songs from young men under a starry sky, not a care in their world.

The gravesite became known as Dog Hill, villagers by common understanding forbidding the use of that land for building houses or shops, because the dogs had caused Guillaume's death, but as brute animals they had not deserved to die either, and the mutual wrongs typified the inhumanity of war.

Marguerite did not die that night, though it appeared as though she might well lose a leg. Odette, who could neglect the café for a day if need be, provided such medical care as she was able, while hoping the old woman's fever would pass.

The morning after the burial, the two soldiers who had held Guillaume's arms appeared at Marie's door. They brought with them a friend, a redheaded corporal with his arm in a sling. When she answered the door, the corporal grabbed her braid, pulling her roughly outside toward the shed.

"Fleur," Marie yelled, following her hair across the yard. "I order you to stay in the house. You must stay in the house."

A few mornings later, the villagers saw that someone had stretched a rope between two trees that stood atop Dog Hill. Midway across the span, this someone had hung two broken branches knotted together to make a *V*. Thalheim sent marksmen to shoot the rope down, but bullets only caused the *V* to dance in the air. He dispatched the strapping soldier with his chain saw, and both trees came down in short order. Dog Hill was now bald. Later, Monkey Boy's mother planted the hillside with sunflowers, their bright yellow faces following the sun all summer long.

Once Marguerite's fever broke, she recovered quickly. She was no longer able to smuggle tobacco, however, because her supply came from a farm several kilometers from Vergers and now the older woman struggled to visit her nearest neighbors.

Emma left a mahogany cane on her doorstep, though no one knew where she had obtained such a thing. In return, Marguerite gave her small jars of lanolin to distribute among the women forced to dig Dog Hill, to ease their blisters. There was a jar for Marie, too. When Emma came to deliver it, Fleur stood in the doorway and accepted the gift on behalf of her mother, who did not emerge from the house's dark interior to say either thank you or hello. Emma was not sure if she heard whimpering from within, or only imagined it.

Chapter 17

Darkness lasted months in Vergers, a melancholy that infected each person, all moods, every leaf in the hedgerows. When the light returned, it took the unexpected form of a nighttime butchering.

The pig was Emma's crowning achievement, everyone agreed, the pinnacle of her cunning. In a single night she fed the village, outfoxed the army, and concealed the conspiracy so well, by morning everyone insisted that the pig had never existed.

The incident began with two corporals on an off-duty lark, one skilled with a repeating-fire rifle, one determined to learn the use of that weapon, and both of them drunk as lords on Calvados purchased at an absurdly overpriced cost from Odette's café. Dark came so late to the north country, especially in the height of spring, that it was still mild daylight when they brought the gun out to the hedgerows for target practice.

Emma happened to be wheeling her cart homeward, unable to ignore her stomach's growls of hunger, and she passed the drunken soldiers with her head down to discourage conversation. Occasionally she wondered what she looked like, bowed low and pulling that wagon. She imagined herself as something ancient, an archetype of all women during all occupations, dragging along the weight of survival just as women had pulled similar carts with comparable contents and identical reasons, for as long as human nature had led men to make war, which is to say as long as there was history.

The first corporal, thin as a whip, instructed his stouter fellow junior officer, pointing at components of the weapon with the tip of his cigarette. Though he spoke a different language, Emma could tell that his words were slurred. She slowed behind them, with the growing feeling that something—drunkards, a gun, a pleasant evening—was about to go horribly wrong.

The corporal moved a switch on the gun and raised it to his eye. "Bums," he said, jerking the rifle as though it had fired. His arms moved in an arc, a pantomime of using one shot to see where the next should go. "Bumgens, bums."

The other corporal, the larger one, asked a question, and Emma listened as the thin one answered at great length, holding the gun to the side, the other hand on his hip. Was there a tone of superiority in that garble?

The second officer reached with both hands, but the first one wagged a finger and stepped away. He had more to say, and since he possessed both the gun and a knowledge of its proper use, he would not permit his dissertation to be abbreviated.

Emma's sense of approaching disaster grew, and she began pulling the wagon again, hurrying herself out of range. A moment later, however, she heard the second corporal shout. Emma turned to see a quick tussle, then the student overpowered his teacher and stepped aside holding the gun. He raised it, bracing the stock against his hip, and with a cry of glory he fired a rapid volley into the trees.

Instead of silence, however, or the whine of a ricochet, the gunfire was followed by screams. Both soldiers froze. Had they shot someone by accident? Emma shuddered to think that her premonition of tragedy had been accurate.

But the screams sounded inhuman, so high in pitch and coming so rapidly one on another, as if the person did not breathe between peals, that she was puzzled about who could make such a noise, until she saw a wild boar come charging out of the hedgerow, squealing like the end of the world, a bloody wound in its right rear shank. The boar, plenty quick on three legs, dashed between the corporals, who by then were leaning on one another laughing uproariously.

Before the wounded animal darted back into the woods, Emma had a better look. He lacked the tusks she would have expected. He was not bristled with coarse hair either, but had skin a bonny pink. This was no wild boar. It was a farm pig, as plain as bacon, escaped from his pen once upon a time and surviving since then by feral foraging, but unfortunately doing so on a spring evening in the wrong place at an unlucky time.

The surprise had sobered the corporals sufficiently that they straightened themselves, such as they could, shouldered the gun, and marched back to their barracks for an extended off-duty nap. Emma marked well where the pig had run into the hedgerow, calculating how he might find a less tangled path, and therefore where he might choose to rest and wait for his bleeding to cease.

She hurried the wagon home, leaving it in the barnyard without disturbing Mémé, then hastened to the rectory. The priest was not there, and neither was he fetching a new corpse over which to pray. Thus his wheelbarrow leaned against the cottage's back wall, idle. Emma helped herself, vowing to return it shortly, and wondering if it was a sacrilege to carry a pig in a device that delivered human bodies to the sanctuary. Hurrying in case the animal proved to be less wounded than it had seemed, Emma decided she was already guilty of far worse blasphemies, and broke into a run.

No one knew the hedgerows better, not even a pig living

amid them. Emma dodged machine-gun placements, a mortar pit, soldiers on guard duty or reading or smoking or cleaning their weapons in an atmosphere of palpable boredom. Had she been a spy, Emma could have delivered these units' locations to the Allies in half a minute. This time none of the soldiers saw her, or heard her, or noticed the wheelbarrow rushing through the underbrush as she made use of all the routes she'd learned in nearly two years of operating her clandestine network.

The pig was still alive, lying on its side and panting, but its eyes had gone glassy. They did not so much as turn in Emma's direction when she trotted past, then caught herself and wheeled back to stand beside the wounded sow.

"Oh my darling," Emma said. "You gorgeous thing."

It was a wrestling match, loading the pig. She tipped the wheelbarrow on its side, then grabbed all four hooves and rolled the pig into the basin. The animal grunted but did not protest. Emma knelt, pig blood soaking into her dress, dirt grinding into her knees, and hooked her hands under the wheelbarrow's bin. Pushing with her legs, straining her back, she had to press her face into the warm side of the pig for greater leverage, and with the grunts of a workhorse she lifted one side of the load. After she'd achieved a certain angle, gravity helped and the wheelbarrow fell into its normal stance, one passenger aboard.

Emma attempted to wipe blood from her face, but only smeared it onto her neck and ear. Then she grabbed the handles and tested the weight. One hundred kilos at least. More than any man in the village, and no one near to help. Philippe, she thought for the thousandth time, where are you? The trees made no answer, only a wren calling from somewhere concealed. But Emma would not abandon such a prize for so small a reason as not being strong enough. She lifted with straight arms, pushed with her thighs, and the wheelbarrow began inching homeward.

By the time she reached the eastern well, it was almost dark and she was drenched in sweat. The pig had ceased breathing, which made her somehow heavier. Did the body, Emma wondered, change its substance in death?

Who should be drawing water at that moment but Odette, who set down her bucket in awe. "Don't tell me," she said, eyes bright. "Did you really kill him with your bare hands?"

Emma answered by emptying the bucket over her head. An hour later, Odette returned with all the essentials for their plan.

Many of the officers had Calvados on the shelves of her café. They would buy a bottle, the label marked in ink with their name, and work at it over several visits. Since Emma insisted that the only successful crime was one that no one knew had occurred, she instructed Odette to steal no more than half an inch from each bottle, too little for an officer to notice, especially given that the last time he had seen it he also had a bellyful of the brandy. The cumulative effect was a near magnum of the drink, which she corked and carried and placed in the center of Emma's table. Beside it she set two clean glass tumblers.

When Thalheim returned that evening, Emma was busy scrubbing her soiled dress in the yard. He strode past without a word, at which she flipped the dress over to clean the other side. It made a loud noise, wet cloth slapping down on a washboard. An air-raid siren could not have delivered a clearer advance signal. Thalheim pushed open the house door as if it were his own home. And, as an hour's rehearsal had prepared for, at that exact moment Mémé rushed the bottle downward out of sight.

"What was that?" the captain said, pausing by the stairs.

"Hmm?" Mémé said it in a singsong way, at the same time examining her fingernails with great interest.

"Something you hid just now. What was it?"

Mémé studied him, her expression addled, and did not reply.

"God save me from the simpletons," Thalheim said. He pointed. "That thing you are now concealing. Bring it out."

As though she were a cat being commanded to fetch, Mémé stared at the tip of his finger.

"Damn it." Thalheim moved past her, muttering to himself. "Why do they permit of your kind to continue to live?"

Mémé slid her chair aside, and the captain found the bottle. "Oho," he cried out. "What have we here?"

Immediately he removed the cork with his teeth, spitting it out on the floor. He sniffed the mouth of the bottle, then used the nearer of the glasses to pour for himself. When Thalheim put the bottle down and raised his tumbler, Mémé filled hers as well.

"Is that so?" he asked, then threw the drink back. Mémé responded by doing the same. When she brought her glass down on the table with a hearty whack, the captain took it to mean that he should refill both glasses, though it actually signaled to Emma to put aside her washboard and make further preparations.

Normally the captain was not one for alcohol. Odette knew this about him, because the other officers often teased. He sent his pay home to his mama, they said, keeping enough for razors and sundries but not for gambling or drink. Still, this Calvados was free, and he poured himself another tumbler. So did Mémé.

When he'd downed the second shot, Thalheim started for the stairs again. But Mémé banged her glass and he hesitated. Then she poured into both glasses and put the bottle down.

"Well, aren't you the souse?" he said, ambling back to the table. He picked up his glass, but before he drank Mémé used her foot under the table to push the other chair backward, and without thought or dispute, the captain sat.

It took a full hour and more to intoxicate him sufficiently. Mémé matched him glass for glass, sometimes rushing him.

"Why are you in a hurry?" he slurred.

"Death," she said, throwing back her drink.

"Not anytime soon," he protested, but he emptied his glass.

Mémé growled at him, and slapped herself in the face, both sides. Then she poured again.

Eventually Thalheim's head began to sway, his words to make less sense to Emma eavesdropping outside. He spent some time with his chin on his chest, Mémé knocking on the table beside his full glass though he was slow to respond. After one last shot, he crossed his arms on the table and lowered his head into that cradle.

Mémé pushed his shoulder, but the eyes did not open. She thwacked his skull. No response. Though there was half a drink left in her glass, she slid it away and rose. With slow dignity she opened the front door, marched past her granddaughter, and threw up in the flowers.

"Oh, Mémé," Emma said, placing a hand on her back.

"There," the old woman answered. "There—"

But another wave of nausea interrupted, and she vomited on the bushes again. So it continued until her belly was empty, and beyond. By the time Emma had given her water to drink, a bit of bread to absorb, and led her to the couch—a mixing bowl nearby in case Mémé needed it later, Pirate meanwhile closed in the baking shed to keep him quiet—a group of neighbors had clustered in the barnyard with torches, Odette at their head sharpening her butchery knives over the pink carcass.

Yves had built a crossbar of rough lumber, tied the hooves in pairs, and hoisted the pig till it hung upside down. Odette brought her blade up to the sow's throat.

"Wait," Emma said. "If you gut it here, we will have to explain blood and innards in the dirt tomorrow morning. Not to mention the crows that will assemble to pick at the mess."

The people murmured, but no one offered a solution. Then a voice called from the barnyard wall. "I have something that will work."

They turned as one, and saw the Goat standing with a knapsack on his back. "Give me a minute," he said.

No one had seen the Goat in weeks. He looked thinner, a waif struggling with the weight of his pack as he staggered into the hog shed. They heard him drop his load on the floor.

"I don't know how he can stand the smell of it," Odette said to no one in particular.

"Or how *we* can stand the smell of *him*," Emma replied.

The people laughed. The Goat heard it all, too, standing in the stench and gloom. But it did not merit a reply. With the two boxes in his knapsack that night, his task was at long last complete. Not once had the occupying army come near this shed. Why would they bother to investigate now?

He pulled away a large canvas tarp, revealing two hundred of those wooden boxes. The Goat had not seen them all revealed together, and he was struck by the magnitude of his feat. Twenty stacks, each ten boxes high, a cache the Resistance would be proud to see, and eager to use, when the proper day came. He half folded the tarp, dragging it behind him into the barnyard.

"Perfect," Odette said, helping others spread the green canvas under the hanging pig. Then she brought the tip of a blade to the animal's jugular, and with a hand as swift as a finch, made a deep, perpendicular slice. The pig's blood poured out in a gush.

By midnight the villagers were lined up, everyone who could be trusted. In recent weeks people had seen DuFour wheeling around the village on Guillaume's blue bicycle, which offended everyone's sensibility because the man whose outcry had condemned the veterinarian deserved least to benefit by that betrayal. Yet he rode the blue bicycle everywhere, and on days with clear weather he parked it right in front of town hall. By common assent, no one told DuFour about the pig.

Likewise the priest was omitted, because the dictates of his conscience were so mercurial. No one knew with certainty where his sympathies lay. He slept undisturbed, therefore, while everyone else made a queue that stretched across Emma's dirt yard, out the door in the barnyard wall, and halfway past it to the eastern well. Pirate hid in the baking shed, overwhelmed by the number of threats, and pacing like an expectant father. The villagers brought buckets or pans, cloth sacks or wooden boxes, into which Emma portioned pork that Odette had butchered and divided with the care of a surgeon.

"Remember, boiling only," Emma instructed. "If the army smells even one ham baking or rib roasting, they will come salivating, and we will be revealed."

The people waited without a murmur, and passed not with their eyes lowered in shame as when receiving rations, but upright, and solemn nonetheless. Only Monkey Boy made mischief, blowing into one of the pig's lungs to inflate it like a balloon, though the moment his mother yanked it away from his mouth, the organ went flat again. Otherwise the villagers took their bundles of meat in silence, saying perhaps a word of thanks or perhaps not, then sidled away, risking a curfew violation in order to receive more meat that night than in a month of rations. When everyone's portion was gone, Odette collected the remains for sausage. The cleanup took hours, concluding close enough to the time Emma normally rose to make the Kommandant's bread that she did not bother lying down at all. The wheelbarrow, which Fleur had given a thorough rinse, Emma returned to the rectory during morning Mass.

Mémé rose in unexpectedly fair humor, much of the alcohol purged from her system before Emma put her to bed. A pair of swallows had nested in the barn eaves, and the old woman stationed herself nearby to watch their comings and goings.

By contrast, the baguettes were browned on top and turned once in the oven before Thalheim presented himself at the baking-shed door. As ever, he had shaved as smooth as the back of a spoon, but his eyes were red and his face pale.

"You people are barbaric," he announced.

Immediately Emma thought they had been discovered. He must have stirred during the night. He had seen, all was lost.

"Whatever do you mean?" she replied, still as a statue in front of the dough she was mixing.

"Drinking such filth. Any liquid that leaves a man feeling this ill in the morning is a poison."

She could not help smiling to herself. "I'm told it takes practice."

"Well," he began, but then stopped, and wandered away.

Emma watched him shuffle across the barnyard, holding himself like something breakable, until Pirate burst out from behind the old hog shed in full disaster, a long night's frustration fueling his passion, crowing for all he was worth. Thalheim winced, hands to his ears, kicking in the bird's direction, but the rooster darted out of reach without pausing the fierce defense of his territory. To Emma, seeing the captain in retreat from that noisy annoyance tasted better than bacon.

The villagers obeyed her cooking instructions, neither smoking, roasting, nor frying the pork, enticing though the flavor would have been. For a culinary people, who in another time could have made a two-day village feast out of that pig, boiling was a masterpiece of restraint. Any regret at making that compromise, however, was overcome by the unfamiliar pleasure of a belly temporarily full of meat.

Toward midday, Monkey Boy reached the special sycamore at the edge of the bluff above the beach, its trunk wider than the full stretch of his arms. He had already taken his daily drink from all three of the town's water supplies: the eastern well just outside Emma's barnyard door; the central well, which fed the village fountain as well as homes and shops along the square; and the western well, which offered the most dramatic views but could turn salty after especially fierce storms at sea.

The special sycamore was not inviting to a climber, having no branches for the first three meters of its trunk. One limb spread wide over the bluff, however, sculpted by unrelenting ocean winds, and if Monkey Boy leaped his highest, the tree's extremity hung just within his fingers' grasp. He wrapped his hands above that limb, hooking his heels as well to hang beneath like a sloth, then shimmying arms and legs up that branch to the trunk. From there it was a scamper, laddering into the highest boughs. The perch he chose leaned this way and that, like the crow's nest atop a sailing ship. He held the trunk with one arm, and observed.

Here a crew on the beach below measured the height of the previous night's tides. There the occupying army was driving steel beams into the sand, their jagged edges pointed out to sea, fitting mines to the tips. He counted two hundred and two. The evenness of the number pleased him. To Monkey Boy's left, a gunnery officer instructed his men in something, pointing and pantomiming. To his right, villagers under armed guard built wooden forms and set steel rods for a future concrete pouring to serve as an antitank wall. This barrier stretched serpentine along the base of the bluff like a physical expression of the word "no." Above it all stood a group of officers—nine of them, he tallied; Monkey Boy loved to count—overseeing the work, all of them shielded from the weather by a makeshift canvas canopy.

In the distance the village rooftops showed through gaps in the trees, slate or tile or cedar shingles and a chimney, all organized around the spire of St. Agnes by the Sea. Monkey Boy tore off a handful of leaves and threw them in the village's direction. They did not go far, though. Floating this way and that, they parachuted down through the branches. He thought he had never seen anything so beautiful.

But in the next moment, Monkey Boy realized that he had forgotten his body business again. It was exactly like whenever he'd found a hiding place as a little boy, and his mother was looking for him: the moment he had settled into his perfect secret spot, an urge to empty himself would arise, with no regard for the quality of his invisibility. Now it had happened again, and the ground below looked so far away. Not to mention the effort of climbing back again.

Oh, it was urgent. All that drinking water, plus the gorging he had done on pig all night, his body unaccustomed to so much meat. Now it growled in his gut. There was no alternative. He undid the drawstring of his pants, opening the buttons in front. He slid the trousers down.

A half-track of the occupying army motored under the huge

tree, stopping directly beneath his bare bum. The vehicle idled there while two soldiers conferred before choosing the direction in which one of them had pointed, the engine rattling as the half-track clattered away. Gripping the trunk with one arm, Monkey Boy hung his backside over a limb above where the machine had paused. He began to giggle, smothering his mouth with a forearm. The mirth of his naughty idea erupted out of him, a guffaw in spite of himself, and he spoke to the branches surrounding him. "Bombs away."

A week later, Emma asked the Goat where he buried the tarp soaked with pig's blood.

"Where crows may go sometimes, but the occupying army never," he replied. "Dog Hill."

In her café Odette deflected all praise of her butchering, instead spreading the legend that Emma had wrestled the pig to death. A success so great deserved a story as unlikely. From that night forward, everyone treated Emma with respect. Her age and gender no longer mattered; they had eaten well because of her.

The priest stopped her on a lane in the village to remark upon it. "It would appear, Emmanuelle, that your sinful influence has prevailed among the weaker-willed of your neighbors. Fewer of them come to St. Agnes to confess."

Emma paused in pulling her wagon the opposite direction. "Maybe that's because I'm not saying prayers with the enemy."

"The occupying soldiers, like us, are children of God."

"Then some children of God are murderers." She began wheeling the wagon past. "Besides, I give our villagers something more nourishing than faith."

"There is no such thing," he answered, limping alongside, trying to keep up. "Life without faith makes a hell on earth."

Emma shook her head and said no more. The Monsignor gimped a few more steps before stopping. "A hell on earth," he yelled. If he added anything more, it was drowned out by the wooden wheels' clatter on the village cobbles.

But that conversation came a week after the butchering. On the day immediately following, everyone stumbled around as if in a daze. Moving at half speed, with soldiers of the occupying army scolding them for sluggishness, the sleep-deprived villagers nonetheless possessed a secret, and therefore a new power. Emma stood at the center, but everyone shared in it. Despite their fatigue, all day they winked or grinned at one another, as if the entire village had stayed up late making love.

The hangover arrived one week later, in the form of the most terrifying man on earth.

Part Four

UMBRELLAS

Chapter 18

In *April's last days* the apple boughs were flamboyant with blossoms, hundreds of varieties in rows a thousand trees long, pinking the hills and hollows, the world perfumed with softness and humming from the attentions of bees. The officer supervising construction of the seawall provided a prickly counterbalance, braying at the local men performing forced labor under his command.

"When the Field Marshal visits tomorrow," he bellowed, his face reddening as he struggled to be heard over the surf, "you will remove your caps out of respect. Failure to do so is unacceptable, and will bring severe penalties."

The men paused with their shovels and hoes, several reaching unconsciously to touch the brim of their caps. All men wore hats in those days, berets as common as pants.

"Back to work," the officer said, sauntering down the line of laborers. "And tomorrow you *will* remove your caps."

When the Field Marshal arrived the following afternoon, a caravan of cars and security officers preceding his open sedan with flags on all four corners, not one of the laborers was wearing a hat. They had come to work bareheaded, and that is how they toiled all day in the spring sun.

As lackeys hovered on either side, the Field Marshal conducted a preliminary review, ordering measurements in one place, adjustments in another. Toward the end he peered down on the laborers and said a single word. "Sunburned."

"They are not wearing caps today," the supervising officer said. "Out of respect for you."

The Field Marshal raised one eyebrow, whether out of pleasure or skepticism it was impossible to tell.

"Sir," the officer said, bowing and backing away, then turning to shout at the men to step lively and work harder.

The next day dawned gusty with rain, metal-gray clouds hanging ponderous and low, and the Field Marshal in a comparable humor. Following an impulse of either courage or folly, the Kommandant suggested a diversion on the way to inspections farther up the coast. It might lift everyone's spirits to meet the local woman he insisted was the finest baker anywhere. "An artist of flour," he called her. The Field Marshal made a face, which the others took for affirmation, and the caravan detoured into Emma's soggy barnyard.

As the cars and truck stopped and the Kommandant explained himself to the assemblage, Emma fretted over whether a person unaccustomed to straw in his bread would notice. Either the Field Marshal would discover her subterfuge, or her baking would receive its highest compliment yet.

But that was a fool's vanity. If he tasted straw she would die, and her death would cause others to starve, Mémé first among them.

Dry under an umbrella held by an aide, the Kommandant in his aristocratic lisp professed her praises to the waiting troops, his minions, his visiting superior officer. Emma said nothing, and knew what she knew.

"Give the Field Marshal a taste," the Kommandant said in her language. "Let him judge for himself."

Emma observed the Field Marshal frankly. He was a handsome man, with sharp cheekbones, his eyes soft as though they had witnessed great sadness, and a tentative manner that she decided might be a form of humility, because every person those gentle eyes fell upon was instantly seized with fear.

"I apologize," Emma said. "The bread is still baking."

"Mademoiselle, make me look good," the Kommandant urged, his smile hardening.

"Your aide normally comes at eight, and it is seven fifteen," she explained. "I put the loaves in the oven only a moment ago. They must bake for nineteen minutes and cool for ten."

"You are saying this commander cannot have a sample?" The Kommandant stiffened. "I order you to give him bread."

"With respect, I cannot obey. All he will taste is hot dough."

He turned and said something to the Field Marshal, laughing, but it was a strange and strained sound that came out and the Field Marshal's expression did not change.

The Kommandant grabbed his aide's green canvas bag and threw it at Emma's feet. "You will bring the loaves to the command post on the bluff the moment they are done."

"That is six kilometers from here. Will you be sending a car or motorcycle?"

By way of reply, the Kommandant climbed into his staff car and tapped on the roof. The vehicle sped away, the retinue of other cars and trucks close behind, splashing puddles and dirtying themselves with mud.

After the last vehicle had lumbered down the lane, Pirate came charging out of the barn in full crow.

"Oh, *now* you show up," Emma said. But the bird only preened and pecked at the ground, pretending not to hear.

As the loaves baked, Emma knew that there would be no satisfying the Field Marshal. If she made new dough, it was two kneadings and three risings away from the oven—hours upon hours. There was the beauty of baking and the frustration of it: the process could not be hurried, any more than a calf could be forced to grow or a tree to take root. Bread takes its own time. Therefore, if she made a new batch, without straw, she could not deliver loaves to the Kommandant till midafternoon, which would generate all manner of suspicions.

No, she would have to bring compromised loaves to the command post, and pray that the Field Marshal's taste buds were as undiscerning as the Kommandant's. Donning oven mitts, she slid the baguettes one by one out of the heat and onto a cooling rack. The *V*s were nearly invisible, fading as the bread torpedoes had crusted and browned.

Emma was not concerned for her own well-being any longer. She had already accepted the losses inevitable to living in that difficult time. There would be no marriage or children, no home comforts or taste of prosperity. Pleasure had ended with her youth and it was not coming back. Philippe—how she ached for him, his affection, his innocence—would never return from conscription. Or if he did, it would be as a broken shell. The Allies would never invade; the occupying army was a permanent fact of life. Emma's concern therefore lay with those who depended upon her, whose lives leaned on the crutch of her network. For her to die would be an act of abandonment. Somehow it was easier to worry about Mémé's survival than her own.

The command post was not that far. Emma covered a greater distance in her rounds every day. Nor was she concerned that it had begun to rain in earnest, coming down like a cow peeing on a rock. Wet weather was something the villagers adapted to from birth, as readily as desert people to blazing sun and arctic people to ice. Primarily Emma felt the pressure of time: she had connections to make, trades to accomplish, and needs to satisfy before the evening curfew. The extra walk would compromise everything else, and fish on the dock would not keep unrefrigerated any more than chickens could lay without feed.

She dug in a cabinet and found an umbrella—not for herself but for the bread, which she slid loaf by warm loaf into the green canvas bag of the Kommandant's aide, hooking the umbrella handle in as well to keep the bread dry.

Two baguettes remained on the drying rack. Could Mémé be trusted to deliver them? Not without risking much more than the bread. Could Emma leave the loaves for later? They might harden, or be seen by anyone passing by. Perhaps if she changed her route, asking certain people to make deliveries on her behalf.

That was it. There were no alternatives. She eased the extra loaves in beside the others, threw the bag's strap over her shoulder, and set out into the rain. She angled the umbrella to spare the bread, as if the end of the loaf were the face of a baby.

Chapter 19

E*mma trudged down muddy lanes,* angling against the rainfall. She had brewed extra tea to keep Mémé sedate while she was gone, though it was actually ground chicory and rose-ends, supplies of real tea having run out years before.

Perhaps, Emma considered, she was walking to her execution. She had no alternatives, possessed no weapons. All she had was rage—which might be the better half of courage, but it had never won a war—and fourteen cooling loaves.

Her plan was to drop one baguette with Yves, if his boat was in the harbor, and another with Fleur, who babysat her broken mother in a house near the sea. Each of them was capable of dividing and delivering a loaf, while Emma continued with the remaining dozen to the command post north of Longues.

The Kommandant would see his order obeyed. The Field Marshal would have his sample. Either he would like the bread, allowing her to live, or he would taste the straw, and her days would end. In a few hours Mémé's tea would run out, she would call for help, and no one would come. Gradually everyone who depended upon her network, from Pierre to Fleur, from Michelle to Marguerite, would lose the necessities that Emma provided. It was not a long walk to the command post, but a slow one with the roads so soggy.

Along puttered a motorcycle of the occupying army, splashing through the puddles. Emma stepped aside for it to pass, but the rider slowed. She gritted her teeth, ready to parry a flirtation or absorb scorn, as the motorcycle came to a stop. The rider lifted his hood and she saw that it was Captain Thalheim.

"Hello, Sergeant," she said. The days of rapport, of morning visits to the baking shed, were long gone.

He did not so much as blink. "The Kommandant commands me for to give the baguette woman a ride."

"He doesn't want me to get wet? What a gentleman."

"He doesn't want the Field Marshal to receive soggy bread." He thumbed at the space behind him. "Climb on."

Emma had too many loaves. The two extras would give her away before anyone took a bite. As she deliberated, the rain fell sideways across her face.

"The Kommandant's patience is thin today. Climb on."

Emma had no alternative. There was no sidecar either, only the back half of his seat. "Look away," she said, and when he did, she hiked her skirts and threw one leg over the saddle. Angling the umbrella to shield the bread, Emma leaned forward enough that she hoped not to touch him any more than necessary. But Thalheim revved the throttle and popped the clutch so that she nearly fell off, and she was compelled to grab him.

"No talk," he said, bouncing through the ruts toward the command post, where there awaited the unsuspecting taste buds of a man who could end her life with a nod.

A guard lifted one hand, keeping the other on his machine gun's trigger, and Thalheim slowed the motorcycle to pull back the hood of his slicker. The guard saluted, which tipped rain off the brim of his helmet, and waved them on. Emma held the captain's shoulder, still shielding the bread, as they wove through the trucks and outposts to a wide wet field rounded by barbed wire. Finally they arrived at a guarded gate.

"Off," Thalheim said, halting. "From here we walk."

Emma dismounted, attempting to smooth her dress, though it was sodden. He led the way through a maze of wires, until they reached a tent in which there was a desk. A soldier there put down his cigarette to salute the captain. While they exchanged words Emma tried to sidle out. Perhaps she could drop two loaves behind a tent flap. But they finished their business quickly and Thalheim hurried past.

"Stay close," he muttered.

As she followed, another guard tagged along. He sniffed his runny nose, and Emma observed that he was young, perhaps fifteen. He was carrying a strange gun, too—like an ordinary rifle but sealed in all openings except the barrel. He labored under its weight.

"What is happening?" Emma asked.

"An escort, in case you try anything foolish. This area is secure."

Thalheim's comment caused Emma to lift her gaze and survey the land around them. Vision blurred by the sideways rain, she could tell that it was vast, two wheat fields in addition to the unmown hay field they were marching across, but what stopped her midstride was the discovery that the farm had been converted into a massive battery. Steel-gray guns, their barrels easily ten meters long, poked out of fortifications that were shaped like giant helmets, but made of concrete two meters thick. Their roofs covered with branches and leaves, the pillboxes arced around the field so that the guns pointed out to sea in all directions, especially the long beaches that interrupted the bluffs and cliffs of coastline.

"Don't delay," Thalheim snarled. "No one here is in good humor."

He stormed ahead, Emma trotting to catch up. But after a moment the young guard fell into step beside her. "I speaks your language," he said. "I only needs practice of."

"What is this place?"

"Brilliant, no? These guns can hits a target twenty kilometers away. And their shelters can takes a direct hit from guns as big as they."

"Don't talk to her," Thalheim barked. "Don't give her any kind of information."

"Yes, sir."

But the captain could not help speaking himself. "You are a pathetic, weak people," he said to Emma. "We are the greatest military power in the history of mankind, and you are insects. We can crush you at any time."

She trudged through the wet grass, her dress heavy, the bag of bread an awkward burden with its umbrella. But the exertion warmed her, as did the annoyance of Thalheim's blabbering. With the young guard huffing alongside, however, Emma could not see any way to shed the spare baguettes.

"Of course our leader knows the waters are narrowest between Dover and Calais," Thalheim continued. "He built there the launching sites for our new rocket missiles, like inviting an invasion. That is how certain we are of superiorities. The one bad element is that if the Allied attack comes there, we here will miss the action. We will be deprived of the opportunity for glory."

"There is no such thing as glory," Emma said.

He laughed at that, one harsh bark. "Not for you people, no. But our E-boats engaged with your Allies in April, very near to here, and sank all their ships, every one. That was glory."

Emma did not reply. The young guard with the big rifle did, though. "Glory for our navy, perhaps yes, sir, but not so much for we soldiers here on this lands."

"If your friends attack here," Thalheim told Emma, "it will be at high tide, when the beaches are narrow and the exposure is limited. I personally heard the Field Marshal say so."

They were nearly across the field. Emma could see officers clustered beside a construction zone, a rain canopy over their heads. They kept their backs to the wind, and to the men laboring with shovels a few steps away.

"You people," Thalheim continued, raising his voice against the weather, "are lazy, passive, and weak. The wine, the climate, the women." He shook his head in dismay. "But we have the wisest commanders, the greatest discipline, the best armaments."

"Begs to differ on that last item, sir," the young guard said.

Thalheim pulled up short. "Excuse me?"

"This weapon I carries here, sir, for example."

"Gewehr 41, excellent rifle. Very powerful, very accurate."

"But heavy, sir. Almost impossible to runs with."

"Which makes it ideal for these circumstances, defending high ground."

Emma marveled at the debate between them, conducted in her language and therefore somehow for her benefit, though why they would care about her opinion was a mystery.

"Well, what about the single-shot bazooka I were issued at my regular post, sir?"

Thalheim nodded. "The iron fist."

"Impossible to aim and therefore useless for guardings. From what I see in training, it is nearly suicidal to operate."

"Nonsense. Your comments are treasonous."

"But I've heard you yourself, sir, speaks of problems with using captured weapons, and our less excellent models."

"Naturally our best matériel must go to the Eastern Front, where the enemy is stubborn and strong. Nonetheless . . ." Thalheim recommenced striding, chest out as they crossed the last of the field. "Nonetheless, I say, our weapons are finest of quality. Our leaders make no wrong decisions, provide no wrong leadership. And you. Be careful what you say. You are very disloyal."

The three of them reached the edge of the canopied area. At the last moment Thalheim stopped, adjusted his helmet, tugged down on the ends of his sleeves, and cleared his throat. As the officers turned and cleared a path for him, Emma deduced what this moment was actually about: impressing people. Thalheim had brought her quickly in order to impress the Kommandant, who in turn had commanded Emma to bring the loaves in order to impress the Field Marshal.

That man, however, stood aside, not speaking, his trimness and stillness a form of contained menace, like a land mine. He turned to an aide, who provided a set of field glasses without the Field Marshal needing to ask. Emma recognized the aide with a surprising surge of venom: it was the officer with the pencil-thin moustache, the one who had struck her father with a club. Emma marveled that he could not feel the heat of her yearning for vengeance. He merely bowed and moved away. The Field Marshal raised the binoculars to his face and inspected up and down the coastline. Emma wondered if there was anyone whom *he* needed to impress.

"I have brought the bread woman," Thalheim announced.

A murmur of approval went through the cluster of men, a space opened, and Emma stepped beneath the canopy. At once she experienced how much pleasanter life was out of the downpour.

She scanned the soldiers despite the close quarters, till her eye lit upon the Kommandant. Emma slid the canvas bag from her shoulder. Perhaps his desire to impress the Field Marshal would mean that he did not notice the extra loaves. Perhaps she would not be revealed.

"I tried my best to keep them dry," Emma said, setting the umbrella down without taking the time to close it. Trembling all over, whether from fear or the chill, she took a moment to imagine herself still alive in an hour, walking home in the rain.

"I'll be the judge of that," the Kommandant growled, handing his gloves to Thalheim without a word, as if the captain were a side table, placed there to hold house keys or the day's mail.

"I brought her as quickly as I could, sir," Thalheim said.

The Kommandant made no reply, sliding two baguettes from the bag and passing them to an aide. "Distribute these," he ordered. "The Field Marshal first, of course."

"Sir," the aide said, bowing.

Now, Emma thought. Now he will pay attention to his superior's appreciation of the bread, and I will be safe.

But the Field Marshal held up a gloved hand, making the aide wait while he continued to study the equipment and defenses on the beach below, taking time to deliberate. Emma suspected he was imagining a battle down there, probing his plan for any weakness. She wanted to tell him, "Don't worry, don't bother. They will never come."

The Kommandant removed two more baguettes, slid them out like swords from scabbards, half turned to give them to Thalheim for distribution, then caught himself. Emma watched his face as he calculated: two loaves to the Field Marshal, plus one now in each of his hands, plus the baguettes remaining in the canvas sack, one for each finger, poking out like the noses of ten popes.

With an expression of honest perplexity, the Kommandant looked into Emma's rain-drenched face for the first time since she had arrived.

"Fourteen?"

Chapter 20

T*he Field Marshal chose just that moment* to call for the Kommandant, who stared at the baguette in each of his hands as if they were grenades, then pressed them against the chest of the guard with a gruff order. The young man took the loaves with wide eyes, as if he were being chastised, while the Kommandant hurried to present himself at the Field Marshal's elbow, announcing his arrival with a clack of boot heels.

The Field Marshal was explaining something in soft tones, his hands relaxed while he pointed here and there, as if it were a casual conversation rather than preparations for savagery. The aide with binoculars at the ready stood by his side as tense as a violin string, and another remained a single step behind, holding one of Emma's baguettes. The Kommandant listened intently, his back taut like a drawn bow, eyes darting wherever the Field Marshal gestured, leaning closer so as not to miss a word.

"Come," Thalheim said, speaking from the side of his mouth. "See how strong we are."

Emma found that it took an effort to look away from the Field Marshal, wondering when he would eat her bread, and whether he would taste the straw. For the moment he continued to gesture up and down the beach.

"Don't mind them," Thalheim said. "They are discuss gun sighting, and the need to finish building of observation platform. Come observe, and despair."

Emma followed him to the side of the tent nearest the bluff and the slate-gray water below. It teemed from the rainfall, a billion eyes winking. The captain lit a cigarette, then spoke in low tones, a billow of smoke appearing with his words.

"See the iron barriers, there in the shallows? They have artillery shells attached to their tips, which we removed from the armories of your defeated army. Anything that touches them will be explode. The waters conceal at present, but likewise one hundred meters past low tide, we have driven logs into the sand with mines at their tips. Also railroad ties cut in half, rough end up, to rip the hull of any craft lucky enough to miss mines. We expect few if any ships to reach shore."

He pointed while he spoke, in unconscious imitation of the Field Marshal, continuing as coolly as if he were reciting the alphabet. Emma glanced at the Kommandant, who hovered at the Field Marshal's elbow, nodding every few seconds. The Field Marshal noticed the aide with a baguette, which he took without interrupting his speech. Rather, he continued lecturing, but instead of using his hand to gesture, the Field Marshal pointed with the long loaf of bread. Emma found it comical, that her life was at stake and the bread was serving as a pointer.

"Down there observe a section of the Atlantic Wall," Thalheim continued in her ear. "If anyone through miracles should survive our obstacles, the wall stops them. This barrier spans from Norway to Spain, four years of work thanks to our highest commander's brilliant vision. Thousands of tons of concrete, hundreds of thousands of steel rods. Also we have hundreds of kilometers of trenches, thousands of kilometers of barbed wire, millions of mines strung along the coast like a necklace of pearls. This requires manpower, materials, leadership." He squeezed one hand into a fist. "Above all else, discipline."

He drew on his cigarette and held the smoke in. Emma realized he was waiting for a reply. "Formidable," she said.

"Formidable? It is impenetrable." He exhaled, pointed over one shoulder. "The invaders deserve your deepest pity. Around this command post we have build twelve strong points, armed with 88s, 74s, and mortars. Those holes in the ground with tank turrets in them, those are Tobruks, and we have dozens. We place artillery in pillboxes above the beaches, concrete two meters thick. We have made install guns at angles to the beach for flanking fire. Most important, we have soldiers who are all educate and drill in following orders. They will not improvise, or feel fear, or leave their posts. They will do precisely as told."

Emma swallowed audibly. "Like a machine."

Thalheim put his hands on his hips, smoke from the cigarette in his mouth causing him to squint. "Right now the Field Marshal is ordering for 88s to be presighted, for maximum lethality. Rather than calculating a shot, gunners will use those wooden posts—you see? there in sand?—to know their range in advance. They wait for target to enter their sights. Then they destroy."

Emma noticed that Thalheim had never spoken her language with greater fluency. His chest was puffed out, his head high.

"This is entirely horrifying," she managed to say at last.

"You begin to understand. I pray your Allies attack here, the more to our greater glory. This is the place our enemy commits an extravagant suicide."

He waited, thumbs hooked in his belt. "For one time the smart miss has nothings to say to Captain Thalheim?"

"They will never come," she answered. *"Sergeant."*

He raised a hand as if to strike her, but an exclamation from his right interrupted the impulse.

"Exzellent," the Field Marshal was proclaiming, his mouth full and his words spewing crumbs. "Exzellent."

The Kommandant broke into a huge smile. Emma thought it looked like he had peed himself with relief.

The Field Marshal waved one hand in a circle—a magnanimous gesture she recognized from Odette's café as signifying that the person will buy a round for the house, but which in this case the aides and guard understood to mean that they should distribute the rest of the bread among everyone under the canopy. Thalheim ground out his cigarette and bulled past, Emma's impudence forgotten as he muscled toward the Kommandant to receive his share.

The young guard handed away the two loaves in his hand, then waved Emma over. She weaseled through the men, all large and wearing bulky foul-weather gear, to hand him the canvas sack. He tried to pull out a baguette, but it was too long to remove completely with his gun in the same hand.

He glanced to the side, spotted a table covered with maps, and leaned his rifle against it. Then he turned and began working his way forward through the crowd of officers, holding baguettes up so that they could tear portions off for themselves.

First, Emma felt relief. The fact of fourteen loaves was forgotten, the straw undetected. But as the men began eating, laughing and jostling one another, comparing the size of their portions of bread and bragging if they'd received a larger one, she experienced a second realization: they had forgotten her.

Emma was female, one of the local people, too weak to be feared, too small to notice. So sure were the men of their power, she had become invisible. No one was looking, no one protecting. Meanwhile the young guard's rifle leaned against a table not two steps from her right leg.

Emma had never fired a gun before. She could remember

holding one on three occasions: once assisting Philippe when he bagged a deer and wanted to dress it where it fell, and twice when her father had managed to shoot a rabbit in spite of his bad eyesight, and needed both hands to put the carcass in his hunting sack. But she also remembered the lesson the drunk corporal had been giving to his friend when they accidentally shot the pig that never existed. It was a matter of aiming and squeezing, and using the impact of one shot to decide where the next should go.

She lifted her gaze. As if by design the men had lined up for her, left to right: Thalheim, the Kommandant, the Field Marshal, the officer with the pencil-thin mustache. Here stood every one of the men that she wanted to die. Forget the knife on her thigh. It was messy and slow and she would be overpowered. One grab of the rifle, however, one lift to her shoulder, one long squeeze on that trigger, and she would lay them low.

Nothing could stop her, until it was too late.

Of course the other officers, after a stunned moment, would annihilate her, a dozen guns, a hundred bullets, her existence blasted upon the bluff above where she had played childhood games and learned to swim and sometimes strolled with Philippe for romance. But then, what better place? It would happen too quickly for her to feel pain. All she needed to do was seize it: the gun, her destiny, the opportunity, and she would change the course of history. All she needed to do.

Yet Emma did not act. The scene of slaughter replayed itself in her mind, the power of it, the certainty of success, while her arms hung dully at her sides. Despite years of occupation and oppression, despite the deaths of people she loved, still her desire for revenge remained frozen. Emma genuinely wanted those men to die, but she lacked the capacity to kill.

The moment passed. The young guard returned to collect his weapon, handing Emma the empty canvas sack with no idea of the danger that had passed. The officers recommenced their tasks, arguing over maps or attending to the Field Marshal, while Emma thought of Uncle Ezra, of Guillaume, of Philippe and her father and the others taken away, of the many villagers who had shown so much courage, and knew with lacerating shame that she herself possessed none.

Thalheim swaggered back, speaking with his mouth full. "I'll grant you have talent in bread, but our nation's rule will last one thousand years. What do you say to that?"

"I think you are probably right," Emma said, the first words she had uttered to him without bite in her voice. "I think that from here on, everything that happens to me, I deserve."

As she spoke a gust of wind swept in from the east, driving rain under the canopy so that the officers turned away. The air also caught Emma's umbrella, snatched it tumbling across the bluff.

As she hurried after it, Thalheim called out, "I wouldn't chase that if I were you." He chuckled. "That whole area is mined."

Emma halted where she stood, at the height of land, rain pelting her back. The umbrella cartwheeled twice, then toppled over the side.

"Ha." Thalheim chortled. "Are you upsets at losing your umbrella?"

"No." Emma continued to gaze over the bluff. "I am upset at being so weak."

As she watched, though, Emma had to admit that there was an elegance to the umbrella's fall: like a trapeze artist, swaying close to the bluff and then away, a flower thrown overboard from a ship, smoothly back and forth, a feather fallen from a nest, gliding down to a place on the sand, where it landed without a sound.

Chapter 21

T*he laboring men received sunburns indeed*, some more severely than others depending on complexion, but which swiftly became symbolic. Within days, people far from the construction site, farmers and shopkeepers, janitors and magistrates, had left their hats at home and cultivated a burn. Red skin manifested solidarity. Freckles became fashionable.

As May arrived and the sunlight strengthened, people standing in the rations line could not resist the temptation to compare their tans. Odette was least darkened, because of her hours in the kitchen. Pierre had mottled skin, perhaps due to age. Monkey Boy was golden from his days in the trees. Mémé's face had grown dappled, which made her eyes seem brighter.

The darkest arms of all belonged to Emma. Her circuit of the town, its farms and forests, placed her in daylight hour upon hour, every day. Yet her most important work, the fuel that powered her entire engine of deceit and survival, took place before the sun was up.

On each day following the Field Marshal's visit, Emma continued to knead and shape and mark with a *V* her dozen compulsory baguettes, plus the two that were the baker's secret. As the weeks passed, had the loaves been stacked together, they would have made a pile to feed multitudes.

But then the fifth of June arrived. At dawn, Emma roused

herself from a sleep so deep it allowed her a respite from hunger. As she crossed the barnyard, silenced Pirate with a bribe of barley, and put herself to work, she had no way of knowing that this day's baguettes would be the last ones she made in her life.

Straw is sinewy, like gristle. It takes strong wrists to grind the grass down. But Emma had mixed the dough so many times she barely noticed the effort. She paused now and then, only to tuck back a rebellious strand of hair. Soon the baguettes lay in their places, tanning as they baked, and Emma noticed the first daylight leaking between boards in the barn's eastern wall. She went to the doorway, saw the pinking sky, and allowed herself a brief wander down the lane for a better view.

At just that moment, the sun found an opening in the clouds. Daylight poured down on the barnyard, illuminating the old stone house, casting shadows through the hedgerows, making grass glint and crows rise, flooding the village square and every house along the way. It brought the warmth of awakening.

The Goat stirred in the hog shed, having slept so hard on the shelf the planks left an impression in his cheek. The stink of the air was enough to make his eyes water. But around him stood all those wooden boxes he had smuggled there, two by two, for months. His legs lay across one stack as a miser sleeps atop his gleaming hoard. The captain in the house would never find these boxes. He was too concerned with keeping his fingers clean. The Goat sat up and rubbed his face with both hands.

Pierre finished sharpening a pencil, packed the curls of wood into his pipe and wished for fresh tobacco as fervently as he had once wished for a bride. He squinted in the morning light, accepting that neither desire would be granted that day. Ambling into the side yard, where his girls stood awaiting milking, he held a match to his pipe and blew gray smoke into the sky.

Fleur, the veterinarian's daughter, dressed without speaking, tied the blue apron around her waist, and plunged her hands into the patch pockets to confirm that certain somethings were still in there. Then she went to wake her mother. Marie had all but ceased eating, ever since the day three soldiers took her behind the woodshed and she ordered Fleur to stay away. Perhaps a rind of cheese would appeal to Marie today.

The war could not prevent an early June morning from glistening with dew. Hedgerows rang with the gossip of birds. In later years many villagers insisted they could not remember hearing any birds during the occupation, but of course they were there, flitting through the branches and calling over the fields.

Cats prowled barns, Apollo wandered in search of Neptune, and Mémé clasped a pottery bowl with both hands, trying to recall whether her grandmother had made it, or her granddaughter. Time had grown so untrustworthy.

Monkey Boy was skipping down the lane by the western well when he entered a tunnel of light, his shadow tall on the ground at his feet. At once he made his gait stiff-legged, lumbering like a giant, arms spread as though he were a tree. "Whishhh," he sang, flourishing his fingers like leaves.

The clouds closed, the sun vanished, and Emma broke from her reverie. She crossed the barnyard, knotting her hair. Pirate strutted alongside, quieter now that day had begun. She peered into the house to see Mémé at the stove making tea, the sight calming Emma for a moment.

Then she heard a noise from the baking shed, realizing with a start that she had not yet put certain things away. She dashed across the barnyard, and there was Captain Thalheim, squatting beside her basin of ground straw. Emma pulled up short, skirt bunching around her legs.

"Good morning, mademoiselle," he said, straightening. As usual he was freshly shaven, his uniform neat. He nudged the mortar and pestle with his boot. "What we have here?"

"Grain," she said, swallowing hard. "A special grain. I use it to add body to the loaves."

The captain bent to pick up the bowl. "A special grain."

Emma's heart fluttered. "A kind of grass, like wheat."

"To add body? What does this mean?"

"So the loaves travel well, with a toothy crust," she said.

He sniffed the bowl's contents. "You add this every day?"

"If the dough feels weak, I do."

"We cannot be giving officers of weak bread."

"Of course not."

He nodded, considering. "You will eat some."

"Excuse me?"

"I do not know if it is poison, or filth, or some clever idea, but I do not trust this special grass. You will eat some now."

Emma had not swallowed one sip of water yet that day. Her throat was already parched. There was no way she could swallow straw, no matter how finely ground. She would gag, or possibly choke.

But the captain had a spoon. Where had he found it? He motioned for her to sit on the stool where she'd been grinding earlier. He held a heaping spoonful in front of her face.

"Now," he said.

And Emma opened her mouth.

Chapter 22

N*o deception lasts forever.* Truth rises like good bread dough. Emma collapsed to the baking barn's dirt floor, her breath blocked by a knot of yellow powder. Captain Thalheim stood with the spoon in his hand, his expression blank while the straw choked her. Emma's vision became a tunnel, surrounded by gathering dark. Finally she hooked a finger in her mouth and scooped the dry knot out, coughing, wheezing relief through a cramping throat.

"As I thought," Captain Thalheim announced, his voice flat. He squatted beside her. "I must now report for duty. When I have made return, we will hear more about this special grass that chokes the baker."

His motorcycle gargled into life, and sped off with a flatulent clatter. Emma staggered to the barn door, and who was standing there but the Goat. He held a bucket of water.

Emma wobbled past him toward the house, then fell to her knees. In an instant the Goat was beside her, one hand on the back of her neck, the other ladling water into her mouth. She swallowed and rinsed and spat to one side, then gulped greedily. Finally she caught her breath, and worked herself back to her feet. "Your hands are filthy."

He remained there on the ground, not answering.

Mémé appeared at the farmhouse door. "Gypsy? Do we Gypsy now?"

Emma scooped herself more water. Without turning her head she asked, "Do you have shoes on?"

Mémé looked down at her stocking feet and laughed in surprise. "Shoes," she said, holding up one finger as she vanished back into the house.

Emma collected herself, scrutinizing the Goat as he knelt. His sleeves were worn at the elbows, his beret streaked with mud. He stank of pig. He fixed his gaze on the bucket, as though it would be wrong to look at her. Yet he had shown the audacity to offer help, and in a moment of weakness she had accepted it. At the notion of being indebted to the Goat, Emma reared back as a horse does from a snake in the road.

A windup timer rang in the barn. The Kommandant's loaves were ready. Emma swatted dirt from her dress as though it were an old rug, splashed her face from the bucket, and assessed the Goat once more. Still he knelt at her feet.

"Do you have anything to say?"

He touched his beret. "At your service, Emmanuelle."

"Oh, stand up," she said, turning away. "Where is your self-respect?"

Not an hour later, Emma had composed herself sufficiently to hand the Kommandant's aide his dozen loaves indifferently, and he puttered off on his motorbike. The dust from his departure still hung in the air as she organized her daily cart of tricks: containers and loaves, items for barter or salvation, tools and necessities, all under a pile of cloth and jackets and means of concealment. She had nearly choked, and the captain had found her out, but the work could not wait.

"Gypsy Gypsy," Mémé cried, rapping the knuckles of one

hand against the other, harder and harder until Emma reached over to calm her.

"Are you coming with me today?" she asked. "Or do you want to water the garden?"

"Garden," Mémé said with a fierce expression.

"Lovely." Emmanuelle lowered a tin watering can from a hook inside the barn and handed it to Mémé. The old woman hugged the can to her chest with both arms. Emma caressed her grandmother's cheek. "Can you keep out of trouble? I'll be back for the noon dinner."

"Come. I want."

"Then please do," Emma said. Shoving the cart's clutter aside, she placed a pillow in the middle. Mémé settled her rump there. Emma went to the front and slipped the harness around her shoulders, Mémé's feet dangling half a meter off the ground.

"Gypsy," the woman sang to herself, squeezing the watering can with her thighs. "Gypsy."

And they set off to keep the village alive.

Emma's habit was to distract Mémé during the actual exchanges, lest she blurt something later in front of Thalheim. It meant inventing games to occupy the old woman's mind—*count-the-birds* proved a favorite, as was *how-many-flowers*. It would have been pleasant if Emma had not possessed such strong memories of her grandmother at the peak of her intellect. Wise Mémé had gone simple, aged Mémé had become childlike. Sometimes Emma returned from a transaction to find her grandmother sitting straight-legged on the ground, petting a frog or contemplating a grasshopper. Once Mémé was toying with a wasp, yet inexplicably went unstung.

That June day there were no birds in sight, and the hedgerow lacked blooms for anyone to count. At the base of a knoll, Emma poured a bit from her canteen into the watering can in Mémé's lap. Swirling the liquid within, she tapped the side with her fingertips. It made a wobbling, musical sound. Mémé's face brightened. She hoisted the can near one ear and tapped it for herself.

"That should keep you for a bit," Emma said, kissing her grandmother's brow, then hurrying up the rise to see. Yes, the red scarf flew from Michelle's upper window like the national flag of indecency. The motorcycle stood in the yard, leaning on its stand like a braggart on a lamppost. Emma angled a small brown egg into the cleft of the chestnut tree. Then with one hand she raised her dress a few inches, the easier to bustle up the hill. With the other hand, she held a large glass jug. In a swift motion she uncapped the fuel tank, poked one end of the black hose she had stolen from the army's truck into the opening, covered the other end with her mouth, and sucked.

There was an art to siphoning which Emma had yet to master. Sometimes she pulled exactly long enough, moving her mouth away at the perfect moment while pointing the tip of the hose at the jug. More often she sucked for too long, earning herself a sip of the petrol. No amount of spitting, nor any food she ate for the rest of the day, would rid her of the rancid flavor. It tasted like deceit.

That morning the fuel had just reached her mouth when she spun the hose away, only a trace touching her lips. Good thing she had no kissing planned, Emma mused, wiping her mouth on her sleeve. The jug made a musical tinkling as it filled.

Faintly, too, she could hear Mémé tapping the watering can down the hill. It provided a reassuring rhythm. By contrast the bungalow behind her remained silent. Emma did not bother to imagine what might be taking place within. It served her purposes and that was enough.

The other technique she had not yet learned was how to stop the flow before the tank was empty. After all, the lusty lieutenant needed to drive several kilometers back to the motor pool, where the motorbike's next rider would fill the tank not knowing the machine had sat unused nearly the whole time it had been gone. If Planeg ran out of gas on the way back to duty, it would reveal what had been stolen. But Emma had no way of telling how full the tank was, or when to stop. Eventually she settled on draining it completely, then pouring a portion back in from the jug. Better not to arouse suspicion.

Emma straightened, rubbing a sore place on her neck. Was that the sound of an airplane? She squinted north, the sky blank, when the source of the noise revealed itself: another motorcycle, burning a trail of dust uphill toward the place where she stood.

She yanked out the hose—no time for a partial refill—capped the tank, and scurried for the woods. Had the rider seen her? Emma could not run with the jug, but she hugged to the edge of the brush, working her way down toward Mémé. This motorcycle was larger than Planeg's, and roared up to the front of the bungalow. The soldier hopped off, leaning the bike on its stand but leaving his engine running.

"Planeg?" he shouted. *"Plannn-eg."*

There was no response. Emma inched farther down the hill, fringing the rough bracken. If she were caught, how would she explain being in this place? With a jug of petrol? And would there be enough in the tank for the lieutenant's return trip?

"Damn it, Planeg," the soldier yelled. He pounded the blue door with the side of his fist.

An upstairs window opened and the lieutenant's head poked

out. His arms and shoulders were bare. He and the soldier exchanged bursts of words, the new arrival's gestures expressing urgency and Planeg's tone one of reluctance. The soldier outside gave a last volley of anger, scuffing his boot in the dirt before climbing on his machine and barreling down the hill. He did not notice Emma, bent small at the edge of the woods.

Moments later Planeg burst out of the house buckling his belt. He wore his uniform jacket but the shirt beneath was open and untucked. Kicking the motorcycle into life, he popped a helmet on his head. Michelle appeared at the doorway, but whatever she called to him was lost over the engine's grumble.

Worried that the commotion would pique her grandmother's curiosity, and assuming she had time yet while the soldier finished dressing, Emma sidestepped through the steep brush toward Mémé. But no, the motor revved and here he came already, one hand holding the throttle and steering while the other fumbled with the buttons on his shirt. Emma froze.

It was too late. Planeg zipped past, glancing at first, then turning to look again, directly at Emma. She felt it like cold water thrown in her face. He had seen her plainly and without cover. The hose in her hand, the jug. He buzzed away, not pausing, a black comet trailing brown dust. Whatever he had been summoned for mattered more than her presence in the trees, but he would certainly remember seeing her there. Emma sat on the ground, the jug to one side. For the second time that day, she had been found out.

The motorcycle's whine dwindled and then the woods were quiet. Emma waited a bit longer, in case Michelle had lingered to gaze after her lover, before rising to continue downhill. But there was noise in the brush. Emma leaned past a fan of ferns to see Michelle, tiptoeing up to the chestnut tree.

Her dress hung loosely open, not one button fastened, but with a webbing of lace beneath. Emma pulled a fern aside for a better view. She knew women's bodies, of course—her own, Mémé's—but strictly in matter-of-fact fashion: washing to avoid illness, dressing for durability and work. This attire, this allure, was something different, brazen, arresting.

Michelle reached for her egg, and her breasts were revealed to broad daylight, pink and full. Emma immediately thought of Philippe, his warm lips on her skin, his kisses on her nipples, and she felt a sudden private kinship with Michelle. This woman's affair with Planeg was not so foreign after all.

Michelle stepped back from the tree. Her hair was wild in disarray, yet the more beautiful for it, her lips swelled as from mad kisses. Showing immense care, she cracked the egg with her fingers and split it, slowly pouring from one half to the other. Emma recognized this old baker's trick. Uncle Ezra had called it hand-by-hand, a way to separate an egg's whites from the yolk without dirtying a bowl. Emma herself never dared do it without something beneath, in case she spilled. How had this woman learned such a skill?

Before she could imagine an explanation, Michelle tilted one half of the shell, gliding the yellow into her mouth. She swallowed the yolk whole, an audible gulp. Then she raised the other half, unceremoniously pouring the raw whites onto the top of her scalp. Emma watched dumbfounded as the woman tossed the shells aside and used both hands to work the ooze into her hair, making it thicken and glisten.

Emma felt a flutter in her insides. It was frightening and strange, and she was unable to look away. What Emma felt was not desire, but fascination with another's desire. She and Michelle were the same age, they had been schoolmates. Yet never in her life had Emma lavished such rich attention on her hair, or any other part of herself. She had spent so much energy striving, she had forgotten entirely about delight. For a moment it seemed as if she had never had a childhood. The one concession she made to vanity, the hair bows Philippe loved to untie, she had stopped wearing on the day he was conscripted. Since then, the occupation had turned her nearly into a farm animal, concerned with practicality and the next meal. But Michelle had kept pleasure in her life, had made it key to her survival. It was an entirely opposite response to the occupation, arguably a superior one. For one lonely moment Emma could not deny it: she contained a great reservoir of sadness.

Michelle finished combing the whites through her hair, working from the crown to the ends, then turned to climb the hill toward her bungalow, open garments trailing, blue door open, red banner flying.

Chapter 23

Yves stood on the dock, watching soldiers load his day's catch into their truck. Bitterns stood at the water's edge, their feathered heads raised as though they were supervising. An officer swaggered over to the fisherman.

"You are less good as before," he said. "You used to catch more."

"That was when I could go farther out to set my nets," Yves answered, bristling. He bent to coil a rope. "I need more fuel."

"Everyone around this place," the officer said, shaking his head. "Forever holding your hands out. Give me this, more of that. No pride. If we did not need they fish, I say shoot they all."

"That may happen anyway, right?"

The officer laughed. "You have a dark humor."

"Was I joking?"

A private presented himself to announce that the last of the fish was loaded. "Right in time," the officer said, nodding in Emma's direction. "Your girlfriend is now arrive."

She pulled the cart aside to give the truck room as it lumbered up from the docks. By the time she reached his boat, Yves sat on the bow massaging one hand with the other. "I am running out of patience with these people," he said.

"Likewise," Emma answered, drawing back a cloth to reveal her jug. "Yet it continues."

"Fishing is hard work. It galls me to do it for them."

She nodded. "Baking is not hard work, but it galls me, too."

Yves took the fuel to the stern. "Maybe they will run out of patience as well, and do us the favor of shooting one another."

"You have the imagination of a poet."

"Or a clown." Yves tipped the jug's contents into his tank. "The wind is nothing today, so this sip will get us ten or fifteen kilometers out. More for everyone, if all goes well."

"Let us hope so."

"Where do you find this fuel, Emma?"

She shrugged. "Who knew Monkey Boy peed gasoline?"

Yves chuckled, returning with the empty jug. "You know, I had a decent run this morning, not half bad. But they took everything. Every single fish."

"Yves, people are taking risks to provide this fuel. They are counting on me to bring them something in return."

"So I kept something the soldiers didn't want." He disappeared into the cabin, returning a moment later with two lobsters, their claws spread wide.

"Nasty." Emma recoiled. "Uglier than spiders."

"They're delicious, believe me."

She wrapped each of the lobsters in cloth, placing them in her cart, and returning with one third of a baguette. "Do I come later for more fish?"

"I owe you so much." Yves took the bread in both hands. "I will return only when I have caught something."

When Emma brought the first of the ocean spiders to Odette, the buxom woman clapped her hands together. "Excellent, excellent. A perfect way to celebrate."

Emma stood in the doorway of the café, which was deserted in that hour between late lunches and early dinners. "What on this battered world can there possibly be to celebrate?"

"The fall of Rome."

"I beg your pardon?"

"The soldiers were blabbering about it at the noon meal. The Allies have taken Rome. Mark this day, the fifth of June. The Fascists are in retreat."

Emma lowered herself into a chair. "Rome."

"You see? The Allies have retaken the capital of an occupied nation. When the soldiers were discussing it, all doom and disaster, that was more delicious than a banquet."

"Odette." Emma dug a thumbnail into the tabletop. "How long did it take?"

"From Sicily to Rome? Two years, I believe."

"Do you think we can survive that long?"

Odette nodded. "Easily."

"Easily," Emma echoed, and they both laughed. But when they finished, their silence was long.

Odette took a bottle of Calvados from the shelf and poured them each a small glass. Lowering herself into the other chair at Emma's table, she folded her pudgy fingers. "You know what this means," she said. "We are next. They have to come here now."

Emma shook her head. "They will never come."

"Oh, you." Odette threw back her drink in one gulp.

"Too many people use hope to hide their misery."

"That is the pessimism of the fortunate."

Emma interrupted her swallow of Calvados. "Excuse me?"

"You, for example, have Mémé out there in the wagon, happily fidgeting while you sit here. That is all you require to get out of bed in the morning. You are needed, as simple as that. But those of us with no family, no such luck, we go for the cheap stuff. We settle for having a sip of hope."

"Tell me again how fortunate I am, please." Emma spoke through gritted teeth. "Uncle Ezra dead, my father gone, my innocent Philippe taken who knows where. Oh, lucky me."

Odette stood, taking the lobster into the kitchen. "Be as grouchy as you like. I am going to celebrate."

Emma considered her empty glass. Apparently her supply of retorts was drained, too. Hearing pans banging, she called out. "How does one cook those ugly things?"

"Many methods," Odette answered from the kitchen doorway. "But for once the best way is also the easiest: boil twelve minutes, perhaps with a diced onion."

"What should I do with the other one? Who would eat such a thing?"

Odette scanned the ceiling as if counting something up there. "The Argent couple, I suppose," she announced at last.

"I thought you disliked them."

The café owner shrugged. "Not them. Their money. But the woman must be near her time. She'll need meat to nurse."

Three mansions stood apart on the hillcrest, the land sloping away in broad lawns to the bluff, then steep to the sea below. Two of the buildings wore crowns of thorns, wires strung in all directions, trucks and half-tracks parked on the grass, giant flags curling and snapping from the balconies, a bustle of officers in and out like hornets from a nest.

The third one, between the others, sat dark and quiet, a great face of stone and ornate windows, its sole sign of habitation a thread of smoke spiraling into a June sky that was as gray and lumpy as the underside of an abandoned mattress.

Emma leaned back against her shoulder harnesses, to prevent the wagon from gaining momentum and careening off the bluff. Mémé hummed to herself in the back, wagging her feet back and forth in large shoes with their patchwork of repairs.

But there was Monkey Boy, oddly enough, prancing outside one of the command posts like a caprice, until a soldier turned and spoke, at which the lad bolted like a colt.

Emma slowed to observe. There was something about the boy's manner, something more than the usual oddness. He turned sideways and began a skipping circuit of the mansion, sidestep, sidestep, from the seaside terrace to the bluff.

For a moment it appeared as though he would go all the way off. The guard called out, and Monkey Boy turned at the edge and smiled. He reached into his bag and produced an apple, which he held toward the soldier at arm's length.

The guard spoke again, and Monkey Boy returned to the terrace in the same sidestep fashion, tossing his head side to side like a rag doll. Reaching the soldier, he offered him the apple.

By then Emma had pulled up to the third mansion, but her suspicions were fully aroused. Placing a block behind one wheel to keep the wagon from rolling, she moved toward Mémé but scrutinized the boy. She knew the local apples were cultivated for Calvados brandy, making them far too tart to eat.

The soldier accepted Monkey Boy's gift, and took a hearty bite. He winced then, puckering from chin to forehead, while the boy clapped his hands and skipped away. Once he had rounded the corner of the great house, the capering changed again, back to that methodical sidestep. As he tottered out of sight, Emma wondered what it was all about.

"Silly boy," Mémé said.

"Yes, dear one," Emma answered. She untied both of Mémé's shoes, sliding out the laces and placing them in her lap. "You put these back together, and I'll return in one minute."

Mémé scowled. "Work."

"Sorry," she said, kissing her grandmother on the crown. "I'll try to improve."

The old woman did not answer. Already she was threading one lace through a shoe's eye, her tongue poked out in concentration. Emma grabbed the sack with the remaining spider, marched to the mansion's door, and swung the great brass knocker.

The young man Argent pulled the door open with a finger to his lips. He wore round spectacles and appeared deeply tired. Emma stood in the foyer for a moment, adjusting to the gloom, aware of a quiet so deep it felt as though someone had recently died. Although it was the fifth of June, the place was chilly and damp: those high ceilings, all that stone.

She followed him to the kitchen, where coals glowed in the hearth. He stirred them with a poker, then reached to a ready pile of broken chairs, backs and legs and arms pointing this way and that like debris from something violent. He took pieces and triangled them on each other in the hearth, and in a moment the wood caught and the room began to warm and brighten.

Then Emma noticed, on an intact chair, a woman wrapped in a blanket, her hair down and face beatific, a bundle in her arms. Emma approached, and saw that the woman was nursing.

"Two hours old," the young man said. "Our miracle."

Not a miracle in the least, Emma thought. All it required was mating, for which, based on the evidence, humans apparently possessed an abundant appetite.

"She's dozed off," the mother whispered. "Here, you must hold her."

"No thank you," Emma said, backing away.

"But yes," the father said, lifting the baby, placing it in her arms.

The infant weighed nothing and did not move, yet Emma struggled, elbows awkward and shoulders raised, until her hands found their place and settled. She had never held a newborn before. The mother rose from the chair with fragile dignity. As the blanket trailed behind her, she waddled to a wide chaise by the window and lay down.

Emma thought this was the most exhausted person she had ever seen. Tucking the blanket around herself, the mother curled up like a dog after a long hunt. Emma studied the miniature being in her arms, a little eggplant, bones and a wrinkled brow like an old man, yet possessing such a powerful calm. A deep, deep quietude.

The father stood at Emma's elbow. "Isn't she beautiful?"

Emma gazed at the baby, her tiny upturned nose. One hand curled outside the blanket, little fingers with tiny fingernails.

What were they thinking, to bring a child into a time of war? What did they imagine her life would be like? An impulse surged in Emma, to murder the girl then and there, to smash her head against the fireplace stone, or wring her neck like one more chicken destined for the pot. Spare her a lifetime of misery. Save her parents from the folly of hoping for good things on her behalf. Protect the whole village from wanting something as unlikely as an infant's well-being.

"You are the first person other than her parents to hold our baby," the father continued. "Her name is Gabrielle."

Emma found it difficult to speak. "Is that a family name?"

"No, mademoiselle. After the archangel Gabriel."

"Why did you choose him?"

"Because she will be the one who tells our story," he said, adjusting his spectacles. "Gabriel was God's messenger, who delivered news of salvation. Long after you and I are gone, the child who was born into this broken world will be our messenger to the future. She will describe how it was in this time and place, what happened, and how we survived till the Allies came."

"They will never come," Emma said.

"She will tell it better than you or I could," he continued, as if Emma had not spoken. "Because she cannot recall, as we do, what life was like before this war. These circumstances are all she will know. Thus she will be the perfect voice for our time."

Emma held the bundle out, handing the baby to her father. "That is quite an expectation of someone so small."

"But she will have her own private professor," the mother called from the chaise. "Her own schooling, here in this kitchen."

"Also," the man added, one finger raised. "This is the size at which all of us begin. Fools and heroes, paupers and kings. All were babies once." He lowered his face till his nose touched the child's. "And so lovely."

Emma could not imagine any of this happening for her: Philippe returning home intact, the means and opportunity to marry, a secure home, the lovemaking, a healthy pregnancy. Every stage of the sequence was impossible, the whole of it inconceivable. No, Emma thought, she might as well be barren.

"I must go," she said. "But I brought something for you." She dropped the sack on the table, a sound like castanets. "Boil it for twelve minutes and you'll have decent meat."

The professor bowed. "We are grateful."

But he did not open the bag. Instead, Emma watched as he

crossed the room and climbed onto the chaise with his wife, who slid her hips back against him, the child snuggled between them like a cat. Emma wanted to shake them all, slap them awake, pull them outside and make them see. The hornets in the mansions next door were proof enough of what lay ahead. This child would not be an angel, delivering news to the future. She would suffer, she would be hungry. How did these parents not understand?

No, they sighed with contentment, murmuring to each other on the chaise. Emma turned away, hurrying through the chilly entry, back out into the day.

A squall of rain hit her face like thrown water. After threatening all morning, the clouds had finally opened. But no, that was a stray gust. Emma realized the weather was more like a fog. Mémé sat on the wagon yet, ignoring the drizzle, growling with frustration at her shoes.

"Are you all right?" Emma asked.

"Almost," the old woman answered, fidgeting, thumbing a lace through the last remaining hole.

"Let's see how you've done," Emma said, examining the finished shoe. It was fully laced, but Mémé had done it in the opposite direction, top to bottom rather than bottom to top. Emma laughed in spite of herself. "A beauty, that's what you are." She wrestled the shoe onto Mémé's foot, tying a knot at the base of her toes.

Mémé leaned closer to see if she recognized this person, uncertain but also not afraid. There was something about the confident way the young woman handled the second shoe, a competence, which earned her trust.

For a moment sun winked through the teeming clouds. Emma raised her head to see if there was a rainbow—no such

Chapter 24

They propped the door open always, in all seasons and weather, so that they could see in advance who was coming. Marie would speak to no one but her daughter, and then only in murmurs. Fleur—so beautiful at fourteen that most men and many women could not help pausing their conversations as she passed—kept house, kept watch, kept her hands buried in her patchwork apron's pockets.

On the afternoon of the fifth of June, Emma steered the wagon to make sure its wooden wheels crossed the cobbles at the edge of their lane, which rattled Mémé in the back but meant that people inside the house would hear the rumble of her approach.

Fleur appeared, an apparition in the doorway, so there was no reason for anyone to enter, nor any way to see inside. Slipping off the harnesses, Emma reached into her pocket for a stone, the one she had picked up when Guillaume was executed, and handed it to Mémé for a plaything while they did their business. The old woman passed the stone from hand to hand, then reached a bent arm backward to balance it on her wrist.

"Good day, miss," Fleur piped. Her voice rang as high as a bird call.

"Good day," Emma said, eyeing the girl sidelong. She was pale, a blue vein visible on her neck. She was also, Emma had to concede, even more stunning than her reputation: an earnest face, high intelligent brow, a cascade of hair on her shoulder.

Emma marveled at how the occupation squandered the beauty of youth. No men but occupying soldiers would see this girl. No boy of the village would admire her from afar, in silent torment before working up the nerve to say hello. Emma knew her own moment of blossoming had passed with the departure of Philippe. Here was this young creature, no doubt in need of a hearty stew and a month of sleep, but possibly as lovely a vision as the village had ever known. Yet it would all go to waste.

Not an hour after holding a newborn and feeling despair, Emma tasted renewed bitterness like vinegar. Fleur as yet had no breasts, flat as a boy and with no hips, but these would come with time. What would not come was a suitor, or the dozens of them that this beauty deserved. No infatuation, no courting, no stolen kisses. All she had was a broken mother.

"How is Marie today?" Emma marshaled the self-control to ask while rummaging in the bags of her cart.

"Like a saint, thank you," Fleur replied. "Always silent and mostly at prayer."

Not knowing how to answer, Emma kept to business, producing an egg and one third of a baguette. "I brought some things for you."

"You are so kind, miss. No one has enough, yet you always have extra. How do you come by these things?"

"Like a saint, with silence and prayer." Emma smiled. "Plus the occasional dodge."

Unlike every other person in Emma's network, the girl did not reach for the food. She plunged her hands into her apron pockets and stared at the ground. "Everyone else has shunned us."

"They have no reason to do so."

"No?" Fleur spoke in low tones. "My father executed, my mother disgraced? And those women's hands ruined in the making of Dog Hill?"

"Those evils are not your doing. They were caused by the occupying army. All of the wrong lies with them."

The girl raised her beautiful face. "Are you with the Resistance?"

"No. I am simply trying to survive, and to help those I can."

Fleur removed one hand from her apron pockets, holding it out. "I thank you sincerely, miss. We will take the egg, please."

"You have no use for bread? You are the first person to turn aside any food I have offered."

"Please don't think us ungrateful, but I am sure someone else can enjoy it. For myself, I eat only what my mother will eat. And, no offense intended, she trusts no food other than eggs."

"Why is that?"

Fleur answered in a whisper, "The shell." She glanced left and right, then leaned forward. "It means no one has entered it. It has not been poisoned. Only an egg is safe."

Emma felt a pain in her chest. She would gladly have offered the girl the entire contents of her cart, if they were not already promised to others. But she did a bit of mental math: if she gave the girl two eggs, there would still be one left to share with Mémé. Scrambled with herbs—atop the third of a loaf Emma had learned months earlier to leave at home, to prevent herself from giving everything away on her rounds—that would suffice for a day. Besides, if any female was to carry the lineage of their people forward, it would not be the one whose life had become utilitarian, like an ox under the yoke. It was this young one's task to create the next generation of beauty.

"Wait," Emma said. She pulled another egg from her bag. "Take this. You need it more than anyone else."

Fleur's eyes went wide. "Two eggs, miss? You give us two?"

"From now on. Whenever I can, that is."

There was a murmur from within and the girl turned her face. "One minute, Mama." She curtsied to Emma, which was awkward in the narrow doorway and with one hand still in her pocket. "I am so grateful. And I hope you can find some hungry villager who needs that bread."

Emma slipped on the harnesses. "It will not be difficult."

Chapter 25

A*s the fifth of June reached high afternoon,* and Mémé slept like an innocent in the back of the wagon, Emma passed soldiers digging in the stream beside Pierre's fields. She could not imagine why. There was no drainage problem, and the property possessed no military value. Perhaps the work was disciplinary, she speculated, because the clay of that region was heavy on the shovel.

Then Emma saw: across the stretch of planted wheat, pale new stalks poking out of the dirt like the fingers of children playing in mud, the river appeared to have backed up somehow. It spilled over the banks though the day's rains had been lighter than expected. But in regular floods—the kind nature inflicts periodically and without mercy, scouring the fields, snatching cows, and leaving homes ruined with mildew and mud—people built dikes or dams to stop the seepage. These soldiers were shoveling hard, almost with urgency, their shirts dark with sweat, to accomplish the opposite. Emma watched them open a sluice from the stream to the field, creating a path for the water.

This was worse than switching road signs. This was using nature as a tool of propaganda. Pierre's field would become a pond, but to what purpose? Who would be deceived, and for what benefit? Whoever spent his days devising false road signs had reached another level. Now he was using the landscape to lie.

One of the diggers straightened. The officer in charge brayed at him, some harsh, back-to-work command. But the man with the spade did not obey. Instead he straightened his arm, pointing past the officer, his finger aimed directly at Emma. It was an accusation, though of what she had no idea.

But when his commanding officer snapped at him again, the sweaty, muddy digger puffed up his chest like a rooster. All at once she recognized him: Lieutenant Planeg, who had seen her at Michelle's at noontime as he sped past on his motorcycle. Clearly he remembered, since he answered sharply to the officer, who turned to follow where that finger pointed. It was Thalheim, whose expression changed from crimped annoyance to a steady, cold smile. Thirty meters away, Emma felt the chill of it in her bones. She turned her cart homeward. Her mouth was dry, tasting of worry.

An hour later in her rounds, hunger overtook Emma. One glass of Calvados with Odette when dropping off the lobster was not enough fuel. The pangs became unbearable, the remaining distance to home too great, the weight of Mémé in the back too much. She had to eat something.

Emma braked the wagon, slid the harnesses down, and turned to dig out the half baguette that Fleur had declined. Too famished to slice a piece off, she bit hard into the loaf and ripped.

Mémé stirred. "Gypsy?" She rose on one arm. "Gypsy?"

With a mouth barely able to produce enough saliva for her to swallow, Emma offered the loaf to Mémé. The old woman turned her face sideways, using her good teeth to gnaw off a portion. Chewing in silence, she handed the loaf back.

In that moment, with those few bites of food, Emma's mind cleared and she knew where she stood: at the foot of the steps leading into St. Agnes by the Sea. Was this where her day of effort was to end, then, on the fifth of June with the rain done and her rounds almost completed, and in the distance the drone of an approaching aircraft?

There was no sign of activity in the church itself, no noise from the rectory across the way. Just that airplane, now loud enough that Emma squinted at the sky and discovered there were two. And then three, three large aircraft coming from the north. Well, and so what? They flew from the north all the time, on their way to more important targets. What need had she of worry? The day already had provided more than enough.

The planes passed overhead lower than usual, so that Emma could see their wings were painted white. A black mouth opened in the metal underside of the lead aircraft. Emma continued to watch, the note of their engines bending downward as they arced away, until that dark mouth spat out an aluminum tooth, roughly above the rail station, tumbling over itself as it fell.

Seconds later the air rang. Something different happened to the trees: they swayed in a way that was not wind. Air-raid sirens began whining, but they sounded different. The airplanes were not passing over this time. They were bombing the village.

Emma felt seized by the desire to be home, absolutely as soon as possible. One more chore and day was done. She tore another chunk off the baguette and handed it to Mémé, then jogged up the church steps wishing that her stomach would enjoy the bread it had received, instead of what felt like wrestling with it. She pulled the handle of the church door, entering to the gentle scent of incense.

Emma heard the bombers passing again, low and bold, not bothering to conceal themselves, but then the door eased closed and she was stilled by the silence. Dim daylight filtered through stained glass. The pews were empty, the pulpit bare. As always, a single candle burned beside the altar.

She started down the aisle with bread in her hand. Where

could she leave the loaf so that no one would see it but the priest? She reached the front pews, hearing the rumble of another bomb, but the side chapel was quiet and the door to the sacristy in back stood open an uninviting inch. Women were not permitted in that area anyway.

At last her eyes came to rest on the proper spot: inside the Communion rail, where the faithful knelt to receive the sacrament. None but the Monsignor was allowed within that rail.

Emma considered what she held: one third of a loaf, perhaps less. The moment the priest noticed it, he would know that she had committed a misdeed, by entering where she was forbidden. He would also know that Emma had answered his demands of her. Nor did she worry about mice; a church was no ark. It contained food too infrequently to sustain inhabitants however small or meek.

Perhaps that was one of the flaws of the faith: life's pleasures were all sins, as if the senses were the enemy of the spirit, the body its soul's adversary. The villagers used to worry about such things, argue about them, weigh them in their consciences, but only in the time before. Once the occupation began, pleasures became too simple and rare to consider them sins: a decent night's sleep, a taste of wine not turned to vinegar, a slice of boiled pork eaten without the army finding out. Emma stood at the center of the church, trying not to become angry. If these were sins, damnation was hereby invited to the table.

She opened the gate in the rail, the one the priest used when he came forward to baptize a newborn, to shake holy water on a casket, to brandish the incense snifter back and forth before the congregation, a cloud of scented smoke passing over their heads and upward. Emma hastened to the front, and without pause or ceremony left the bread in the center of the altar. Then she quit the place at a run, before God or anyone could catch her.

Chapter 26

T*he meaning of Planeg's finger* became clear when Emma had pulled the wagon past the crossroads and saw, there at the roadside, the lieutenant's motorcycle. He had left the gas cap on the seat so that anyone—a passerby, a stranger, a commanding officer wanting to know why his lieutenant was impermissibly slow in responding to orders to report—might see for themselves the reason for the machine's abandonment.

Emma peered into the tank: as dry as the inside of an oven, the fumes sharp like the memory of a moment of shame.

A cascade of realizations came to her one by one: Planeg having to walk all the way to his barracks, with all of that time to wonder why he had run out of fuel, recalling the woman in the bushes carrying a jug, suspecting he had been played for a fool, reconsidering his arrangement with the brittle but otherwise generally satisfactory tart in the cabin at the top of the hill, re-evaluating the entire comfortable circumstance he had devised for himself for the duration of the tedious occupation.

Worse, once he had arrived, and explained the empty gas tank to his superiors, as a result of their predictable displeasure Planeg was assigned to the shovel detail, work far beneath his rank, under an officer he didn't respect and in fact had planned one day soon to surpass. Now he would have to flood the croplands first, for a purpose no one had disclosed. Every dig of the spade into a clay as thick as the skulls of these backward rural gas thieves sharpened the lieutenant's resentment of rank, of menial tasks, and above all of that woman with the jug, until his hands hurt and she became an emblem of misplaced trust, his arms grew sore and she was a symbol of his deception, his back ached and he was no longer an officer or even human, but some animal force distilled by frustration into a sweating, smoldering, vengeful thing.

Who should happen along at that very instant, refueled herself by recent bread and an act of generosity, but the one person responsible for putting him in that soggy ditch doing the work of privates. It seemed as if his temper had called her forth, drawing the wagon past that ditch as a magnet pulls at a pin. Planeg had pointed his rigid finger in her direction only because at that moment he chanced to be unarmed.

All of this possibility Emma understood as she placed one hand on the motorcycle seat, the leather damp yet from the day's earlier rain. She glanced north to see Apollo the draft horse ambling up the lane, his head low as if lost in thought.

Yet Emma's attention next turned west as she heard, and then saw, more bombers, again with their wings painted oddly white. This time, however, there was enough treeless sky for her to see that only one of the aircraft possessed that black mouth in its belly. The others were smaller and quicker, guards of some kind, darting above and beside the big one. Behind that trio came another three, close on its wake, though they did not stand out against the gray sky until they'd drawn close.

Something fell, then, some small, parachuted item swinging side to side in the air, its landing place hidden by the hedgerow half a kilometer ahead. Prompted perhaps by the continuing angers of her belly, Emma's immediate thought was: food.

By the time the second wave passed, the thunder of the first crew's bombs had reached where she stood. Another sound responded, not an echo but similar in volume and growl, and Emma wondered if these were the antiaircraft guns Thalheim had spoken of so proudly that day upon the bluff. Regardless, it was still her village under attack, still the railroad station that seemed to be the target. But nothing came by train anymore, and the rails had already taken away Philippe and the other conscripted men. Why were the bombers bothering now?

As quiet returned Emma continued to imagine the afternoon from Planeg's perspective, how he disobeyed Thalheim in order to explain himself, to identify her with a righteousness that outranked rank, and how the impatient captain had squinted at her, but upon discovering the identity of the fuel thief, what pleasure it had given him. His smile had turned her stomach.

"Here," Mémé said. She had climbed down from the wagon and tiptoed up beside her pensive granddaughter. "Watch."

She grabbed Emma's shoulder for balance, pulled her dress up to the knee, raised one foot against the side of the motorcycle's seat, and shoved. The machine tipped, then toppled, falling on its side with a torqueing of handlebars and the sound of things breaking on the underside. The gas cap tumbled off its perch, rolling into the ditch and the grass below, where it came to rest somewhere out of sight.

"Home now," Mémé said, marching to the wagon's stern and hoisting her buttocks to drop heavily aboard. "Hungry."

Emma considered the motorcycle, there in the ditch. Apollo arrived at her side and seemed to contemplate it, too.

"I guess we can't get in any worse trouble," she told the horse. "Right?"

Emma slipped her arms back into the harnesses, which by this time had formed the leather into the exact shape of her pulling body. Leaning toward home, she started the wagon rolling, planning a route that would keep her on as level a terrain as possible, all the way to the barnyard gate.

"Do you know what, Grandmother?" she called back over her shoulder. "Everything is about to change."

Mémé stroked her eyebrows with both hands. "Change?"

"Yes." Emma pulled with her head up while the horse, snorting his nostrils clear, fell into step beside her. "Everything is about to fall apart."

Chapter 27

I*n early evening on the fifth of June,* Odette stood working in her kitchen when the café's front door swung open, pushed so hard it clattered against a table.

"Not open for dinner till six thirty," she called, chopping an onion. "And go easy on that door, would you please?"

"Here she is," a familiar voice snapped. "As I told you."

Odette turned to find DuFour standing at her kitchen's entry. Two soldiers hovered behind him with rifles. "Oh, you," she said. "What are you sniveling about? Or have you finally come for that free dinner I offered you?"

"You are under arrest for spying for the Resistance."

"Go shuffle your papers," she replied, returning to her cutting board. "I have soup to make."

DuFour strode into the close room, clearing a way for the soldiers. "Arrest her," he told them. "The Kommandant will want to hear everything."

Odette pointed the knife at him. "I'm busy, I said. Now get out of my kitchen."

One of the soldiers lowered his rifle. He did not speak. Odette sized up the three of them, only one in stabbing distance. Oh, the pleasure it would bring, to bury that blade in DuFour's poochy potbelly. But he was not worth the repercussions.

After wiping the knife, Odette placed it on the cutting board, raked the diced onion into her palm, and dropped it into a pot of steaming broth. Inside boiled a good-sized lobster, and Odette had intended for it to draw a high price that night.

Now it would more likely go to waste. But hadn't this moment been coming for months? Still, as she switched off the heat under the pot, Odette was surprised to find her throat tightening. So many foods for so many mouths, customers in fact expected within the hour, regardless of the bombing of the train station. Yet interrupting that meal's preparation felt like an act of loss and surrender. It felt final.

Odette knew what it was to relinquish something precious: throwing a handful of dirt on a casket, releasing the hope of ever marrying and having children. By placing a top on that pot, she felt as though she were taking leave of her oldest friend.

"Go ahead," she said to the soldiers. "I'll behave."

Odette kept her buxom chest out and shoulders back as she followed the soldiers out into the street. Rather than the garrison, they turned toward town hall, and she understood that she would not be facing the Kommandant right away. More likely, she would be locked in the cell that had held Emma's father. Odette cast her gaze about, wishing the sky were not so gray, nor evening coming on, while she took a last view of Vergers for what could be months. Allied planes buzzed in the distance, as they had all afternoon, and she suspected that this arrest was DuFour's doing entirely. If she managed to survive, she would roast him on a spit.

The town clerk shouted from behind, telling Odette to hurry, and she duly picked up her pace.

"Aha!" he cried, rushing forward. "You did it."

"What did I do, you insect?"

"You hurried."

"Yes, and so what?"

"I said it in their language." He pointed at the soldiers. "Not ours." He seemed almost to skip beside her. "You know their language. You have been spying all this time, in your café."

At that, Odette felt her first flush of doubt. DuFour might be a first-class fool, but he had put her in serious trouble. "I don't know what you are talking about."

"Deny all you like. You have already revealed yourself."

They marched off together in silence toward the jail.

Chapter 28

T*here was unusual traffic* on the dirt roads on the evening of the fifth of June as Emma pulled for the last stretch home. First she happened across the parcel that had dropped from the airplane. It sat in a field to the left, on land that had been plowed but not planted, which struck her as a perfect metaphor for the condition of her country: fertile, ready to continue the cycle of seasons, but thwarted by the endless occupation. Mémé hopped off the wagon before it had come to a complete stop.

"Gifts," she cried, feet wide for balance. "Sky gifts."

Emma considered ignoring the salvage opportunity, and continuing home. A reckoning with the captain was coming soon enough. She should feed Mémé, hide the fuel jug, and make other preparations.

But seeing her grandmother excited like a child made Emma hesitate. Nothing she did now would alter what lay ahead. She slid from her harnesses and wedged a block behind one of the wagon's wheels.

Mémé paced at the edge of the field. The package lay a few steps down the embankment, but the slope was steep and the grass wet. Stepping sideways, Emma inched down. When one of her shoes slipped, she caught herself with a hand on the ground, and after a few steps more she reached the field's roiled soil.

The parachute lay flat on the dirt like the lung of a slaughtered pig. But a parcel wrapped in canvas lay alongside, making a strange sound. There was nothing remotely bomblike about it, so Emma began untying the cords. Anytime she jostled the basket it made that odd sound, familiar though she could not quite place it. She carried the package back to the wagon, fidgeting loose the canvas until at last she could see.

A dove. The parcel was a bird cage. Inside, a small gray-and-white bird, head bobbing, skittered back and forth on his pedestal. His cooing she recognized from the belfry of St. Agnes by the Sea, where scavenging pigeons congregated more frequently than parishioners. The bird clambered about in its cage, clinging to the bars with tiny red talons.

"What in creation?" Emma asked.

Mémé did not answer, busying herself with something at the roadside.

Emma unwrapped the package more. It also held parchment paper thinner than a blade of grass, two molded tubes as long as the tip of her pinkie but as thin as a fingernail, plus a cube of seeds pressed into fat that she understood at once was bird food.

By instinct she unwrapped the cube first, sliding it between the bars. The dove immediately began pecking at his feed. Emma sat back, facing Apollo. "Why in the world would they drop a bird to us?"

"Help me," Mémé called from the field's edge.

Setting the basket aside, Emma peered at her grandmother. She had clumped the parachute into a ball in her arms, rendering her unable to climb back up the bank. Yet she was grinning wider than Emma had seen in years.

"Oh, dear one," Emma said, hurrying over. "What have you gotten yourself into now?"

"Silk," Mémé answered with a laugh, raising her arms to hold the parachute high. "For your wedding dress."

Chapter 29

E*mma had barely concealed her find*, the basket tucked beside Mémé in the wagon, the parachute under a blanket, when the Monsignor appeared on the road, coming from the direction of their home. At first she did not recognize him, the man had aged so much recently. In another era she would have guessed cancer, and might have felt pity. But in the time of occupation, she bristled and prepared her defenses.

"Emmanuelle, I have been searching for you."

"Once more your prayers are answered. What do you want?"

"So unfriendly, after all this time."

"Our conversations lately have not been what I would call delights."

The priest stopped where he stood, as Emma saw that he was leaning on a cane. "I have always been a poor evangelist." He coughed into his hand. "I daresay you've won more people to your viewpoint than I have won to God's."

"Perhaps that is because God has deserted us."

"Blasphemy," he said weakly, shaking his cane. "Why must you always speak sinfully to me?"

"Do you see God anywhere around here?"

"Well." The Monsignor's hands revealed a bit of a tremor. "His works are far between, I concede." He darted a tongue over his lips. "But only if you do not consider the air in your lungs, the ground you stand upon, or the stars at night in the firmament."

"Creation happened a long time ago," Emma said.

"Please," he said, raising an open hand. "It is difficult enough to sustain my own faith in such cruel times. And your deeds reveal faith more strongly than your denials refute it. I did not seek you for another argument. I came to bring you news."

Emma folded her arms on her chest. "I'm listening."

"Your friend Odette has been arrested—"

"What? When? How do you know this?"

"—accused of eavesdropping on the officers in her café, for the Resistance. DuFour caught her, and apparently he has proof."

Emma stumbled backward, the wagon following her steps, so that she had to pull to recover her balance. Glancing back, she saw Mémé listening to everything with wide eyes.

"What will they do to her?"

"What they do to everyone." The priest tapped his cane on the ground. "Why do you think I own a wheelbarrow?"

Emma considered the trinkets in her wagon, the bird, everything suddenly trivial. She had delivered the lobster to Odette not two hours earlier. "Is there anything we can do?"

"Pray."

"I mean anything real," she snapped. "Where are they keeping her?"

The priest sighed. His head seemed too large for how thin his neck had become. "The town-hall cells. They would have shot her already, if not for the bombing of the train station. It has given the Kommandant, for now, more pressing concerns."

As if to confirm that observation, another wave of bombers swept in from the north, at the far edge of sight but approaching at high speeds. The sound of their engines grew as another wave followed close behind, then a third and fourth. The gathering dusk made them barely visible, but the sound gave a sense of their place in the sky.

The priest, Emma, and Mémé stood watching for a full minute, Apollo dipping his head into the wagon to satisfy his curiosity about the bird cage. They could not tell where the bombs fell, but they heard the explosions, as well as the subsequent report of antiaircraft fire. In one or two places they could spot a flash of light from the blasting guns.

"I suppose, Emmanuelle," the Monsignor continued at last. "I suppose I am here to warn you. If they have arrested Odette, they will come for you, too. It is a matter of time. You should flee."

"But I have told you. I am not a member of the Resistance."

"Do you honestly believe that it will matter?"

"I cannot abandon the people. It's not only Mémé. They all depend on me now."

"I suspect that will not make a difference either." He gazed at the ground, nodding to himself. "Our uninvited guests may be God's children, but they do not seem to place much value on the needs of people here. On the lives of people here."

How defeated the Monsignor was, Emma thought. She liked him better when he was full of vinegar and damnation. "Why are you suddenly so concerned with my well-being?"

"One hundred and two," Mémé called from the wagon.

"That's right," the priest said, lifting his face again. He pointed a shaking finger. "That's it exactly."

Emma turned to her grandmother. "What are you talking about?"

"That is how many people I have baptized since the bishop

assigned me to this parish," the priest explained. "One adult, one hundred and one babies. It is a bond the likes of which you will never understand. But for a man whose vows forbid him from knowing fatherhood, it is the sacrament that brings me nearest. Many have moved away, because of the war. Thirty-one were conscripted. Twenty-six have been killed, and to my unending heartbreak, I personally witnessed one of those deaths."

"Thirty-four," Mémé said, licking her thumb and making the sign of the cross on the brow of an invisible child. "Thirty-five."

The Monsignor's face wrinkled and Emma thought he was about to cry, but then he smiled. "Your grandmother never misses a baptism."

"What?" Emma asked. "How is that possible?"

"Marguerite brings her, I assume while you are busy with your affairs."

Emma faced Mémé with hands on her hips. "Is this true?"

By way of reply, the old woman cradled an imaginary baby and whispered to it, "Thirty-six."

"You are among my one hundred and two." The priest switched the cane to his left hand, raised his right arm, and although it shook with palsy, he made a sign of the cross. "God bless you, Emmanuelle. May He grant you the wisdom, in your final hour, to seek His grace and beg His protection."

On hearing that word, Emma remembered that she was wearing a knife, snug against her leg, inches from her fingers. She hooked a thumb under the wagon harness. "Sorry to give you the bad news, but my final hour is a long way off."

The Monsignor made no reply, only lowered his arm and returned the cane to that side. Then he shuffled past, heading for the crossroads and the lane back to his rectory, across the road from St. Agnes by the Sea.

Emma watched the old priest go, and saw Apollo make the choice to amble after him. They made a picturesque pair, she thought. Those once powerful, marching into the twilight.

Oh, but wait: the Monsignor had not mentioned the bread she left on the altar. Perhaps he had not been to his church all afternoon. In that case, a surprise was awaiting him at seven thirty Mass the next day. Let him repent of his judgments then.

Emma pulled away at her harness. She could hear more planes in the distance, and she wanted to be home. An old fantasy returned—that Philippe would somehow be waiting there for her—but she pushed the idea out of sight.

"Grandmother," she called over a shoulder. "Did he announce the count at the end of each baptism?"

Mémé had circled her arms around the bird cage, cooing to the creature within. She nodded to the cage, as if the bird had asked the question. "Yes."

Emma took several steps, thinking. "What number was I?"

"You were . . ." Mémé furrowed her brow.

She examined her hands, she searched the sky. "You were. You were." Mémé scratched her head, fidgeted her clothes all over, wiped her face with both hands. Only then did Emma see that the woman was crying. She hurried out of her harnesses, back to her grandmother's side. "Dear one."

"Can't remember," the old woman chattered to herself. "Beautiful baby. Can't remember."

"It's all right," Emma said. "It doesn't matter."

Mémé yanked off her shoe and threw it in the road.

"Grandmother, really." Emma trotted back for the shoe. "We need to be getting home now."

"Can't remember," the old woman roared. "Damn it."

Monkey Boy and the Goat lurked by the eastern well, glancing around from time to time to make sure no one was watching. As Emma trudged her slow approach, it seemed as if they were playing a game. The boy was prancing, making the strange two-step he had done around the mansion on the bluff, the one with a guard outside. But as Monkey Boy hopped sideways, the Goat crawled along with a strip of tailor's tape, attempting to measure the width of each step.

"Please slow down," the Goat chided. But the boy could not contain himself, and polkaed halfway up the lane. The Goat hung his head, then noticed shoe prints in the dust. "Oh, now there we go," he called out, stretching the measuring tape between four or five prints, then sitting back on his heels to calculate on his fingers. "Good lad."

Monkey Boy came skipping back, followed closely by Emma towing the cart, her grandmother in the back banging the side of the wagon with the flat of her hand. The Goat straightened and addressed Monkey Boy.

"And you say there are seventy-seven of your hops between the mansion and the bluff? And you're certain you measured the one with the army inside, and not the young couple, correct?"

Monkey Boy skipped in a circle large enough to contain the Goat, the well, and the wagon. Day was done and Emma's head hanging, but he showed no lack of energy. "Seventy-seven," he sang, as though it were a nursery rhyme. "Seventy-seven from the bluff. One hundred sixty-four from the road."

"What's going on here?" Emma demanded, straightening, pressing both hands at the small of her back.

"Coordinates," the Goat replied. "Targets."

"Seventy-seven," Monkey Boy chimed, skipping past Mémé.

"Grrr," she replied, making her wrinkled hands into fleshy fists.

"One hundred sixty-four," he sang, bouncing out of reach.

"Give her room or she'll brain you," Emma warned. "Mémé's in a foul humor. And you—" She pointed her chin at the Goat. "Is that my measuring tape?"

"I confess that it is," he answered. "But I needed it for an extremely important reason."

"You entered my house and stole it."

"I cannot claim innocence of the crime. But you see—"

Emma snapped her hand out. "Give it back now."

"Let me explain, please." He placed the tape in her hand, immediately bowing backward a few steps.

"If you ever enter my house again"—she stuffed the tailor tape into her pocket—"I will wait till you are asleep in the hog shed and then I will set it on fire. Do we understand one another?"

"Emmanuelle." The Goat shook his head. "Don't you see what is happening? Don't you feel what is coming, any minute now? Our possessions—tape measures, anything—are not going to matter anymore. Not when our lives are at stake. Believe me, if only because of our long friendship. We need to join—"

"We are not friends." She slid back into her harnesses. "We have never been friends."

"You are mistaken, Emma. All we have left is one another."

She started pulling the wagon. "I want you out. Pack your things and vacate the hog shed tonight."

The Goat flapped his arms against his coat. "For God's sake. What would it cost you to give me half a minute to explain?"

Emma paused, staring at the ground for a moment, the soil of her home and origin, trodden by the ages into hard-packed clay, and one day, the place her dust would spend all eternity. All at once she found herself struggling not to cry. Odette was in jail, her father gone, so many killed.

And what a day she'd had, the fifth of June. It felt as long as a week. She had nearly choked to death on straw, the army confiscated all of Yves's fish, the little girl could trust only eggs, there was no one to help Emma, no one to protect her, and meanwhile this very minute another wave of bombers was droning closer to pummel the train station—which, in addition to whatever military value the Allies awarded it, happened also to be Philippe's means of someday coming home. The wonder was that Emma did not cry all day long.

But no. This was her life, her only life, and so it would always be. The occupying army would never leave, the Allies would never come, and all a person could do was endure. Emma collected herself, steeled her spine, made a spiteful face at the Goat. "I am too damn hungry to listen."

She pushed against her harnesses, and was surprised to feel the wagon considerably lighter. Emma looked back and Mémé had climbed off. She was holding the bird cage, its cover removed, the dove swinging on his perch like a little ornament.

"Grandmother, please. Can we go in now? You'll feel better when you've had your egg."

Mémé ignored her, inching toward the Goat with the cage held high. Monkey Boy came to see as well. "Coo," Mémé said. "See the coo?"

Now it was the Goat's turn to dance, hopping from foot to foot while he held his head with both hands.

"Perfect." He stomped his feet. "Mémé, you are perfection, thank you, God in heaven." He seized her hand and kissed it. "I heard rumors that they were dropping messenger pigeons to us, but did not believe it. This little fellow could not come at any better time."

"See the coo?" Mémé said.

Monkey Boy poked his smallest finger between the bars of the cage. The bird sidestepped closer on its perch, and pecked the boy's fingertip twice.

"Bit me," Monkey Boy cried, leaping away. His face alight, he held his pinkie in front of Emma's face. "Bit by a bird."

The Goat sidled up to Mémé. "I know this is a lot to ask. But could I *please* have that dove? I promise to take good care of it."

She turned sideways. "Mine."

"Of course it's yours, Mémé. Yes. But this is a special kind of bird. It needs special care, because it can do special things."

"Mine," Mémé said, taking several steps away.

"No, no," the Goat said. "You can trust me. I won't take it from you, not a chance. But I am asking you to give it to me."

"Mémé," Emma said, sighing in her harnesses. "I'm not interested in what he wants. But we don't have anything to feed a bird like that."

"You see?" the Goat said.

"You feed?" Mémé asked him.

The Goat shuffled his feet a moment. "No. To tell the truth, I won't be feeding him. What I will be doing is setting him free." He spread his arms wide. "I will do some special things with him, and then I will let him go home."

Mémé narrowed her eyes. "Let him go?" She marched past him, toward the barnyard door.

"Mémé, wait." The Goat jumped ahead, holding her arm. "You have known me since the day I was born. You knew me when I was Didier, back when I had a name." He fell to his knees. "Please."

"What is this ridiculous drama?" Emma asked.

But Mémé's expression softened. She laid a calm hand on the Goat's shoulder, as if she were knighting him. "Baptism."

"That's right." He nodded emphatically. "My mother said you were the only person at my baptism who was not a family member."

Mémé smiled at him. "One hundred and two."

"I know you want a pet to keep you company," the Goat persisted. "But I promise, there is an excellent reason for you to give me this bird. Please. It could help us defeat the occupying army."

"Enough exaggeration," Emma said. "This day has been endless, and I need badly to eat and lie down. Can we please go home?"

Mémé lifted her hand, and the Goat did not speak further. Then with great dignity, she set the bird cage on the ground.

"God bless you," the Goat cried, jumping to his feet and kissing her on both cheeks. "Thank you."

Rolling her eyes at Emma, Mémé waved a hand in front of her face, as if to fan away the odor.

The Goat snatched the bird cage and scampered off into the hedgerows. Monkey Boy grabbed a low limb of a nearby chestnut and began to climb. Emma could hear him cooing as he vanished upward into the leaves.

Chapter 30

B*y nine o'clock that night*, Pierre had heard all he needed to know. The familiar thing, oddly enough, was not the noise of explosions, though they had been roaring every minute or so since the sun sank into the sea, and though he recognized the sounds from memories he had tried to bury as deep as his ancestors' graves. No, it was the feel of the earth, as bombs tore into it. It was the electricity of the air, as if lightning were about to strike. He remembered.

But to be certain, he needed to see. And of all his riverside acreage, only one spot would do. It was no place for an old man, but in those times, the same could be said of his entire country.

The ladder was rough and dusty in his hands, when Pierre carried it from the back of the barn. Once he turned Apollo free, he had no further need to climb for hay. Now he tucked his pipe into a pocket of his old wool vest and set aside a tin of rat poison. When the dog bit Marguerite, when Guillaume killed the dog, when the captain killed Guillaume, how could Pierre not poison the dogs? He regretted their suffering, and that of the women forced to shovel Dog Hill. But this was a war, and he had never stopped being a soldier.

Still, he said a quick prayer for the animals of war, who neither took sides nor carried guns, yet suffered a share of the hardship nonetheless. He wiped his hands on his pant legs and lifted the ladder upright. It leaned against him, the weight nearly toppling them both, but he set his feet wide and pushed with his arms, and the upper end fell against the hayloft.

At various times in his life, Pierre had mistrusted people—a feed salesman from Caen who spoke too fast, a drunkard from whom he bought a field, knowing the man would spend the money dissipating the remainder of his days—but rarely had he mistrusted himself. And now? How long since he had relied upon his balance? How steady were his legs?

There was one way to find out, and the double report of a bomb exploding nearby and its echo off the hedgerows put steel in his spine. He gripped the sides of the ladder and began to climb, the gap between rungs larger than he recalled, though he raised his knees right and left and wiggled his boots after each step until the crossbar underneath felt secure. When he reached the hayloft, Pierre saw that he would have to stretch one foot way out to step aboard, and the distance was farther than his legs had parted in years. How does a man get so damn old?

A fall from the top would be the worst sort of injury, and it could be days before anyone discovered him. Or no, Emma would find him, because she checked each morning, even now when she no longer had tobacco to deliver.

Pierre extended his leg and pressed, making a swift transfer of weight onto the loft. Before he could celebrate, though, he sneezed hard. All around him the bales were dusty, pulled apart by mice or the feral cats who came to hunt them. A man could easily trip.

"You old fool," he muttered, lowering himself to all fours, remarking to himself not for the first time how aging returned a man to infancy, as he crawled to the loading door. In a lifetime now past, this door had swung wide to accommodate bales thrown from a loaded wagon below, with room for a man to catch and haul them inside, where another man would stack them to keep the horses fed through the winter ahead. How much strength did it take? As much as the task required, because there was no alternative, and the men who helped would need extra hands to barn their own hay in another day or two, and so the wheel went around.

Pierre unlatched the door and swung it back, his land and the surrounding country opening to view. The first thing he saw was that his fields had been flooded. They glistened in the dark. An entire season's crop planted, and now destroyed. What would everyone live on, when winter came? Who knew why the occupying army had done such a thing? It seemed wanton, done solely to inflict pain, and primarily on the animals, too.

A man who has lived to see his neighbors taken away by force, and to witness the execution of friends, already has the measure of his adversary's character. All Pierre wanted to know now was how severe the retaliation would be.

Because that is what he saw under way, from his perch in the hayloft: the beginning of a retribution, a strike against the entrenched and mighty. The horizon gave off an unmistakable glow. The waves of bombers had become nearly constant, striking inland, pounding the ground. The occupying army's antiaircraft fire likewise sounded continuously, tracers arcing into the sky to guide the gunners' aim until the next wave of bombers roared over Vergers.

The time had arrived at last. Pierre felt glad to have lived to see it. He wondered how bad the devastation would be. Young men were lucky to survive such clashes of might. Old men should not dare to imagine that they would, too.

At that, he knew he had two tasks to perform, if he could get himself safely back down that ladder. Only two, but each was an act of conscience. A man of finite days should not ignore such opportunities.

Pierre left the loft door wide. He climbed down with cautious feet and shaking hands, and when he reached the ground he patted his pocket, confirming that the pipe was still there. He left the ladder in place and the barn door open. If what was coming rivaled what he had seen before, there was no point in closing or locking anything. It would ravage everything in its path.

Entering his house, Pierre removed his old beret and hung it on a hook. He dragged an old trunk out from a closet, searching through its carefully folded contents until he found what he was after: a sergeant's cap from the Great War, gray blue, round at the crown with a black bill sticking forward. The sight of it straightened him, and he pulled the hat onto his head the same old way, back to front, using the stiff bill to set the correct angle.

The hat still fit after all these years. Pierre smiled: a man's head does not change size, regardless of the rounding of his stomach or the bending of his back.

His plan required violating curfew, but Pierre suspected the usual guards would be busy elsewhere. He fetched his walking stick, then turned his girls out in the side yard. If no one came to milk them, they would suffer. But he knew from personal experience that hunger would hurt them first.

No one knew the hedgerows better than Emma, with her barters and gambits, but Pierre had learned a few tricks himself over the years. Dogs barked and he could hear people outside their homes, discussing in worried voices the red haze to the east, but he kept to the edges of the road. A military truck roared up suddenly, one poor private with a flashlight strapped to the hood, the rest of a long convoy following in the dark. But they were in a hurry and Pierre hid behind a tree until they had passed. He managed to reach the village undetected. Seeing a thin line of light around the blackout shades of his first stop, he paused to rest a moment. Then, adjusting his hat and with a deep breath, he set out across the square for the home of DuFour.

Pierre rapped on the door with his cane. "Do not shoot. I am not armed." He listened, but could not be sure if anyone had replied. He gripped the handle. "I am coming in."

DuFour sat in an armchair by the cold hearth. A bottle of Calvados sat empty on the table. The town clerk lifted his head, recognizing the old farmer, then raised a glass stained pink with the drink. "Here's to the great noisy world," he said, and tipped the last sip into his mouth.

Pierre stood evenly in the doorway, feeling strength and a long-forgotten sense of cleanness as he beheld the town clerk. "I am here because I pity you," he said. "This bombing is the beginning, and I believe an ugly time has come."

DuFour inspected the Calvados bottle, tilting it to confirm that it was empty. "Why is that my concern?"

"I should not have left you alone with my injured horse. You were young, and weak. I should have mastered my grief and finished Neptune myself."

"What are you talking about? You are speaking in riddles."

"I felt it only decent to warn you. I have seen times like these, I lived through them before you were born. Regardless of who prevails, I do not believe tomorrow will go well for you."

DuFour sniffed. "Pish. Don't you know who I am now? Whose favor I enjoy?"

"If you stand in the middle, both sides will be shooting at you. My advice would be for you to gather a few things, and several days' food, and get a head start."

DuFour set glass and bottle down on the table and folded his hands on his belly. "I am expected at the offices tomorrow. People are depending on me. The Kommandant."

"He will be too busy trying to stay alive to notice your absence. If he is not gone already. Save yourself while you can."

"The old ways are done, you know. The new ways are here to stay." DuFour ran a fingertip around the mouth of the bottle. "And you are the worst kind of fool: boring, and old."

Pierre drew himself up, tugging on his wool vest. "Think what you will of me. I have warned you. My conscience is clear."

Outside the nightfall was complete, vague moonlight as the last of the day's rain clouds lingered overhead. Pierre was glad he had brought his cane. He held it ahead almost as a blind man would, feeling his way around the village, across a hedgerow gap and past the crossroads. The walk to his second task took nearly an hour, though normally it would require one quarter that time. But when the eastern well came into sight, he paused to lean against it, wiping his face with a handkerchief.

What would he say here? How could he be more persuasive than he had been with the clerk? Pierre put a pinch of tobacco in his pipe bowl and struck a match on the stone of the well. In the distance, the bombing continued. The answering fire had become more intense. Pierre could not say for sure, but he thought he had seen a plane with no engine, gliding silently across a bit of cloudless sky. But that would be impossible, and he cursed his old eyes for playing tricks.

Soon the pipe was smoked and no better words had come to him. Pierre followed his cane to the barnyard door, which he eased open, its hinges making a rusty complaint. A rooster perched on a shed perked up his head, but Pierre tapped his pipe out on the boards and the bird, instead of crowing, hopped over, pecking to see whether the ashes were something to eat.

The old man heard the murmur of two women talking. Through a side window, he saw them sitting at a table, lit by a stub of candle. Mémé was carrying on while Emma mended something, a sock, while giving her grandmother half an ear.

He knocked on the door and heard chairs scraping. Emma swept the door open. "Philippe?"

"Ah, no, it's only Pierre," the old man answered. "Only me."

"What are you doing out at this time of night?" She drew him inside. "You could be shot."

"I'll only be a moment," he said, removing his military hat. "I wanted to warn you."

"You are sweet, Pierre," Emma said. "But I could be warned about everything I do all day."

"This is different."

"I like your hat," she said. "I wish I could offer you something to eat or drink."

"Emmanuelle." Mémé brought a finger to her lips. "Listen."

"Yes," Pierre said. "For one moment, please. I know these sounds. I heard bombing like this in the Great War." He took Emma's hand. "The true battle has arrived. You must leave at once."

Emma pulled her hand free. "With all respect, who are you to speak to me like this?"

"An old fool, as I have recently been reminded. But one who cherishes your well-being." He saw that he still had his pipe in his hand, and he looked for a place to set it down, settling on the near windowsill. "Emmanuelle, who I have known since the afternoon of your birth. For once please put aside your pride and use your ears." He sighed. "I am too old to leave, and my girls need me for morning milking. But you have a wagon, and I imagine some foodstuffs saved. You could get away."

Emma would not look at him, but Pierre glanced at Mémé

and she was listening. "If anyone from our poor village deserves to survive this war, it is the woman who has kept us alive."

"That is exactly why I will not go," Emma answered. "There are people who depend on me for more than tobacco. If I leave, they perish. I will stay until there is no one left to care for."

Pierre leaned his cane against the table. "The war has arrived at our door, and I am a veteran. I know what that means." He tottered forward and hugged her with both arms. Emma's hands hung at her sides, but when he did not let go she raised them and hugged Pierre back.

"Your father would be mightily proud of who you have become," he said. "I am going to miss you."

"You are very kind, Pierre. But I will be bringing you freshly smuggled tobacco in a few days."

He collected his cane and opened the door. "I wish I could believe that." And the old man wandered out into the night.

Emma stood in the doorway, watching until he had crossed the barnyard and disappeared in the dark.

As she closed the door, Emma heard her grandmother growl. "What is it?" she asked. "What's wrong?"

Mémé pointed at the windowsill. "Pipe."

Pierre had left it behind.

"I'll bring it to him tomorrow," Emma said.

Mémé looked off to one side. "Tomorrow."

Emma lay awake for hours, the thrum of bombs distant and then frighteningly close, until she concluded that no degree of exhaustion would bring her the relief of sleep. Even on ordinary nights, real rest did not begin until Thalheim had tromped up the stairs and kicked his boots off without regard for the thumping he'd made.

Finding herself bolt upright sometime later, however, Emma knew she must have slept. The candle had burned out and Pirate was in full cry, though it was still deep night and outside there was some form of commotion.

Mémé lay on the couch like a pharaoh in his tomb, face inscrutable and breathing so slow it seemed almost as if she had stopped. But her grandmother was fully dressed, Emma noticed, which meant she expected to be awakened before the night was through.

Again the outcry from the barnyard, a confusing tumult as Emma splashed water on her face to clear the fog of sleep. Surely it was not time to knead the dough already.

She stepped outside to what appeared like two men dancing. Back and forth they parried by the hog shed, until one of them flung a wooden box on the ground. "Explain this, you lying spy."

The box broke open on impact, spilling shining cylinders. Emma drew closer before she recognized them as bullets, hundreds of rounds, dull brass casings and their bright steel tips.

"I am as surprised as you are," answered the Goat. "I wonder who stored ammunition in that shed."

"What kind of an idiot do you think I am?" shrieked Thalheim, giving the Goat a shove.

"Oh, a complete one, I'm sure," the Goat cackled.

"A comedian," Thalheim snarled, and he surprised the ragamuffin with a kick in the groin that dropped him groaning in a ball to the ground.

From there the Goat noticed Emma and made a hand motion, warning her away, but it caused Thalheim to spin on his boot heel and shout, "You." He pointed at her. "You'll have to answer for this as well."

"For what?"

"Your shed is filled with ammunition, and don't pretend to know nothing about it."

"But I don't. I haven't been in there in years—not since your army took my father's last pig."

The captain unclipped his holster. "I should shoot all of you."

"For what possible reason?" Emma asked.

"She knows nothing about this," the Goat said at the same moment. He had come to his knees and was working to regain his breath. "We would never confide in her. She is too proud."

"I am what?"

"Don't bother trying to protect her," Thalheim said.

"Why did you look in the sty anyway, after all this time?" the Goat asked, coming to his feet, reclaiming the captain's attention. "That stockpile took months to build."

"So you admit it?"

"Why deny what you can see with your own eyes? I am not without some pride myself."

Thalheim seemed to relax a degree, resting a thumb on his pistol grip as though he welcomed the conversation. "One of our excellent snipers bagged a homing pigeon at sunset, headed north, back to our enemies. Its papers showed exact location of our communication center. It also had mention of ammunition supply near the eastern well."

"God in heaven." The Goat shook his head. "All that work, lost because of a bird."

"You will tell me more," Thalheim said. "And perhaps I will spare your life. How did you get that matériel here?"

"On my back," the Goat said, having regained his swagger.

"I already recognized you as a donkey," Thalheim scoffed. "I meant to this region."

"Why not tell you?" the Goat said, scratching his battered coat. "On trains."

"Our army searches every railcar thoroughly."

The Goat smiled. "No one opens a cabinet that says 'Danger: sixteen thousand volts.' Once I'd carried the ammunition here, I could count on your obsession with order. Racist cleanliness is a weakness, you know."

"It is a strength," Thalheim said. "As valuable as discipline."

"No one from your army searched this completely obvious hiding place, including you with it right under your nose, because you didn't want to soil your boots. All it will take to defeat your so-called excellent army is people willing to endure a little dirt."

"You are see our army's weakest element here," Thalheim insisted. "Boys who have never thrown of a punch, and old soldiers sent to recover from the Eastern Front. All they do is fall in love with the sun and ocean and wine." He wagged a finger at Emma. "And of you harlots. An army built to blitz grows bored easily. This is why we need discipline, to protect the fatherland's high ideals."

Something about that last phrase caused Thalheim to recollect himself, standing in a barnyard, pistol drawn, carrying on to the conquered about his nation's supremacy, while the man smirked and the woman calculated her escape so visibly he could hear her wheels turning. "Also you never bathe, any of you. It is disgusting. Why am I speaking to you?"

"I'm finding it educational," the Goat said. "Please continue."

"Enough. The guns that belong to these bullets, where they are hidden?"

The Goat made a face. Perhaps it was intended to show courage or scorn, but to Emma it appeared as if he had finally become aware of his own scent.

Thalheim advanced on him. "Conversation is ended. Now you tell me location of guns."

"Not in a hundred thousand years."

Thalheim cocked his pistol. "I am out of patience. And I am due at the command post to report."

The Goat made a little sweeping motion with his fingers. "Better hurry along, then."

The captain waved his gun in the air. "You think this is some joke?"

"No." The Goat shook his head. "Not in any way a joke."

"You tell me of where guns are, or I shoot you now."

"That's it?" the Goat said, nearly a whisper. "This is the moment?"

"Tell, or die."

"What the hell." The Goat shrugged. "It is a small thing to leave an unhappy life."

"Damn you stupid bumpkin fools," Thalheim said. He raised the gun, holding it inches from the Goat's nose. "Contemplate your mortality."

Emma knew this moment too well, the horrible pause. But the Goat did not blink, nor scowl, nor squint at the pistol barrel. He only looked at Emma until their eyes met, his expression revealing the inner softness he had attempted to conceal all of his life, and with frank knowledge of what was about to happen to him, no escape, that softness contained their full history, the lifetime of it, how they had nursed while their mothers sat together, how they grew and fought and strove like brother and sister, and now in the moment when it all fell away, all of that time was reduced to this strange, powerful, tender sibling affection, one fraction of a second of recognized love, a thunderbolt, then the pistol's trigger pulled, obliteration, the maroon splash of his existence on the barn wall and a body crumpled on the earth like one more ruin.

"Dear God," Emma said, rushing forward but helplessly and too late. And Thalheim had not holstered his pistol yet.

"You were colluding with him."

"No. I know nothing about these bullets."

"I saw the look he gave you."

Emma could not help seeing the Goat's body, his legs in an awkward position. "It was old friendship. Not conspiracy."

"What about the poison powder you put in the officers' bread?" He stood squarely. "Explain."

Those legs were distracting. She wanted to put them in a comfortable posture. "It wasn't poison. I was—"

"I saw you gagging on it with my own very eyes. Also explain of the rations you stole, which made extra loaves when the Field Marshal was here. Don't think I didn't notice."

"That was for my neighbors—"

"And the fuel you stole today?" Thalheim interrupted. He holstered his gun. "From an officer?"

"I can explain all of these things. But the Goat—Didier, that is—Didier and I grew up together." Emma waved a hand at the hog shed. "Honestly, I had no idea about—"

"You lie." He advanced on her.

Emma retreated, talking faster. "Our mothers were friends. We were schoolmates. I am not in the Resistance. I am just trying to keep people alive."

He poked her chest with a hard finger. "I said you lie."

"The powder for baking is not poison." She backed into the barnyard wall. She was trapped, pinned.

Thalheim grabbed both of Emma's arms and shook her. "Tell me the truth," he shouted into her face.

But if he had intended to frighten Emma, or persuade her, it backfired because he had touched her. That contact brought forth the full measure of her disgust, rising like bile for this man who taken so much from her: food, home, loved ones, peace of mind for two years. But he had never possessed her obedience, and she was not going to oblige him now.

Emma looked down her nose and spoke in a voice dripping with contempt. "You are not worth lying to."

His stung expression showed that her insult found its mark, but she had not expected him to answer it by punching her in the face. The force of it sent her spinning, her body a vine winding around itself though he grabbed her chemise before she hit the ground, jerking her halfway back.

"Your smelly friend was right," he growled. "You are too proud." And he smashed her forehead with the heel of his hand, snapping back her neck. It hurt spectacularly. She raised an arm to shield herself as the captain punched her face again.

The man was wearing gloves, Emma noticed. What kind of a man wears gloves in June? A breakthrough had arrived for Thalheim, though, some dam of restraint broken, and he surrendered to its flood, pounding her repeatedly, relentlessly, so that Emma was reminded of a thresher crossing a hay field, blades spinning to pummel the wheat. No one would save her, no one would stop his hard-knuckled hand, because no protectors were left and her only friend was the ground below, yet the captain refused to let her fall against it.

After two years of frustration, two years of enduring her sarcasm and scorn, he needed four fists to express the frenzy in his heart. Instead one of his hands gripped her torn shirt, keeping her in ideal range, while the other went left and right on her face—but untidily, wildly, sometimes striking her neck or ear, the ear stung especially.

But then Emma could not distance herself any longer, because of the pain. Out of the mayhem of blows an idea came, a recollection. She reached down for the knife against her thigh. The handle felt solid in a world of blurred confusion, the knife seemed to jump from its sheath, and she managed to slash sideways once.

Thalheim grabbed at his shoulder. "You monstrous bitch," he cried, tromping his boot on her wrist.

Then his gloves were throttling her throat and the knife fell away as Emma felt for the first time in her life the weight of a man on her body—while she thrashed till her strength turned to vapor, and the hands wrung her life away, and the world closed down to a small dimming darkness.

Yet he let her live. A motorcycle had come into the barnyard and the strangling paused. While Emma gasped for air a young voice spoke rapidly, it was a message of some kind, and she recognized the word "Kommandant." Thalheim opened his hand, dropping her as he snarled a reply. The young voice answered, and the motorcycle rattled away.

Thalheim bent over, yanking Emma up by her hair. "Am I a sergeant tonight, clever bitch?" His face leered close, eyes bulging like a horse in panic. "Say my rank or I kill you now."

Emma tried to answer but her tongue was stuck in her throat. A strained garble came out.

"Say it or you die."

"Capt—"

"Yes." He threw Emma's head back. "Yes." He stood, brushing dirt from the knees of his pants. "Lucky for you I am called

to important duty." Thalheim took out his pistol-cleaning cloth, pressing where she had cut his shoulder. "Now you listen: when this air attack has passed, and failed as it is certain of fail, *Captain* Thalheim will return, and he will take his pleasure from the clever bitch. Yes he will. Then he will finish of her, and of her idiot grandmother, and burn this filthy peasant place to ashes."

Emma shook her head, gurgling, but the captain had stepped away. He lit a match, and she could smell tobacco. Thalheim put on his helmet, neatened his gloves, straightened his uniform to perfection—taking his time, the pride of his kind. Emma lay unmoving.

Eventually he ground the butt out in the dirt. "Consider it kindness, that I give you longer than the others," he said. "Contemplate your *mortality*."

With the final word he stomped again on her wrist, all of his weight. It made a snapping sound like kindling for the fire, a lightning bolt of pain and Emma knew that a part of her was damaged inside, though to her numbed mind it seemed to be somewhere far away.

Thalheim climbed aboard his motorcycle and roared off, a spout of gravel thrown in her swollen face. Emma lay there, her mouth full of blood and dirt. It tasted like dread.

Chapter 31

O*dette paced the rectangle of her cell,* corner to corner to corner. She was dismayed to learn how much confinement galled her. Life was all about constructive use of time: minutes left in a recipe's broiling, hours till the café opened, days till the beet greens sprouted. Before the occupation, when women wore tight belts and dandy hats, she had favored blousy aprons and a big watch on her wrist. She was a person of activity, working every waking moment. Between the café, caring for older villagers, and relaying information gleaned from overly talkative soldiers, Odette had not experienced a stationary moment in years. This forced idleness felt like claustrophobia.

Now that she had passed the better part of a night, inactivity goaded her like five too many cups of tea.

Worse, the basement contained neither window nor clock. Odette knew by the grumbling of her stomach that the dinner hour was long past, and she shook her head to think of all the hungry customers arriving at her café to find the windows dark, the lost revenue, the lobster now spoiling in its pot. At home she slept by the window, and waking at any hour could estimate the time by the light in the sky, and where the moon hung. But in that cell, night stretched long. Dawn might come in a minute, or two weeks. With the air rumbling from bombs, the ground trembling, Odette felt like she was being held in a tomb.

Yet the guard seemed nothing other than bored. He inspected every inch of his rifle, polishing certain favored spots with the cuff of his sleeve. He examined his fingernails. When the lights flickered after certain bombs, his reaction was limited to raising his eyes to the fixtures. Once the light stabilized again, he wagged his boot side to side while observing closely, as if trying to decide which angle showed it to greatest advantage.

"You aren't quite the army's brightest, are you?" Odette asked him at last.

"You speak my language."

"You noticed." She crossed her arms. "And they had told me you were as clever as a cow."

He did not answer. It was difficult to appear strong while caged, but Odette felt power rising from the soles of her feet. This war seemed a decidedly amateurish affair: the guard was present, for example, because the cell lacked a proper lock. From a certain point of view, he was as imprisoned as she. "My mother's people were from Düsseldorf."

"Ah."

"Yes, a conversationalist of rare ability," she muttered. "Where is your home town?"

He remained on his stool, sliding a hand up and down the stock of his rifle. "Munich."

"I've been there. Lovely cathedral."

He shrugged.

"Not a churchgoer? Well, I also remember a square flooded with ice, and my grandfather rented me a pair of skates."

The soldier stood. "How about you stop talking?"

"I think your Kommandant wants me to do a great deal of talking."

The guard wandered down the hall. "Save your chatter for him."

The lights went out, simultaneously with the roar of a bomb

quite close. The building shuddered. Odette felt dust fall from the ceiling onto her face. Something in the manner of the darkness gave her a sense that this outage would not be temporary.

The soldier remained in place, waiting. Odette watched his gray silhouette. When the lights did not return for several minutes, she heard the knocking of his heels on the floor. A door whined on its hinge, then his boots clanked up the stairs.

He returned carrying something metal, she could tell by the sound it made when he set it down. The soldier poured papers out onto the floor, crumpling some. There was a metallic scratching sound, twice, then a small flame. He brought a cigarette lighter to the paper, and it filled the hall with a cheery orange light. The guard held the crumpled page as long as he could before releasing it into the basket. A glow remained, and he tossed another crushed sheet in on top.

Odette leaned on the bars. "DuFour will burst into flames himself when he finds out you touched his papers."

The guard raised an eyebrow at her, then returned to feeding the fire. For a while the corridor brightened as he burned page after page, but smoke began to roil along the ceiling. Odette found it growing difficult to breathe, yet she did not make any complaint. She felt she was being tested, so she sat on her bunk and kept her head low. The soldier remained upright on his stool. Although he had not said anything, she knew they were in a contest to see who could endure the smoke longest.

Soon her eyes hurt. Her throat pinched. Her nose began to run. The guard rubbed his hands together over the flames. Odette leaned lower, trying to catch the good air below. The guard dropped in several pages at once, his fire tonguing higher than the wastebasket's brim, billows of gray rising and curling down the ceiling. As they clouded around his head, the soldier sneezed.

"Yes," Odette hissed, but he only stood, passed his eyes over her with reptilian indifference, and strode to the hall's far end. There he pushed the door wide till it held, providing the smoke with the chimney it desired, while Odette felt cooler air pour in around her feet.

"What do I get for winning?" she said.

The soldier trod back down the hall. "We will soon see."

Odette stood. "What did I do to deserve this treatment? Serve the Kommandant undercooked eggs?"

"It has nothing to do with deserving."

"Where's the justice in that?"

He lowered himself back on the stool. "Making you people obey is more important than justice."

"What do you think he will do with me?"

He shrugged. "Guess."

It was as though he had dropped a rock into her stomach. Which was worse, her fate or his indifference to it? Odette paced the cell, trying to imagine options. Was there anything she could offer the Kommandant? Would any negotiation be possible? Would he have any interest in the facts?

She knew the answer. She had witnessed the occupying army's methods for four years. There were no exits, no escapes. To be suspected was to be guilty, and to be guilty was to be dead.

She must leave the cell, and town hall, and village entirely. Take the bag of cash hidden behind the stove, and at least until the end of the war, abandon the life she had known. But how? This guard was as simple as a pudding. She guessed his age at twenty, perhaps twenty-one. What did boys that age desire? She remembered all too well what they had desired of her, back in that day. With breasts developed larger and earlier than most,

Odette used to joke that not a fellow in town could say what color her eyes were. Why would this guard be any different, except perhaps to feel more desperate after life in a garrison?

There was one move left to make, and if it failed then the game was over. Odette stood with hands on her hips. "Soldier, what is your name?"

"Kreutz."

"Corporal Kreutz?"

"Private."

"Well, Private Kreutz, I would rather not die as an example to scare my friends into behaving themselves."

He opened the bolt on his gun, squinting into the opening. "So?"

"So." She came to the front of her cell, leaning against the metal until the bars pressed her flesh. "So a woman would do anything to survive. You know that, I believe. In the end, this is what we can offer to save our lives. This is what we can give."

Kreutz stared at Odette directly for the first time, her mannish body, her giant breasts, and he burst out laughing.

"Ha ha," Odette said, tentatively.

But the soldier laughed easily, swinging his arms a bit as he swaggered over to the cell. "What are you offering?"

Odette swallowed hard. She had hooked him, that easily, but with no next step in mind, only to get the cell door open. "Does the captive dictate the terms of negotiation?"

"I don't know what that means," Kreutz said, still chuckling. As he reached the cell door, however, his face grew serious. "When I was ten my grandmother died, and I had to help my mother clean out her apartment."

Odette was surprised by this turn, but she drew nearer. "God rest her soul."

The guard made an annoyed face before continuing. "At one point I moved a table that had stood against the wall for as long as I could remember. Behind it I found a head of garlic, turned black. Who knows how many years the thing had been rotting back there?"

He leaned closer, hooking a finger over one of the cell bars, as though he were playing the low note on a harp. Odette moved across from him. "Yes?"

"That," the soldier said. "That is what women smell like in your country. Unwashed. Disgusting."

Odette winced, but the soldier had grown talkative. "And you?" He laughed again, rocking back on his heels. "Do you even *have* a sex in there, with all of that smelly garlic blubber? Ha."

Odette felt a wave of shame the length of her body. How could she have forgotten that her mother was the only person ever to call her beautiful? Idiocy it was, to attempt a seduction. What had been impossible at twenty was doubly impossible now.

"You don't have to be cruel," she said, retreating. "I am still a human being, you know."

He sneered. "I would rather mate with a dog."

The woman curled up on her bunk, hugging her knees to her chest. No jail could equal the iron bars in the heart.

Kruetz returned to the trash basket and dropped in two fistfuls of papers. He bent forward as the flames turned his face yellow and then brilliant red.

The night was one long fever of hallucination. Emma saw jellyfish in the sky, their bodies like overturned bowls, their tentacles dangling. Next she dreamed of Mémé, who grunted like a sailor hauling anchor as she dragged a body across the barnyard and away. Where had a body come from, to lie in the dirt like that, and who had showed such inconsiderate manners to leave Mémé with the chore of removing it?

Lucid moments visited at intervals. When dawn came, so would the captain and his revenge. What wrong she had done him, Emma could not recall. It did not matter. He would kill her. He had pledged himself to it.

Emma did not dwell on her own extinction. It was difficult enough to breathe through a nose clogged with dirt and blood.

The Goat, Didier, that was the body. Now she remembered. Mémé had found the knife, too, wiping it on her sleeve before tucking it into the folds of her tunic. Emma heard the sound of splashing water. Opening one eye, the other apparently unwilling, she saw Mémé empty a bucket of suds against the side of the baking shed. Why was she washing those boards, how silly, while the water made a rivulet that flowed toward her, another bucket thrown and a little puddle began to form on the ground near her face, it made the shape of a paisley.

We are as temporary as clouds, Emma thought, lolling onto her back. Lovely and high and sunlit, then gone on the next wind to some other place and shape. Oh, the barn was dirty with Didier, that's right. The mess of his execution. So much information in his final glance, too. And then she returned to the darkness.

A jolt of pain startled Emma awake. She sucked air, gasped, felt her lungs inflate as though she had exhaled hours ago, and it brought a sharp stab to all of her left-side ribs. Emmanuelle was not finished yet.

With her second breath came worry. If she died, who would

care for Mémé, putting up with her stubbornness and calming her with tenderness? Who would straw the dough to make extra loaves? Who would bring Michelle her egg and Yves his fuel and Pierre his tobacco and more eggs to Fleur and her damaged mother, Marie, on and on, Odette, the priest, and Monkey Boy? No one. If you want to know your worth in this world, make a list of the people who will starve when you die.

Who should come to mind then, like a memory of school letting out on a child's spring day, but Philippe. How she loved him, Emma admitted it now: his earnestness, his quiet voice, the inability to hide his desire. How they had wanted one another, of course it had always been mutual. It all seemed so small and young and long ago. How frightened they had been of each other. Now they both knew real fear, the ways it changed people, hardened them. Would the war grind all of Philippe's innocence into dust, as it had hers?

Emma remembered the sight of the top of his head, on that night when he bent to kiss her breasts while she watched in excited disbelief. Now her dress was torn wide, her body nakedly exposed. Probably the captain had seen her, but the nearness of death overwhelmed any modesty. Her consciousness faded again for some time.

In the hour before dawn Emma's fever broke. She felt pain for real then, but her mind had calmed and she knew the ground beneath her. One eye was swollen shut, but with the other she saw Mémé, sitting near in the dirt, keeping watch.

The old woman saw the eye open, lifted her granddaughter's head with care, and brought a glass of water to her lips. Although some spilled on Emma's face and neck, she gulped greedily.

What was better than water? Elixir, life-giver, healer. With each swallow she felt the dirt washed not away, but deeper into her body, sluicing the dust and blood until she could breathe.

With a soft cloth Mémé washed Emma's face, jerking away at the least wince, wiping her nostrils clear and dabbing around her damaged eye. The air grumbled from the direction of the village, the sky glowed with fires, but in that barnyard there was a moment's peace. Then Mémé raised Emma's head and scooted her lap underneath, making a pillow of her thighs.

Emma stared at the sky, feeling the return of clarity. Where could she go to avoid the captain? Should she take Mémé, too? How much of a journey was she capable of making?

Before any answers had come, Emma began hallucinating again. Those jellyfish in the sky had returned. No, they were the white seeds of a blown dandelion, swept by the wind. Or no again, they were parasols. Like so many fine ladies had gone boating on a summer's day, parasols here and there all over the sky.

She remembered her umbrella on the beach, how artfully it had swung in the wind, and these hallucinations did the same thing. There were dozens, hundreds, all over the predawn sky.

Something was different, though, in her one-eyed vision. At the end of the handle, in the place of a hook these umbrellas had some unusual shape, what was it?

All at once she knew, and the whole world was revealed. On all of those umbrellas, in the place of a hook, there was a man. Descending ever so slowly in the June night sky, hundreds of men, thousands, each riding his silken jellyfish down to her village, and it was no dream.

And with the advent of these strange angels, the world became exactly as the Monsignor had foretold.

Part Five

HELL ON EARTH

Chapter 32

D*awn on the sixth of June* delivered the loudest day in the history of the earth. Planes, bombs, responding ground fire, engines of tanks and trucks, all created a din so constant it seemed as if the hedgerows were shouting from their crowns.

The last hours of the night performed a departing trickery, too, as fires on the horizon snapped and climbed, and the sky oranged before Tuesday had actually begun. Emma lay on the kitchen floor facing east, thinking the colors were strangely beautiful, a halo on the land, when the sun rose, bringing a day too bright for the flames to be seen across a distance as anything more than wavering air beneath rising billows of black.

With that, the source of the roar appeared to be the sea. What strange monster had been unleashed? What appetite must it possess? Whom would it devour on this day?

Thalheim feared the quartermaster, but then, everyone did. Fat as a zeppelin, unflappable, aware of every nut and bolt in his beehive warren of supplies, he maintained order from his throne—a metal office chair atop a pile of wooden pallets—through sheer intimidating bulk, plus a whistle with which he was famously communicative. Despite the deep-of-the-night hour, soldiers of every need and disposition stood in respectful single file, waiting for the quartermaster's attention. With the air battle under way and the invasion imminent, no one wanted to find himself low on ammunition. Thalheim stepped past them all, pulling rank because of his new assignment. Yet he had never dared to ask the quartermaster's name.

But that whistle shrieked, and the man was scowling down at him. "State your business."

"Message delivery for the Kommandant," Thalheim said, waving the envelope with its official seal. He used his good arm, the other one sore and bandaged where Emma had slashed him.

The man-blimp took out his whistle long enough to spit on the ground, then point with a beefy arm. "Bike R7H has fuel. Return immediately. No joy rides today."

Thalheim reached the armed checkpoint before daybreak, declared his business, spoke the password, and parked his motorcycle by the front door of a palatial villa. Moments later a corporal ushered him into a room with ornate wallpaper and fine furnishings, where he saluted despite the pain in his shoulder.

The colonel sat sipping tea. A bald man, who kept his monocle in place by maintaining a constant sneer, he nonetheless drank with pinkie erect. Setting the delicate teacup in its saucer on a table, he held out his hand for the envelope.

Normally Thalheim would have no idea what the contents of an officer's communication might be, but in this case the colonel made it no secret. His eyes went wide as he read, the monocle falling to dangle from a strap clipped to his collar.

"*Now* he wants tanks?" he scoffed. "*Now* he wants me to bring tanks?"

Thalheim knew better than to speak, especially as the colonel stood and began to pace.

"Does he have any goddamn idea whose permission I must ask before I can do that? Does your imbecile commander have any idea?" He crumpled the paper and threw it on his desk, then spied the teacup, and swept his arm so that cup and saucer smashed on the far wall.

The maroon blotch on the wallpaper reminded Thalheim of something, though he could not say what. He waited until the storm had passed and the senior officer came to rest by the window, monocle restored. The captain clicked his heels together. "Sir, will there be a return communication?"

The colonel spun, as if surprised to discover the messenger still present, but then he spoke quietly. "Tell him it is far too late for such politics," he said. "Tell him I said to go to hell."

Thalheim saluted, and hurried from the room.

The engine of the motorcycle was loud enough that he did not notice anything special on the return trip. But when he paused between two fields to relieve himself, Thalheim heard the explosive roar of battle in the distance. He switched on his staff radio.

At first it crackled and buzzed. Then the anonymous authoritative voice, which he'd heard deliver announcements countless times, now declared flatly: the invasion had begun. While moving his arm in small circles to test where the knife wound was tender, Thalheim listened to the full report. Enemy maneuvers were now under way along nearly ninety kilometers of coastline. All troops were ordered to shoot any person seen cooperating with the invading forces, as well as any person giving shelter to enemy soldiers, sailors, or airmen.

Thalheim expected orders on where to report, the usual instructions unit by unit. Instead the broadcast ended. He waited, but there was nothing more. He raised his head, finding himself astride a motorcycle with broad fields on either side. He checked his pistol to be sure it was fully loaded. Then he started up, riding full throttle back toward the garrison.

Thalheim's first stop was the mess tent, where he found a mystery. Normally at that time of day the area would be crowded and loud, hundreds of soldiers stuffing their bellies before the morning change of the watch. But now? No one present, not so much as a punished private peeling potatoes. One feral cat prowled by the serving tables, then spied him and darted out of sight. Tent flaps rose and billowed in the breeze.

He piloted to the supply depot to return the motorcycle. But the controlled place he'd left hours earlier had descended into chaos. The quartermaster was attempting to bring order but it was futile, his waving arms and shrill whistle ignored while senior officers shouted orders, lower ranks and privates ran like kitchen bugs exposed by an overhead light, trucks, machine-gun-mounted cars and half-tracks left without the driver fueling, or signing out, or performing any of the usual formalities.

The captain stood observing, waiting to see if a line would form or hierarchy coalesce. But no, the quartermaster continued to bellow, and departing troops continued to ignore him.

Thalheim rode past a cluster of arguing soldiers, reaching the place where his unit's vehicles parked. The space, normally filled by three transport trucks, a mobile machine gun, and a command car, was as empty as an old man's mouth. Whatever glory they were to accomplish that day, he would not be part of it.

Riding back to the motorcycle's designated place, Thalheim struggled to stifle a surge of shame. He had done nothing wrong. He had followed orders and done his duty, as a good soldier should. The only question was what step he ought to take next.

As if in answer, a shell screamed overhead, clearing the

commissary and landing hundreds of yards farther inland—but with an explosion so loud it concussed the air.

What could one man do? He could seek his place, and find his duty. Thalheim checked the fuel in several motorcycles, till he found one with a full tank, whereupon he gave himself authority to commandeer it. The colonel's reply contained nothing that the Kommandant needed to hear. And Thalheim had to go to the water. He had to see for himself.

Odette sat in her cell, wishing she had possessed the presence of mind before leaving the kitchen to snatch the cheese cutter. A strong thick wire with wooden handles on each end, it would have made a perfect tool to garrote the contemptible Kreutz. The idea of it gave her a bleak satisfaction as she passed the night awake on the bunk, hours elongated because without a window she could not tell when dawn approached.

Yet she must have dozed at some point, because when a fraction of daylight did sneak down the stairwell into the basement, a new guard occupied the stool, and he with soft cheeks and slender, hairless wrists: a boy. The gun and uniform did not matter. With every detonation from above, she saw clearly, he flinched. What use could she make of his youth?

Pierre sat milking the first of his girls, wondering if a soldier would come to collect the pails that day. He patted his wool vest's pockets again, trying to remember where he had left his pipe. Not in the hayloft, thank heaven. He remembered filling his bowl later, over by the eastern well. But where?

DuFour splashed water on his face, rinsed his mouth with anise, breakfasted on acorn tea. How was it that his loyalty to the occupying army did not merit rationing him some actual tea leaf? He dressed in professional fashion, set his beret in place, all while considering the documents he must process that day, the dispositions and requests, while making sure to allot time for a gloating visit to the café woman in jail.

DuFour paused in the entry of his home, relishing that particular prospect, how humbled she would be. And how pleased the Kommandant, possibly impressed at how his humble clerk had caused the woman to entrap herself. DuFour opened his door with a snap to his step. It lasted only a moment, gone before he had reached the street, as a gust brought thick smoke over the grass, the foul smell of rubber burning. Only then did the old man's nighttime visit return to disquiet his mind. Should he actually go to work?

Monkey Boy dropped a bit of bark through the branches, watching it tumble. He had spent hours in certain trees, keeping watch, exercising his facility with numbers. Five hundred and five, that was how many dead bodies he had seen so far that morning. Before that day he'd seen only four, bringing his lifetime total suddenly to five hundred and nine. Meanwhile an average of thirty-eight men per landing boat, the ramp dropped and out they poured, the first wave falling from gunfire almost as one, others spilling over those bodies into waist-deep water, and on average eleven of them making it out to the sand.

The astonishing thing? The thing which he did not understand? Behind every landing boat, despite all those bodies lolling in the surf, more landing boats waited, foam at the bows as they surged forward. The ramps dropped and their men fell, and yet the next ones poured in immediately like an unstoppable tide of humanity.

Of ships, he had observed them left to right and out to the horizon more than a thousand, which was as high as he could count, and more. But there was a sense to it: behind the boats that carried soldiers, warships blasted away with their big guns. From time to time a detonation came from the distance, some even bigger battleship too far out to see, which flung missiles inland high over his head. The projectiles were huge. It was as though they were firing Jeeps. Long after the shell had passed overhead, there came a roar like a giant opened furnace, like a detonation of the planet itself, the sound of the shell's firing delayed by distance, and Monkey Boy cupped his hands over his ears.

Still the sight remained, extending from the beach below him all the way to the horizon. It was the most elaborate, terrifying, beautiful thing he had ever seen. Someone else needed to witness this, and explain to him what it meant. Monkey Boy clambered down his special sycamore in search of someone to tell. But who?

Fleur pulled a quilt over the shoulders of her mother, who lay in bed facing the wall and shivering. Outside the world snarled and convulsed, as if the house sat on a strategic bombing target rather than in a small meadow away from the village center. A fly buzzed into the room; every window in the house was already shattered. Fleur had spent the hour after daybreak with tweezers, picking splinters of glass first from the skin of her mother and then from herself. She had learned patience with instruments from her father, the outspoken veterinarian who hushed while treating the animals. Now Fleur sat on the edge of the bed and rubbed Marie's quaking back as a breeze blew straight through their house. The torn curtains rose and fell like a sigh.

The priest awakened to feed his chickens and prepare for seven thirty Mass. His right leg was worse than ever, almost useless as he dragged it along behind him. There was nothing wrong with his body, he felt sure. The fault lay in his faith, which could no longer be reconciled with the world around him. He prayed constantly now. But the gap between heaven and earth had grown too large.

As if to prove the point a nearby bombardment rattled his house, interrupting his Ave Marias. On such a day, would anyone come to St. Agnes by the Sea? If someone did, what strengthening of faith could he offer? What vision of salvation remained?

Pirate lengthened his neck to crow with all of his might. There was a body rolled against the chicken coop. A person. It smelled unfamiliar, and therefore unwelcome. The rooster declared his discontent, but the body did not obey. Hopping down from the coop roof, Pirate noticed that the barnyard door had been left ajar. Beyond lay a world of potential threats, but a universe of possible meals. Bobbing his head with each step, glancing sidelong, he dashed across the open space and out the door. There was a well, and beyond it a wall of green. Freedom at last.

Mémé snored away on the couch, exhausted after a long night of nursing her granddaughter. Emma stood in the doorway, angling her heel back and forth to put on her shoe without bending over. Pain flared down her right arm, but she only winced and gritted her teeth, then dragged herself out to the baking shed. The Kommandant's aide would arrive at 7:40, which meant she was behind schedule and he did not like to wait.

For once, Pirate failed to make his ruckus around her ankles, but Emma was numb to that information. Pain occupied the full of her attention, forehead to ribs to shins, so that she tossed barley kernels underfoot without noticing the barnyard's silence. One thing halted her, though—the place where the Goat's blood had stained the earth. It made an odd, curved blotch. How much rain would it take to wash the mark away? It did not matter. Emma memorized the shape, in order to keep it forever, before shuffling on into the barn.

In the shed the rounds of dough had grown fat under their cloth covers. Emma set her kneading board onto the table just so. She ran her palm over the smooth wood of what had been Uncle Ezra's execution tree, then lifted the cover from one bowl and with her left hand punched the dough. Her aim erred, though, caving in one side, the other half still risen and rough. She struck again, and the mound fell into itself. As she went to turn the bowl over, the dough nearly slipped and she had to jerk her hip against the table to prevent a spill. Pain shot through her arm and the side of her face like an electric charge, and she had not even begun kneading yet.

Emma took deep breaths, calming herself, trying to bring her right arm forward. But it would not obey, dropping from the board back to her side. If only she had stabbed the captain upward, as Guillaume had instructed. If only she had shot those officers when they stood in a row. She might be dead, but they would have been stopped. Emma started kneading with her left hand, it began well enough, until the board tipped. She jerked forward again, but too late. The dough fell to the shed's dirt floor, the kneading board toppling after.

Emma was on her knees instantly, fumbling the board against her chest and back into place. She scooped the empty bowl under the dough but its white skin was marred with dirt. When she tried to brush it away, the brown spread. A spot of red, her chin cut reopening, dropped onto the mess.

"All right," Emma said, wiping her good hand on her dress. "It'll be nine loaves today. And if he doesn't like it, he can take it up with Thalheim."

Dabbing her chin with her sleeve, she reached for another bowl.

"What is your name?" Odette asked the boy.

He stiffened on the stool. "I am not to speak to you."

"I am jailed and you have a gun. What danger are you in?"

As if her mention of it had reminded him, the boy stood the gun on its stock so that it aimed at the ceiling. With bayonet, it reached past his shoulder. "Kreutz told me you were a witch. He said you would put a spell on me."

Odette sat up on her bunk. "Does this feel like a spell?"

"You are speaking my language. That makes me nervous."

"I am from your country," Odette said. "It is all a mistake that I am here."

"You were arrested for spying."

Odette let that one go. "Where is your home?"

Deliberating whether he should answer, the boy ran his thumb around the tip of the gun barrel. "Grainau."

"At the foot of the Zugspitze?"

He stood. "You have been there?"

Odette shook her head. "I have only seen pictures."

"It is the most beau—"

A bomb landed closer than any before, exploding in the street outside the town hall. The building shook and they both heard the sound of falling stone. Odette could not see the boy any longer. She rushed to the front of her cell, knowing that his injury meant her freedom. He was curled in a ball on the floor.

"Are you all right?" she called to him.

For more than a minute he did not answer. "I was conscripted," the boy from Grainau said at last, and she could tell that he was crying. "I didn't want to come. They made me. And now I am going to die here."

Odette rolled up her sleeves. "Here is what you do," she said. "Take your gun and get away from the village, and if anyone asks, you have a message to deliver to a major. No one will interfere. Once you reach the open fields, get rid of your rifle and present yourself at any farmhouse. They will give you work clothes to replace your uniform. Follow the river upstream to Caen, to the monastery of St. Stephen. It is easily found, watch for the six spires. They will hide you safely."

"You see?" The boy stood, dusting himself off before lifting his rifle from the floor. "A spell, exactly as they warned me."

"Don't you understand, Private Zugspitze? *I* am not the danger. I am nothing at all. The thing you should fear is the order they gave you to stay, when they have all moved to somewhere safe. The thing to fear is out there, falling from the sky."

As if she had conjured it, another shell struck, this time hitting the town hall directly. The northern half of the building was sheared away, caving into itself as though its ancient stones were cubes of sugar. The basement jail, located at the opposite end, nonetheless shook as if in an earthquake, flinging Odette to the floor. She lay there, arms shielding her skull, waiting whole minutes for debris to stop falling and the air to go still. When at last she found the nerve to lift her head, she saw that the explosion had bent the cell door, its base had gouged an arc in the cement floor. Now it stood wide open.

Odette considered it a favorable omen that the door would never close again. She poked her head into the damaged hallway, walls buckled and light fixtures shattered on the floor. The boy, her guard, her captor, was gone.

Chapter 33

"No," Mémé said, arms crossed, feet planted in Emma's path.

"People are expecting me," Emma said, adjusting the wagon harnesses, her right arm now in a splint. She had given up on the bread that day, unable as she was to knead with one hand, but the Kommandant's aide had not come for the loaves anyway. Still, there were eggs to be gathered and given. "I cannot sit idle while our neighbors go hungry."

"No," Mémé said.

"With respect," Emma said, lowering her head, then raising it again with effort. "I understand the dangers. But Odette sits in the same jail that held your son-in-law, my father. We did not act to help him soon enough, and I will not repeat that mistake."

Mémé scowled on, her face cragged with age and determination. "No."

"Look at me," Emma whispered. She could well imagine, with her closed eye and swollen lips, what her grandmother saw. "Would you have me wait here till the captain returns?"

Mémé's lips began to tremble, but she pressed them hard together, wringing out any room for sorrow. "No Gypsy."

"Dear one." Emma laid her good hand on the old woman's crossed arms. "I am stubborn, like they say my mother was. I am almost as stubborn as you. Helping others may keep me alive."

Mémé turned away. "No." But this time she said it quietly.

"I'll return by midday." Emma gave her grandmother a kiss on the cheek. "Noon, and no later. I promise."

Mémé held still as Emma pulled the wagon around her and through the barnyard doorway. Though the straps chafed her shoulders, she felt a measure of relief. If she found the captain somewhere along her route, perhaps he would spare Mémé.

A few steps past the well, however, Emma stubbed her foot on a stone, and a whip of pain cracked from her heel to the back of her head. She stood reeling for a full minute before shuffling on again. Perhaps this plan was a mistake. Either way, she would not be suffering for much longer.

Monkey Boy ventured toward the beaches only as far as the bend in the road, where he could see the mansions on the cliff. The one on the left, with those flags of the occupying army flapping in the wind, looked dead. No one entered or departed, no soldiers appeared outside at all. The one on the right, with wires coming from every corner to reach in seemingly every direction, was fully engulfed. Flames poured from the upper windows, and no one was attempting to put them out.

The center house, where the young Argent couple lived, was gone. Its crumbled stones sat in heaps or lay tossed onto the lawn, as a bored child might scatter his blocks. Two signs indicated what the rubble had been: First, a downstairs corner remained undamaged; the place two walls met and a bookshelf hung gave evidence that this pile of rocks had once been a dwelling place. Second, the chimney remained somehow intact, rising by itself into the sky. Monkey Boy thought it resembled a finger pointing: here; once upon a time people lived here.

The Monsignor was well along in the seven thirty Mass, celebrated that morning for three hardy souls who came to spend the warring hours in the presence of God. The priest was moments away from elevation of the Eucharist, when a soldier no taller than a child burst through the main doors. He ran halfway down the center aisle before slowing, then coming to a complete stop.

"You there," the priest called from the altar, interrupting a prayer. "No guns are permitted inside the church."

"You had better run for it," the soldier said, pushing the rifle behind his back. His face was smudged with dirt and his pronunciation crude. "No one will be spared."

The Monsignor limped down from the altar, leaning on his cane. Was this soldier a child? His voice sounded unusually high.

"They've blown up town hall," the private continued. "And I hear they are winning at the beaches. They will kill everyone."

"You have no authority here," the priest said.

"Leave this place," the soldier cried. "Save yourselves."

The Monsignor felt a swell of power, as if a moment had arrived for which there had been years of preparation. Uncertainty fell away, and he now knew his role for that day's conflict, and for the rest of the war. The waiting and doubting had reached its zenith, faith and reality reconciled at last.

Throwing aside his cane, he strode to the Communion rail and raised both arms high. "This is not a place of men and their wars. This is the house of Almighty God. You may stay, if you adopt an attitude of humility and prayer. Otherwise begone, sinner, and may God have mercy on your soul."

The tiny soldier ran before the priest had finished. He left the door wide, and the noise of combat spilled buzzing and snapping into the church. But the Monsignor returned to his place at the altar, hands trembling with the power and the glory. He glanced at the Mass book to find his place. Yes, the elevation.

He faced the crucifix, while with both hands he lifted Emma's one third of a loaf as high as he could, crying out in Latin: "Do this in memory of me."

Then the priest bowed his head, two of the three other heads in the church replicating his motion exactly.

The third head, in the front pew, belonged to Pierre. He inclined in the opposite direction, eyes raised to the heavens. His hands were folded in prayer, and his fingers—as worn as old leather, but strong like ropes from a lifetime of milking—were interlaced and extended, so that anyone from above could see that they made a *V*.

The town-hall stairway survived the explosion, but Odette had a difficult time climbing them with no railing and a wide opening on one side. Parts of the building dropped randomly from above, keeping her snug against the wall.

The hallway to DuFour's office remained intact, and the door closed. He had always made such a show of locking and unlocking, probably he was cowering in there right now. Out the window he would go, that was her thought. For all he had done to her, to Guillaume, to all the people of the village, DuFour must go out the window. But when she touched the door it swung back on its hinges, and there was no office on the other side. Just open air, and a smashed desk amid the rubble below.

She held the doorframe, scanning the debris. Was DuFour buried in there? One could hope. Odette spat with satisfaction and began to make her way back down. She considered her good fortune at surviving a bomb so near, at being free.

The contentment did not last. As she reached the street Odette could see, despite the litter of downed trees and broken buildings, that the blue bicycle was gone. The scoundrel had run before the bombs fell. Frustration redoubled her anger.

She straightened her clothes and decided: next stop would be the cottage of that whore Michelle. The day before, Odette had listened on her illicit radio to reports from Rome, where the occupying army fell, the Allies gained control, and the people took it upon themselves to punish some of their neighbors' conduct. Yes, Odette hurried across the square to the concealment of the hedgerows. She knew exactly what to do with a collaborator.

Chapter 34

E*mma stood before town hall, stunned.* The right half of the building was gone, flattened, a jumble of rock with pipes and wires protruding like some industrial monster was buried beneath. The left half was intact, but with a gray coating of dust. It was an odd joke, that the building's damage mirrored her own, but she slipped out of the wagon straps and, leading with her open eye, ascended the rubble. From above, she could peer unimpeded into the basement, and see for herself that no prisoner remained in the cell below. Nor, Emma was reassured to note, was there any bloodstain on the floor or walls.

She returned to street level with care, holding her splinted arm out for balance, and pulled her wagon toward the village green, and Odette's café.

When Emma wheeled onto that street, however, she noticed something else first: Uncle Ezra's bakery. A continent of time had passed since she'd last stepped inside. Now the door was broken open, all the windows smashed, and as she saw the shelves tipped against one another, the walls stained with mold, the giant mixer on its side, Emma felt a thousand years old. Her body hurt, Thalheim would shoot her at the first opportunity, the invasion had come too late. An armored truck rattled down the side road, its gun pointed ahead, its smokestack billowing black. Emma considered sitting down right there, accepting whatever might come, inviting the eternal rest that she suspected was not a great distance away.

But then she heard singing. Not a graceful melody or fine voice, but a high piping, somewhere between infant and bird. It was the most innocent sound to enter Emma's ears in as long as she could remember, so she slipped out of her straps and followed it. The singsong came from Odette's café.

Finding the front door open a crack, Emma pushed it wider with her splint. There, at a table for two, doodling with her finger on the tablecloth, sat Fleur.

"I went for water," she sang, almost in a whisper. "I only went for water."

"Is Odette here?" Emma asked.

The girl needed a moment to answer, bringing herself out of reverie and squinting at Emma as if she did not recognize her.

"She told me to come here if something went wrong." Fleur spoke as if she were still singing.

Emma came to the table and sat across from the girl. "Did something go wrong?"

"Only the last part. The last little part."

Emma looked the girl over. "Are you all right? What happened?"

"I went for water," Fleur answered. "That was when the bomb fell into the house. All I did was go for water."

"Oh my dear. And your mother—"

"It's not my fault. She asked me to."

Emma nodded. "I see. I'm very sorry. But truly it's not your fault at all. You had no way of knowing—"

"This was only the last little part anyway."

"What do you mean?"

Fleur made a face. "My mother died halfway when they shot

my father. Then almost halfway more, after what the soldiers did to her. Today was the last little part. I have been waiting for it."

The girl rose and went to the door, which opened onto the village green. Once, this had been a place old men played boules at noon, young men sang during a night of drink, Odette both served and ruled, and now it was deserted. Fleur stuffed her hands into her frock's deep pockets.

Emma sat there, ruminating that the girl might be the most beautiful creature she had ever seen. And now another orphan of the war. She came and stood beside Fleur. "What do you have in your pockets, that you must be fiddling with it all the time?"

The girl shrugged and lifted one hand. It held gardening shears, metal ones with yellow rubber grips on the handles.

Emma took the thick scissors in her good hand. "You've been cutting flowers? How sweet." But then she opened the shears, and saw that the blades were rutted and gouged. "Or what have you been cutting?"

The girl grinned, but it was a naughty smile. "Wires."

"What do you mean, wires?"

"Any wires. My father showed me how."

Emma ran her thumb along the blades. They were ruined. "I don't understand."

"We villagers have no use for wires. But the soldiers, they need wires for everything. Whenever there is no one around, I snip them. My father said it was good to do this, so I cut some wires almost every day. And now I have no family, which is when Odette said I should come here."

"Don't cry," Emma said. "It will be all right."

Fleur drew her head back, as if from a bad smell. "I am not crying. My father and mother are together. And anyway, do you know how hard it is to feed a ghost?"

Lost for an answer, Emma gaped a moment at the shears, then held them out to Fleur. The girl tucked them in her pocket, sidled to the table, and began doodling with her finger again.

"I went for water," she sang, as if no one else were there. "I only went for water."

The radio had gone insane. Thalheim listened with disbelief to reports from all sectors. In one place, hundreds of invading men had assaulted a cliff directly into machine-gun fire, the soldiers continuing to climb despite dozens of their fellows tumbling past them to the ground below. In another location, enemy ships had towed long barges which they scuttled in a semicircle around a village, creating an instant harbor. In yet another place, invading troops had landed accompanied by a corps of bagpipers, the instruments wailing louder than cannon fire as soldiers poured out onto the beach.

Marksmen of the occupying army had thwarted the landing craft, emptying their guns to prevent attackers from reaching dry ground. Some strafed from side angles, too, littering the sand with invaders' bodies. In a few places, the exits from the beach had seen such massive assaults, so many invaders flinging themselves forward, soldiers of the occupying army had abandoned their battle stations in fear. However, commanding officers stood at the pillbox doorways, as ordered, and used their pistols to execute these traitors on the spot. Preparation was prevailing. Discipline was winning.

Eventually Thalheim reached a vantage he knew, stopping the motorcycle to crawl on his belly to the edge of the bluff. His shoulder ached, but he was safe behind barbed wire. The hill was heavily mined, too; he had overseen the work himself.

What he saw excited him: the beach was covered with wreckage, tanks and trucks and transport craft, all burning and bent. Bodies lay in the open, hundreds of men palsied atop their rifles or languishing in wavelets, halfway out of the sea. To his far right a big ship had run aground. It must have carried ammunition, since it produced nearly continuous explosions.

There was a smell to the air, metallic as though he had a coin in his mouth, with a whiff of gunpowder that vaguely resembled a campfire. It was not unpleasant, and Thalheim inhaled deeply: the scent of war.

As he observed, the battle scene made a visible sort of sense, a fine fury along the line of collision below, while a kilometer away the only danger came from sporadic air attacks.

As if to symbolize the invaders' feckless ways, a pilotless landing craft careened across the water, nudging aside other boats, running over bodies in the surf, banging against the wooden obstacles, and impaling itself at last on a steel spike with a mine at the tip, whose detonation ripped away the bow and sent the landing craft down in a wake of bubbles and swirls.

Soon smoke from the ammunition ship had grown so heavy on the beach that shooting momentarily ceased. No one on either side could see to aim. The conflict acquired a strange calm.

Thalheim could hear big guns down the coast, however, the 88s and mortars with their satisfying throaty report. He could smell the acrid smoke that seemed to come from all directions.

This was the moment, the fulcrum of the battle, after which the invaders would lose their drive, and defenders of the coastal battlements would counterattack, turning the momentum and driving the Allies back into the sea like some creature not fully evolved, and therefore not equipped to live on this land. The moment of mighty transition was at hand, and if he was not to be a force in the victory, at least he was a loyal witness, for which Thalheim felt gratitude.

The wind gusted, the view cleared, an enemy destroyer fired from two hundred meters offshore, and the battle recommenced. Yet it seemed as though the next wave of landing craft was delaying, holding back while troops that had already landed fought their way up the sand a few dozen steps, before dying in a squall of gunfire. What kind of leadership would strand so many soldiers here to die? What kind of filth led this army?

Everything in Thalheim's sight confirmed his conviction that he belonged to the strongest nation in history, the fiercest warriors, the greatest race. He felt his heart pounding against the ground beneath him.

From a gap between the landing crafts that held back, a strange floating machine emerged. It was sluggish, wallowing in the surf like a pig in mud. Yet somehow it proved impervious to the firing from the shore. He had never seen an object less seaworthy, but even the 88s could not stop its plodding progress.

Over a span of minutes, while men on the beaches and men on the bluffs exchanged fire, the casualties entirely on the invading side, this piggish behemoth rose up, taking ordnance from both flanks while water poured off of its sides. The onslaught punctured its inflated skirt until gradually the thing emerged as its true self: a tank. A floating tank.

While Thalheim marveled that such a device existed, the armored machine began turning its treads, throwing sand as it labored forward. He watched Allied soldiers scampering down the beach to cower behind the tank, hiding themselves as it muddled inland. Its turret was pointed at the nearest beach exit.

As the Field Marshal had predicted, the pre-aimed guns dropped those soldiers like so many flies, their weapons never fired. Also as planned, the armored machine soon encountered the antitank trench dug above the high-tide mark, a hole as wide as a man and as deep as three, and there it stopped.

"Now we've got you," the captain said to himself.

But the tank carried some sort of contraption on its roof, a scaffold which now rose from hydraulic pumps with tedious slowness, unfolded in its middle due to gravity's pull, and with a screech of metal fell open in front to make a rudimentary bridge.

The thought occurred to Thalheim for the first time that the enemy might not be completely weak after all, that the invaders might also have prepared. While he watched in horror, the tank set out across the bridge, which sank into the sand, but held.

Observers above the battle must have been paying attention as well. The nearest pillbox on the bluff unloaded its power downward, a bellow of shooting that pinned invading soldiers behind the tank—one who was foolish enough to poke a head up dropped instantly in the hail of gunfire.

By then the tank had reached the trench's other side, where, as ponderous and wrathful as a bull, it at last seemed to take notice of the coastal defenses harassing it. With painstaking patience the turret turned, the long gun barrel lowered, and the bull's charge took the form of a single shell, blasting into the bluff two meters below the pillbox. As dirt and rocks tumbled down, the fire from above redoubled, machine guns and rifles, a hand grenade thrown though it did not reach nearly far enough, detonating with a harmless geyser of sand, while with the same sluggish determination the turret adjusted slightly, the barrel rose a degree or two, and the tank fired again.

The shell pierced the pillbox opening, its explosion so powerful the resulting billow contained pieces of guns, helmets, what Thalheim could clearly see was a human leg. With the shot's echo rattling down the coastline, one person spilled out the rear exit, writhing in the dirt and then still.

As the bull pawed the earth onward to the beach exit, the pill-box delivered no additional weapon fire. The remaining Allied soldiers fanned out along the side of the tank, as though it led a wedge of geese.

Thalheim rolled away from the bluff, kicked his motorcycle to life, and fled.

Chapter 35

E*mma left the wagon* at the foot of the knoll, to spare herself the effort of hauling it up to Michelle's door. She had no eggs to hide in the tree, had not visited her chicks yet. Nor did she expect to siphon fuel that day, since the lieutenant was probably battling the invasion. Still she felt compelled to complete her rounds, to maintain the pretense that life was unchanged, and to enable Thalheim to find her. Then he might do as he would without hurting Mémé.

The hill proved too steep, and Emma paused halfway to rest against a linden tree. It was in bloom, the fragrance that surrounded her sweet but musky, a fecund contradiction of the deathly pounding coming from the beaches and the smoky scent everywhere else.

Her ear hurt, her throat, the whole left side of her face. Her right wrist throbbed where the small bones had fractured. She held her splinted hand high to keep blood from adding to its swelling. When it became too heavy, Emma lowered her arm and pushed on. Only then did she notice that the cottage's blue door stood wide. Something was nailed to it, too. A squirrel? The tail of a fox?

"Michelle," she called, drawing nearer. "Mademoiselle?"

There was no reply. Emma reached the dooryard and saw what hung on the door: a ponytail. A long clump of human hair, precisely the color of Michelle's.

Emma leaned into the open doorway. "Hello?"

The kitchen was a shambles, chairs tipped over, broken glasses and plates. On the counter sat a pair of farm shears, as one would use to cut wool from a lamb. On the floor, clumps of hair drifted here and there in the breeze.

"Michelle? Are you all right?"

Still no answer, and Emma grew bold, venturing into the other downstairs room: a settee, a chair by the fire, a footstool. Despite her aches she decided to climb the stairs, the wood complaining under her weight until she reached the landing. One bedroom was plush as for a wealthy person, a four-post bed with sheer linens draped on its frame, a deep mattress and many small pillows. Long gloves and lace things lay tossed on chair backs. All around the room there were candles burned to various heights, perhaps a dozen of them.

When Emma was fifteen Uncle Ezra had taught her reduction, boiling a full pot of beef or chicken stock down to a quarter cup of spectacular concentrated flavor. Now she understood that there was another kind of reduction, and she had allowed it to happen to her: living made small, a way of life diminished and humiliated. Considering the one candle by whose light she and Mémé ate dinner every night, sharing their one egg and fraction of a baguette, Emma marveled that Michelle had managed to create this room of luxury.

As if to complete Emma's thought, the other upstairs room was spare, a pink vanity with a small, matching metal seat. She sat, studying all of the powders and creams, admiring them. Tools of seduction, these artifacts of deception, and her ignorance of such things caused Emma to chuckle.

Then she made the mistake of looking up. The face that confronted her in the mirror was none she had seen before. The entire left side was bruised from throat to hairline. Her lips were misshapen, the lower one split. Her eye was swollen nearly shut, though she mused that it appeared worse than it felt. Her chin bore a cut that had scabbed hard.

Emma spoke to the woman in the glass: "Good God, you are ugly." The woman told her the same thing.

She picked up a brush and a dish of powder, patting a bit on her left cheek. The bruise remained as visible as ever. She selected a lipstick: red as an embarrassment, red as a wolf lifting his mouth from a fresh kill. She ran the smooth stick across her lips, but it hurt to apply pressure.

That pain broke all reverie. This was nonsense and indulgence. Emma wiped her sleeve roughly across her mouth; it stung but she did it again till all the lipstick was gone. She licked her fingers and swept the powder from her cheek as well. The stairs seemed louder on the way down.

Emma stood by the door, considering what the cut hair meant, what kind of retribution it signified. She wondered who in the village had done this. How would that person feel to know that the fish he or she had eaten the day before was caught by Yves because of fuel Emma stole thanks to Michelle's romance with a lieutenant? It was an awkward irony: After this long an occupation, could anyone say they were entirely unimplicated?

Emma gimped down to the wagon. The battle burned at the edge of her vision, a thunder of shelling from offshore. Every noise, she knew it in her battered bones, meant that someone was dying.

The Allies had invaded after all. Emma had never been gladder to be wrong. But if they lost—given that elsewhere a single dead occupying soldier resulted in thirty villagers shot—she figured the entire village could expect execution. If they won, the battle of the beaches would move inland, and every home and barnyard would become a tactical objective, a thing to be fought over. Either way, the bloodshed was barely beginning.

She slid into her harnesses, body aching, mind alternating between clouded and clear, and trudged on like an animal hardened to its chores. From a distance it may have appeared as though the wagon was pushing her.

Emma lifted her head, only to see sun pouring through the clouds over the ocean. Great bright beams from sky to sea; as a girl, she had always called that sight God. What should she call it now? The moment that question arrived, she realized that no one had sent for the Monsignor to collect Didier the Goat with his wheelbarrow. The poor man lay in her barnyard, unfuneraled, unmourned. Emma knew where she needed to go next.

In the middle of a hedgerow near the village she spied something dangling from a tree. It was just above Dog Hill, the grass June-smooth, the sunflowers only a foot high. When she cleared the shortcut she saw that the something was a person, hung up by his parachute perhaps twenty feet from the ground, the easiest target an occupying army could ask for.

The paratrooper had been shredded with bullets. His head hung as if he had no neck bones. One of his legs remained attached only by a thin band of muscle. As he swung in the wind, the soldier's leg moved with a delay: The body turned away, then the leg. The body turned back, then the leg.

Emma staggered sideways at the horror of it. Or was she weakened by hunger? She could not recall the last time she had eaten. But the day was advancing without regard for her. She pressed against the straps and trudged toward the village.

On the way she saw a bridge with a gap in its middle. An airplane burning in a field. A mule dead in a ditch, its legs as stiff as wood. At the train station she saw a locomotive engine on its side, the wheels and gears and underside visible. It looked as wrong as a dislocated joint. But Emma pushed on, not resting till she reached St. Agnes by the Sea. Garbage burned in the street. The giant front doors were open wide, one of them hanging by a hinge.

Emma slipped off the straps and dragged herself up the steps. Hymnals lay scattered in the alcove. Someone had ripped the confessional curtains. She tiptoed farther. The candle beside the altar that was always lit now lay on its side, extinguished. All of the stained-glass windows were shattered, like so many dogmas that could not withstand disbelief.

Then she saw the shoes, black with holes in the soles, in the sacristy, where no woman was permitted. Emma knew whose shoes they were, and she hurried despite her aches and the rules.

A shell had struck the church, reducing the back stones to rubble. Day poured in where a wall had stood. The priest's face looked unharmed, and she felt a second of optimism. But when she knelt to turn his head, and saw the far side ripped completely away, Emma arranged him as he had been.

"Oh, Monsignor." She sat back on her heels. In a place where everyone knows everyone, where no one's history is wholly separate from anyone else's, any death counted as a loss.

Here was the war's strangest lesson yet. All sorts of people—friends and family, yes, but also adversaries and annoyances—all kinds had died. As they left behind everything, work and home and habits and opinions and even hidden chickens, somehow Emma's heart broke for all of them, including the ones she couldn't bear. Somehow their dying made them unhateable.

Emma stood, wondering what to do, who to contact if there was no priest to collect the body. Already flies were circling, she felt a mix of pity and disgust. She could not leave him here to rot.

Sacrilege though it was, Emma opened the cabinet that held priestly vestments. She ran her fingers over the garments, some of which she recognized from the religious seasons: red for Pentecost, rose for Advent, white for Easter.

Memories flooded through her, incense and singing and prayer. Emma remembered her First Communion, when she was more excited about the white dress Mémé had sewn her than about sharing in the bread and wine.

And now the priest was dead, his crime an insistence on his faith, and his punishment the spending of his life's one mortality.

Emma found a purple altar cloth, from Lent or the Stations of the Cross. The raiments of ritual carried too many meanings on a day with so much death. She latched the cabinet closed and bent to her task.

Rolling the priest to one side, she eased him onto the cloth so he could slide on the stone floor. But Emma had only managed to bring him halfway through the doorway when she realized one arm would not be strong enough. She tried using her injured hand, too, but her fingers could not grip. Returning to the closet, she knotted several shawls together, wrapped them around the Monsignor's legs, then looped them over her shoulders like the wagon straps.

Now she could pull with her body, and he slid easily across the floor. Emma brought him to the front and center of the church, as he had done for so many others. There she wrapped the altar cloth the rest of the way around, tucking in his arms and his legs. She used the shawls to secure his shroud so no flies could enter. For the second time in two days, Emma opened the Communion rail, taking from the altar the thick red book from which the priest read during Mass and placing it on his chest.

Then she stood over him. This man had baptized one hundred and two villagers, including her. He had placed that first Communion wafer on her tongue. Though Emma had been too young to remember, he had performed her mother's funeral. She ought to say some sort of prayer. But nothing would come.

"If you see God," she said finally, "ask Him why He stopped loving us."

Emma waited but the body made no answer. She hobbled down the aisle, out to the wagon and its open loops of harness. There she stood in uncertainty. What now? Where could she expose herself to Thalheim next?

Chapter 36

B*y late afternoon* people had begun exchanging stories about their first Allied soldier. A boy told his friends about one as tall as the doorframe who gave him candy. The boy's friends called him a fibber. Marguerite described a man who entered her house with his rifle lowered, but tapped the flag on his shoulder to identify himself, and left a pack of cigarettes on her side table.

They handed out powdered coffee. They climbed poles and cut wires. They seemed loose, athletic, well fed.

They were different from the occupying soldiers in other ways, too. Instead of loud, hard boot heels, the invaders wore quiet shoes, and less snug uniforms. They pointed in their mouths to show that they were thirsty. They looked like walking Tannenbaums, festooned with gear from the first-aid kits strapped to their helmets to the canteens on their hips to the grenades clipped on both sides of their chests.

Some wore branches and leaves on their helmets. Some had blackened their faces with pitch. They seemed disorganized, not in the rigid squads the village was accustomed to, but organizing as they found one another, forming units almost improvisationally.

One woman said a soldier had removed his helmet to take out a picture of a girl, which he displayed while holding his hand beside his thigh to indicate the girl's height. Another woman—her hands permanently scarred from the digging of Dog Hill—was sitting in her kitchen nursing a baby when a soldier burst in with pistol drawn, saw her, and backed out apologizing.

Pierre used his cane to lift the back flap of the officers' mess. The place was deserted, chairs tipped, meals abandoned half eaten. He spotted the confectionery by the exit, and after a moment's searching he was rewarded beyond belief: cigarettes. Packs and packs of them, and under the table a large boxful. Immediately he lit one, savoring the flavor, the relief of it, the deepest itch finally scratched. He breathed out a sweet blue plume.

Pierre began to stuff his pockets with packs, but then paused. He slid the box out, and it was not too heavy. After a pack or two for himself, he thought, the rest should go to Emma. She would know who else was in need; she would have a plan for distributing them fairly. He would deliver the box the moment the invasion ended.

Yves inched closer to the fuel depot's rear fence, which appeared entirely unguarded. One soldier was busy at the front fueling a line of trucks, the drivers all shouting at him while he scurried here and there. The fisherman helped himself to one tall canister of petrol, snaking it through an opening in the fence and out to a hedgerow, then another, then a third that was smaller but had straps so he could carry it on his back. The weight of the three together was just within his capacity to lift.

No point in carrying the containers to his boat, Yves reasoned. The harbor was as unsafe a place as he could imagine. He would hide the canisters near his home, and the next day bring them to Emma. She would know who needed fuel most, and how to deliver it.

Odette held a finger to her lips and Fleur nodded, following her into the occupying army's abandoned commissary. The shelves stood floor to ceiling, stretching back along both sides for the length of the tent. There was so much: flour, sugar, coffee, it seemed endless. A sack of potatoes stood a full meter tall.

"It is like the vault of a king," Odette whispered. Fleur nodded with wide eyes.

Then they spied the eggs, indented trays that held four dozen, stacked twenty trays high.

"Perfect," Odette said. "Nice and light, and we'll return for more when it's safer."

"Emmanuelle," Fleur chirped.

"Yes," Odette continued. "We'll bring these to Emma. She'll know what to do."

With that she lifted a dozen or so trays and hurried away. Fleur paused, snatched four eggs from the next tray to tuck in her apron pockets, and scurried to catch up.

Emma intended to check on Yves, to see if he had managed to fish that day, people would be wanting their dinner, but the war would not let her anywhere near. The battles were like hornets' nests, fierce angers in one place with relative quiet a kilometer or so away. She pulled the wagon numbly along the village's western edge, as close to the fighting as she dared. Perspiration beaded on her brow, a fever from her injuries, and she staggered in the road. Someone was coming, she could tell, skipping toward her—who would skip on a day such as this?—but her head was spinning and she needed water. Slipping off her harnesses, she tried to reach the canteen in the back of her wagon. But her legs felt like lead, her eyes fluttered. Emma dropped to her knees, then tumbled forward in the dirt.

The skipping person was Monkey Boy. At last he had found someone to tell everything. But before he could reach her, she had been shot. Five hundred and ten, and he stopped in the road.

But she was moving, one arm twitching. Monkey Boy ran till he reached her body on the ground. Rolling Emma onto her back, he recoiled at her battered face. He examined the rest of her, and there was no bleeding place. She had not been shot. Also she was still breathing. Still five hundred and nine, then.

Monkey Boy had a secret, which was that climbing trees all day makes a body strong. Arms like ropes, back muscles like cables. He lifted Emma onto his shoulder as if she weighed as little as a puppy, and laid her in the back of the wagon as gently as if that puppy were asleep. She murmured, and he saw her lips were cracked.

Rummaging in the wagon's bins, he found the canteen. The top unscrewed, he poured a splash in her mouth. She coughed, eyes opening with a wince. But when she saw who it was, Emma took the canteen, and drank from it for many loud gulps.

Monkey Boy scurried to the front of the wagon. Spying from high in the branches, he had seen her do this many times. Often he had imagined himself in this very situation, leading the wagon, being important. He slid his arms into the harnesses. While Emma recovered in back, he pulled in the direction of the special sycamore. Instead of telling her, he would show.

As they drew nearer to the coast, soldiers from both armies passed them. At one point they saw three of the Allied invaders hunched around a machine gun, and one of them put a finger to his lips. Monkey Boy froze. Five of the occupying soldiers rounded the corner, bent low and arguing in hushed voices. Before they noticed, though, the machine gun fired a great loud burst, and all five men lay sprawled in the road. Startled, Monkey Boy pressed a palm to his chest. Five hundred and fourteen.

Soon he and Emma reached the sycamore, perched on a promontory so steep and rocky the occupying army had not fortified it, and the invading army had not attacked it. Under the tree's broad paternal arms, Monkey Boy cooed like the messenger pigeon from a day before. This tree was a difficult climb, because the first branch began so far up the trunk. But an idea flashed in his head: the wagon could provide a boost.

Monkey Boy towed it into place. The fighting popped and banged and roared, some of it less than a hundred meters away. He set blocks behind the wheels, as he had seen Emma do. Then he skipped around to the back of the wagon and pulled on her good arm.

"What do you think you are doing?"

"Come see." He raised her up, starting a fireman's carry.

"Get off of me." Emma yanked back so hard her injured arm banged the wagon's hull. She closed her eyes, the pain rising like a fire, then retreating slowly like a coal going dim.

"So sorry," Monkey Boy said, bobbing like a duck in small waves. "So sorry. But you have to see. You want to see."

"What are you talking about? What do I want to see?"

He pressed his hands together as if in prayer. "Please come see. I should not be the only one."

"See what?" she said through gritted teeth. "Tell me."

He jumped away, then back, unable to contain himself. "This." He threw his hands in the direction of the beach, again and again. "This, this."

"Monkey Boy," Emma said, her voice as steadying as she could make it. "Calm down. What must I see?"

He stretched his arms wide and smiled with the whole of his face. "How they save us."

Later that day, Emma herself could not describe how they managed it. Monkey Boy removed the wagon slings and tied them to his shoulders. She slid them up her legs to the thigh, then hooked her good arm around his chest. And the boy she thought of as half simpleton, half elf, stood on the platform of the wagon and lifted them both up into the largest tree on the coast, as hidden as squirrels but with a view as for eagles.

Soon they were standing where the thick first branch met the trunk, and from there he climbed like it was a ladder, hand and foot, up and away from the wagon, Emma's face burrowed into his back while she clung and gritted her teeth and told herself: He will not let you fall. This is not how you die.

"There," Monkey Boy said at last, his back warm and breath hard, but his voice still a youthful chirrup. "Here we all are."

At first Emma could not see. She had to step out of the harnesses, her good arm hugging the trunk, until she was clear of him. Then she pressed herself to the tree and slid inch by inch around to the side that faced the ocean.

When she opened her eyes, Monkey Boy sat five meters out on a limb, swinging his legs. He grinned and pointed. "That way."

Emma turned, and saw the end of the world. A ship larger than any floating thing she had seen before, ten times the length of Yves's fishing boat, listed in the sand, fire bellowing from its middle. Tanks pointed nose first into the beach, their rumps in the air. An airplane, one of its wings missing, perched on its tail as if a giant had planted it. Trucks with stars on their rooftop canvas lay on their sides, or stood stationary with all doors wide. Different hues of smoke rose here and there, light gray to darkest black, some of it so thick she could not tell what was burning.

More than anything, though, Emma saw bodies. They lay in all sorts of positions, clustered at the waterline and here and there all over the beach. None of them were moving. A group of soldiers waded in the surf, collecting more bodies and towing them by one limb or another onto the beach, where still other soldiers hoisted them to lie in a row like a makeshift morgue. A man with a clipboard inspected each new body as it arrived, then made a note on his papers.

From down the beach she could hear machine-gun fire, the *sip-sip* sound bullets made when they entered the sand. A cluster of men dispatched toward the shooting, throwing grenades and using flamethrowers, until the machine gun stopped.

Other men rolled out tracks of wire mesh, a makeshift road on which the few trucks still working now made their way. She heard fighting at one of the beach exits, but it was too far to see. Emma could tell, however, that the Atlantic Wall which Thalheim had been so proud of, those four years of work, had not held the Allies off for more than half a day. How many bodies it had required, though, how many young men to prove a fanatic wrong.

Emma turned to Monkey Boy, heart in her throat, and he was still grinning.

"What in the world can you be smiling about?" She could barely speak. "Don't you see all of this?"

Monkey Boy squeezed the limb with his legs to secure himself, while opening both arms toward the beach. "For us."

Emma looked again. The dead outnumbered the population of the village of Vergers. They outnumbered all the people she had seen in her life.

Yet more machines and men were landing by the minute, trucks with balloons over their heads like miniature zeppelins, tanks, half-tracks, Jeeps, more ships approaching from the horizon, men with red flags directing traffic, an army pouring onto these sands hardly five kilometers from the village.

There was nothing for the invading hordes to gain. With the livestock gone, lands flooded, people cowed, there would be no spoils. Then why?

Emma suffered daily for friends and neighbors. They were doing it for strangers, throwing themselves on that beach, slaughtered till the sea ran dark, and another wave came, and was slaughtered, and another, whole cities of men. They had never met Emma, she would never meet them, and still another wave.

It was so humbling, Emma clung to the tree and did not think she could continue to breathe. The weight of their sacrifice might crush her. Here they had died, and up the beach they were still dying, in flocks and willingly for the idea that she, Emma herself, and her friends and family and neighbors, ought to live in freedom. Who on earth deserved such a gift?

She turned again to Monkey Boy, tears stinging the cut on her chin, and she nodded. "For us."

Monkey Boy pulled the wagon with his chest puffed out. It was easy work compared with climbing. Also the woman who fed everyone rode in back, teaching him all sorts of shortcuts. If he knew trees, she knew forests, and it filled him with awe.

The fighting had moved inland from the beaches, he could tell. But whenever they approached troops of either army, or heard gunfire, or detected suspicious rustling in the leaves, she pointed with a stick and he towed in that new direction.

Soon they arrived at the barnyard of old Pierre. When they called out, no one answered. The river had flooded most of his land, his three cows corralled by water on a rise of grass near the barn. They seemed calm, however, their mouths chewing away at nothing.

Emma climbed down from the wagon, leaning on Monkey Boy's arm, and they tiptoed into the barn. Pierre's morning buckets sat untouched by the door. Dipping a stick in the milk, she saw that a skin had formed on the surface.

"Not good news," Emma said.

Monkey Boy nearly laughed out loud. It was all unbearably exciting. The woman dug in her pocket for a small tobacco pipe, and with a groan from bending over, placed it on his milking stool. She spent a moment enjoying that image—in the dusty barn light it seemed like a painting, an artist's still life—before shuffling out into the yard.

"There's another stop nearby," she said, and after a few minutes' pulling they arrived at a fence of barbed wire, with a sign announcing that the area was mined. Emma climbed down again, sloshing through knee-deep water to the wire, and with a lift of her skirt she had stepped over the fence.

"But the sign," Monkey Boy said, pointing.

"Don't worry," she said. "I put it there."

Emma waded around the hedgerow, but Monkey Boy could still see when her shoulders fell and her head dropped. She raised her arms and seemed to hug herself, swaying there, and he wondered if she was about to fall down again.

Emma turned and waded back to the wagon. "Drowned in their coop," she said. "Every one of them."

She gave no further explanation, leaving Monkey Boy to tow the wagon and ponder what it meant. He had not traveled twenty meters, however, when he thought he heard another cow.

"Wait," Emma said, rising to her knees in the back.

The sound came again, and Monkey Boy knew it was not a cow. He pulled directly toward it, a place they had passed minutes before, but from the other direction so they had not noticed the man lying there, back in the dense hedgerow. He was tangled in ropes, his face smeared with pitch so that his eyes looked startlingly white, his body bent like a question mark.

He spoke in his language, tensely as if breathing hurt him, and pointed at his legs. Emma knelt beside the man, her face still swollen like an overinflated balloon, and instructed Monkey Boy: where to find scissors in the wagon, how to cut away the ropes, when to lift the branch that lay across the man's ribs.

Monkey Boy studied the parachute tangled overhead. As the trees leaned in the wind, he considered climbing to pull the fabric free, which branches he would have to grab. The soldier continued speaking intensely, a ring of dried saliva around his mouth, until Emma pressed a finger to his lips to shush him. After that he only watched them with his strange white eyes.

Emma wrapped his legs in old sacks, using a bit of rope to pull them straight, which caused the soldier to growl and thrash his head from side to side.

When eventually he was breathing normally again, Emma held his legs while Monkey Boy took the rest of him, and they hoisted him out of the ferns. He made a yelp with each breath, and it reminded Monkey Boy of the sounds he heard a dog make once, when an occupying soldier had shot her in the leg.

But this paratrooper went silent, eyes closing as they settled him into the wagon. Monkey Boy held his palm over the soldier's mouth before turning to Emma. "Still breathing."

After nesting the wounded man in among bags and blankets, he strode to the front to take his place again, but found that Emma had done the same thing on the other side. They each slid an arm into a harness.

"We didn't see the captain anywhere," she said. "And I am out of ideas. This man is someone we can help."

She paused, and Monkey Boy waited, marveling at the notion that they would be pulling the wagon together. The greatness of the day was beyond his imagining.

"It's time," Emma said. "Nowhere left to go but home."

Chapter 37

They came with rifles raised, shouting. Mémé made no sound. The invaders pulled her away from the house, yelling as they pointed at her feet and the ground she stood on, and she knew to stay put. Two men guarded her while others charged into the house. She could hear them shoving furniture and pounding up the stairs. It grew silent for a moment, then they charged down and out again. One of them threw a shirt at her feet; it was from Captain Thalheim's uniform.

They began shouting again, pointing at Thalheim's flag on the corner of the house. They waved their arms in front of Mémé. One of them aimed his rifle at her chest. The others spoke to him harshly, but he did not lower his gun.

One soldier quieted them, a short, freckled one, giving Mémé a moment to defend herself. She made a gruff snort, as if suppressing a sneeze. Then she spat on Thalheim's shirt.

A few soldiers cheered, the one threatening her lowered his gun, and they began discussions among themselves. At that moment three more men entered the barnyard, and the sight of one of them made the others straighten and salute. That officer asked a question, then pointed at the others, who answered him one by one. Mémé was astonished: it seemed they were introducing themselves. What kind of an invasion involves men who do not already know one another?

Then the officer was speaking to Mémé. In her language. Yet she barely heard him, the pace of events was so swift. She wanted to go back inside and resume the nap she had been awakened from, the sleep she had entered to avoid her hunger, and to stop her mind from dwelling on Emma's promise to be home by midday, now that the sun was low in the west. Yet the man continued talking while Mémé weighed all of these concerns, so that when he paused, and she realized he had asked her a question, she had no idea what to say in reply.

"We have maps, you see," he said, pulling papers from his jacket pocket and unfolding them. "But the road signs do not agree with them. We don't know where we are."

Mémé stood before him, mute as a mule. To her ears, this man made no sense.

"Am I speaking the right language?" he asked. "And when do you expect the enemy officer to return?"

She began to wring her hands and make a mewing sound.

The officer turned to the men. "Maybe she's deaf."

"Not deaf." Emma stood at the barnyard door, looped in the wagon harnesses with Monkey Boy. "Only shy. I can help, if you'll lend a hand for a moment."

Some soldiers had turned guns on her, but as she wheeled forward they saw the paratrooper in the back.

"We found him in a hedgerow, tangled in the trees."

The man was awake, sitting upright. He said a few words to the others, and they laughed and gathered near the cart.

The officer offered a handshake to Emma. "Captain Arnie Schwartz, McLean, Virginia. Thank you for helping this soldier."

Emma took his hand in both of hers. "You came for us."

"Well, yes."

She continued to hold his hand. "I never thought you would."

The captain smiled. "During training, I sometimes thought that, too. Now, about this soldier here—"

"Both of his legs are broken," Emma said, turning. "And he may have other injuries. He needs a doctor."

"Five hundred and fourteen is enough," Monkey Boy cried.

"Shush now," Emma said, and he shrank as if she had thrown cold water on him.

"Um," the captain said. "Let's debrief for a minute here."

He leaned on the wagon's side and began asking questions. As the paratrooper replied, Schwartz translated for Emma. She knew he was giving only part of the story, but she considered it good manners that he told her anything. Mostly she marveled that he was actually standing there, in her barnyard.

"He says the fires in the village were drawing in oxygen," he said. "So they sucked some of our jump fighters in, too. Others landed in flooded fields—"

"That would be Pierre's land," Emma interjected.

"—where they drowned from the weight of their gear. This man you helped here, Corporal Mark Bronsky from Portland, Maine, saw from above as two dozen men went under."

Emma nodded. That explained the previous day's ditch digging.

"He pulled hard, to pilot away. But bad luck put him in a crosswind, and he wound up in the trees."

"It was good luck, though," Emma replied. She slid out of the wagon harness. "I saw another one caught in trees near the village. The occupying soldiers had cut him apart with bullets."

Captain Schwartz put his hands on his hips, regarding her frankly. "We're a hodgepodge right now, ma'am, I have to say it. Men from different units who've met up in the crazy woods here." He pointed at some of them. "He's a hundred and first like me, those two are eighty-second, we've got three marine companies represented here, a radioman with no radio, a sniper with an enemy rifle. Good fellows, but real scrambled eggs."

He unfolded a map. "If you could explain the geography here, it would be a good start for us."

"I will help," she said. "There is one thing, though." Emma's tongue was sandpaper in her mouth.

"What's that?"

He looked so healthy, eager, worried but not afraid. Emma pictured herself as he saw her: face battered, hair bedraggled, sweat marks on her clothes where the harness straps had been.

"I hate to ask for anything," she said.

"If you're going to do it, now's the time."

She picked at the scab on her chin, saw that her finger came away bloody. There was a chance she might fall over. Instead Emma steeled herself and whispered, "Do you have any food?"

"Oh." The captain straightened with a smile, as if seeing her clearly for the first time. "Oh, sure."

He gave an order, and men came forward with rations. Emma tried to eat slowly, with at least a show of restraint, while Mémé wolfed the food down, glancing sidelong as if someone might take it away at any moment.

Captain Schwartz studied them before turning to his men. "You fellas seeing this?" The soldiers all nodded.

Emma noticed Monkey Boy watching her eat, and gave him her tin of food. She took a long drink of water, then handed the jug to Mémé. "You are outside of this small farming and fishing village, here," she told the captain, pointing with her good hand at a spot on the paper. "Five kilometers from Longues-sur-Mer."

"Then why did I see a sign that said we were—what, eight miles from Honfleur and five from Caen? My map says they must be a good twenty miles apart."

"I don't know miles," she answered. "But Caen to Honfleur is more than sixty kilometers."

He swatted the map with his hand. "Makes no damn sense."

Emma drew herself up. "Your papers are correct, sir. The signs are a lie."

The pleasure it gave her to say that sentence surged through Emma like a blush. It felt as if she were reclaiming her native countryside, the unimpeachable jurisdiction of her hometown.

"I can tell you more than this," she continued. "I have lived here all of my life. I know where their machine guns are located, the mortar installations. I know their fuel depot, where the barrels are stacked three and four high."

"I'm listening," he replied, and indeed all of the men were leaning closer.

"They travel the main roads," Emma said. "But I can show you shortcuts they know nothing about. They possess many weapons and no mercy, so you must not underestimate them. But they are also vain and self-important, and therefore vulnerable."

Captain Schwartz gave her a long appraising look. "Are you some kind of spy? Or with the Resistance?"

"I am a survivor. Who helps others to survive."

He nodded. "What is your name?"

"Emmanuelle."

"I can see what they did to you, Emmanuelle." He gestured at her face. "Maybe you are too smart for them?"

She stood straight, shoulders back. "Let us all hope so."

He smiled. "You are one plucky gal."

"Very," Mémé growled, and when they turned to look at her she glared back as if she might charge at any moment.

The captain began giving orders, directing his men one way or another. As they organized, he turned back to Emma.

"We're going to establish a perimeter east and west on the town road, and in the pucker brush by the well over there." He pointed past the barnyard door. "When we get back, I'm hoping you could identify those forces you described on these maps, and then we'll be on our way."

Mémé pointed at the paratrooper in the wagon. "Him?"

Captain Schwartz scratched his jaw. "Look, we don't have a medic among us, or a radio to call for one. We'll help you get him set up. After that, I don't know. I have orders. If you could stabilize this soldier for the time being . . ."

They did, Monkey Boy hovering as they carried Corporal Bronsky inside and laid him on Mémé's couch. The paratrooper kept thanking everyone, but he grimaced when anyone moved him. As soon as he was settled, Bronsky closed his eyes. Monkey Boy sat by the wounded corporal, taking his hand. And did not leave his side till morning.

Emma and Mémé went back to the barnyard, watching as the soldiers divided in groups.

"We will be back in fifteen minutes," Captain Schwartz told Emma. "And not sixteen."

He gave the command, and one group headed up the town road, the lane by which the Kommandant and his aide always arrived, another marched down the road in the other direction, from which the convoys typically came, and the third struck out past the eastern well and down the hedgerow beyond. In a few seconds, they were all swallowed by dusk.

"They came," Emma said.

Mémé drew near and they fell into each other's arms, embracing as if one of them had spent a year at sea.

Thalheim's timing could not have been luckier, to find them that way. Three minutes earlier or twelve minutes later, and Captain Schwartz's men would have welcomed him. As he slunk through the barnyard door and hugged the wall like a shadow, Emma thought for a moment that the Goat was still alive.

But when he stepped out of the darkness, she eased Mémé aside. "Dear one, leave me with him."

Instead her grandmother moved between them, raising her fists. Thalheim hesitated, his helmet gone and uniform untucked, then clasped his hands as if in prayer.

"Hide me," he said. "Conceal me in the hayloft. Please."

Mémé gave one cold laugh and sneered. Emma shook her head as if to clear it. "You are asking us for help? After all you have done?"

"I was following orders."

"Look at my face." She stuck out her chin. "Was this an order?"

"I lost control. And don't say you didn't provoke me."

Emma snorted. "You said you were going to kill me."

"A threat only. You are so insolent. Any other officer—"

"You promised to rape me."

"I did not want your body, I wanted your obedience." He snuffled. "I could not have done it anyway. I am a virgin."

Emma surprised herself then, by calming, and scrutinizing him. Without his helmet, Thalheim was revealed: a boy. Perhaps younger than she. Now she understood why he shaved with such care: to conceal the fact that he had no whiskers at all. He was too young for a beard.

Mémé paced the barnyard, a scowl darkening her face.

"My given name is Hans," he continued. "Named after my grandfather, a brewer. I was compelled by my families to join of the army, to enlist before I was drafted, and I am their great pride for having attained rank of captain. Before the war I was study chemistry."

Emma marveled to learn after all this time that behind the bravado and doctrine, there was a human being. Did he deserve to die? Was his life without worth or redemption? Perhaps Thalheim had another role left to play. If he surrendered, and repented of his fanaticism, what good might he prove capable of committing?

Or was this speculation a sign of weakness once again, her inability to kill? The way Mémé stalked around them, opening and closing her fists, Emma thought she might just be too soft.

"At least help me escape," Thalheim pleaded. "Dress me in your father's clothes."

The image offended Emma so deeply she drew back several steps. "Absolutely not."

"Do something, please. I am beg of you."

Emma shook her head. "No."

His expression hardened. "You will not aid me in any way?"

She crossed her arms. "No."

Thalheim hammered his fist against her forehead. Again Emma had not seen it coming, and again she tumbled to the earth.

"Enough of this," he snapped, reaching to unclip his holster. The captain drew his pistol and took aim.

Emma had time for a single thought: Philippe.

All at once Thalheim's eyes widened, then went still. He must have died standing, Emma imagined, because all of his joints—

knees, elbows, waist—collapsed at the same time, like a marionette whose strings have been scissored. He fell on his face in the dirt, the handle of Guillaume's knife visible in his back, just below his ribs.

Mémé stood as tall as a monument, tapping her chest with a hand that glistened from blood. "My conscience," she said. "Not yours."

One of the Allied soldiers asked if he could have the dead man's flag. Emma said she would be glad to see it go. He lowered it from the house, careful not to tear, folding it away in his pack.

Captain Schwartz stood over Thalheim, muttering, "We weren't gone ten minutes. What the hell happened?"

"She saved me," Emma said, pointing at her grandmother.

The officer directed two men to remove the body. They dragged it away up the road out of sight.

The invading soldiers were weighted down with gear—canteens, bandoliers, grenades—yet they didn't seem burdened by it. They looked fit and well fed, chatting easily while Mémé ate more of their rations. Emma sat at the kitchen table, penciling hedgerow shortcuts and occupying army posts onto the captain's maps. With her writing hand in a splint, the best she could do was make Xs, and explain what each one meant.

"Here you follow the animal trails, you'll see them in the tall grass, until it opens onto a dirt road."

Captain Schwartz nodded. "How do we take that church? The steeple is visible from a distance, so it's a key rendezvous point."

"There is a machine gun." She tapped the page with her pencil. "It faces the village, so you can surprise them from behind."

She handed him the paper. "If your men are quiet, that is. A map won't do the fighting for you."

"This is all incredibly helpful." The captain sat back, though he continued scratching his chin.

"But?"

He shrugged. "Ammunition. Nothing to be done, but we could sure use more of it."

Emma stood, despite her injuries feeling stronger by the minute. "Follow me."

When the captain saw the stacks in the old hog shed, he danced a little jig. Then he called his men; they opened some boxes and took turns equipping themselves.

Emma stood by, surprised to feel herself moved at the sight. "I am glad this supply will not go to waste."

"It's a gold mine," Schwartz answered. "Bringing this here must have been incredibly dangerous for you."

"Not me," Emma began, her throat tightening as she recalled her disdain for the Goat, years of it, while he had sweated and carried and taken risk after risk. "A friend."

Suddenly four soldiers dropped to one knee, rifles to their cheeks. Emma glanced around, not seeing anything as the captain pushed her into the shed. The stink of pig made her eyes water.

Then they all heard the sound of crickets, and the soldiers relaxed. Captain Schwartz shouted, and a group of new men came forward, with someone huddled behind them.

"I don't understand," Emma said.

The captain held up a wooden trinket, thumbing it rapidly to create an almost cricket sound. As the troops greeted one another, Schwartz interrupted to question the new arrivals. Then he turned to Emma. "I'm afraid I have to leave you with an additional responsibility. These men found one of your villagers near the conflict. Can you please take care of him?"

Emma tried to peer past the officer. "Who is it?"

The soldiers parted, a form stumbled forward. It was Argent, the young professor from the mansion on the bluff. His glasses were gone, his face lacerated on one side. Emma looked beyond, but there was no one else with him.

Though she had never learned his wife's name, Emma felt the loss like a blow. And the baby, barely a day old. Before she could offer comfort, though, or say anything, the infant mewed in her father's arms. He was carrying the newborn after all.

"Ha!" Emma cried, clapping her hands once. The soldiers turned to peer at her, and she seemed equally surprised. What was this rush of emotion? Was it actually a glimmer of optimism? In spite of everything, the child was alive.

"Baby," Mémé said. She scurried to the house's doorway, waving an arm to invite them inside. "Baby."

The young professor turned in the direction of that voice, stumbling into the house, and in his weary arms a bundle of warm cloth: the pink-skinned girl whose nappie needed changing, who needed to nurse but would never nurse again, whose exhaustion had overwhelmed all of her other wants so that she slept even though war raged around her, eyes closed as if instead of chaos and violence the world were a quiet nursery.

Although months of conflict remain, at a cost of thousands of lives, this very second is the moment that the war begins to end, the time that the future commences.

The baby girl, Gabrielle, will not grow up with memories of occupation and invasion. Her childhood and adolescence will contain a treasury of hours—with Emma at bedtime, in Odette's café, playing in the hayloft while Pierre milks his girls—of hearing the story: who survived and how, who outsmarted whom, which people sacrificed and how much.

Their stories were like a cemetery in the mind, naming the dead, mourning what was lost. But they also made a chapel in the imagination, proof that the people were strong enough to endure. Catalog of triumph, relic of redemption; story was souvenir, salve, and salvation.

Gabrielle divined this insight only after the war had ended, however, after the villagers had experienced the merciful tincture of time. On that gusty June night—blood on their clothes, hunger in their bellies, aching in their hearts—the people's future remained a frightening unknown. Gunfire clattered in the distance, a thudding of mortars. Soldiers prepared for battle in the dark. The smell of gunpowder arrived on the wind.

Who should swagger into the barnyard just then, but Pirate. Feathers scorched and disheveled, he strutted before the soldiers undaunted, crowing at them in full volume: get out of his barnyard, get away from his roost. The men laughed.

One soldier said something in his language to the captain, who made a firm reply, and the laughter stopped.

"What did he ask?" Emma said.

"If he should shoot him," Schwartz answered. "I said that scrappy little guy is actually part of what we're here to save."

Then he cleared his throat and called orders. The men assembled, checking their equipment one last time. Captain Schwartz turned to Emma. "Here. Something to remember us by." He handed her a hard square of foil.

"As if I'm likely to forget," she answered.

"Okay, men," the captain shouted. "Let's march." He strode

through the barnyard door, soldiers filing behind him, their bodies hunched and rifles raised.

After the last of them had passed beyond the eastern well, into the hedgerow and out of sight, Emma found herself standing alone. Hell on earth continued all around: flames on the horizon, bombers snarling overhead, people inside the house awaiting her help. But for that brief interval the barnyard was an oasis, a private moment of calm. It felt vaguely familiar, as if from a long, long time ago.

Here was the place Philippe would return to, and bit by bit recover with the help of a woman as steady as rock, and find himself healed by the joyous, exhausting duties of fathering. Here was the place that the future lived.

With her good hand Emma unwrapped the foil around the captain's gift. Chocolate, a fat square of it, and she immediately bit off a chunk. After all those years of eating sparely, she felt her mouth flooded with flavor: rich, milky, sweet.

The taste of hope.

Acknowledgments

No exact undisputed tally exists, but credible estimates say that the D-Day invasion on June 6, 1944, cost the lives of more than 4,400 Allied soldiers. The United States Cemetery and Memorial at Omaha Beach, final resting place for American war dead from the overall Normandy campaign, holds 9,387 graves.

Those battles also took the lives of an estimated fifty thousand French men and women.

Many excellent books and films explore this heroism, and I was most inspired by *D-Day* by Stephen E. Ambrose; *D-Day Through French Eyes* by Mary Louise Roberts; and *D-Day Normandy* (a photographic essay on the invasion) by Donald M. Goldstein, Katherine V. Dillon, and J. Michael Wenger.

My friend Marcia DeSanctis, author of *100 Places in France Every Woman Should Go* (which is infinitely more than a travel book), insisted that I hire Claire Lesourd as a guide in Normandy. It proved to be an excellent suggestion. Claire turned out to be a walking encyclopedia, bringing me to the villages, beaches, and battlefields where history was made. I am grateful for her knowledge, patience, and help. Kenneth Rendell's unique Museum of World War II, outside of Boston, contained thousands of artifacts that made the war experience tangible—from Hitler's uniform to the grappling hook used in the climbing assault on Pointe de Hoc. My sister Casey Kiernan made me aware of that museum as well as the HBO program *Band of Brothers*. My interview with Ron Hadley, landing-craft commander and veteran of Omaha Beach, was about as humbling a conversation as I've ever had.

That interview took place thanks to an introduction by my friend Chris Bohjalian, who continues to help and guide my work with incredible generosity. I am lucky and proud to know him.

The other person who supported this book—from first draft to last, with patience, humor, and wine—is the inimitable Kate Seaver. I am in her debt in many, many ways. Early drafts also benefitted from the wise, clever, and challenging responses of Geoff Gevalt, John Killacky, and Hawk Ostby. I also appreciate the kind help of Peter Heller and Mary Morris, whose works of fiction far surpass mine.

I am especially grateful to the people who brought this novel into being: my trusted agent and friend Ellen Levine, the best ally I can imagine; and my editor and friend Jennifer Brehl, who improved this book from first sentence to last. Thanks too to Mumtaz Mustafa and Leah Carlson-Stanisic, for designing a beautiful book.

If there seem to be a lot of names here, it is because so many people helped me bring this idea from imagination to reality. I could not have done it without them.

About the Author

STEPHEN P. KIERNAN spent more than twenty years as a journalist, winning numerous awards before turning to fiction writing. *The Baker's Secret* is his third novel.